C000008991

# BALMANIE

## TONY LINDSELL

# DEDICATION

For our children and our children's children and all
who may suffer at the hands of climate change

# ACKNOWLEDGMENTS

With thanks to Steve Calcutt and all members, past and present, of the Anubis creative writing group of Leamington Spa for their advice, encouragement, constructive feedback and constant good cheer. Special thanks to Tom Evershed for patiently reading chapter after chapter and for his invaluable input; and to Steve Ward and Patrick Kincaid for reading specific chapters. Many thanks also to Peter Shipton, Murthy Buddhavarapu, Martin Been and Grace Pink for their advice on medical matters; to Peter Claisse for advice on nautical matters; and to Russell Allen for advice on certain 'other matters'. Any errors in interpretation are entirely the author's.


*Cover design — Molly Vincent of Image IT Ltd, Daventry*

# CHAPTER I

A COBWEB glistened with dew on the ivy that shrouded the bay window. A droplet formed at its lower edge. It grew and grew, like a balloon, until it could cling on no longer, and fell to the sill below. A faded orange petal, attached by a tiny filament to the foliage, spun aimlessly in the still air.

A spider crawled across the web. Henry watched as it reached the orange petal and disappeared. He looked behind him to the kitchen. The gurgling of the percolator had stopped. A power cut.

"Can't a man have a decent cup of coffee on the first day of his retirement?" he grumbled.

"It'll be on again soon, darling," said Josephine quietly.

She was etched in silhouette, the morning light pouring in behind her. How beautiful she looked, Henry thought, even after all this time and all she'd been through. A wren burst out of the ivy. It looked briefly around and then dipped its head back in. He wondered if it ate the spider.

His mobile vibrated. A text.

"Am OK…so far," it read. It was from their son, Sam.

"What the hell does that mean? Why wouldn't he be OK?" He punched the remote on the TV, defying it to work without power, then picked up his tablet.

"Dammit, no Wifi."

He connected to the mobile signal and flicked to the BBC news app. The circle went round and round. He switched to Sky News. 'Reports are coming in of an incident in...' The screen went blank. He shrugged.

"London?" Josephine asked. But she could only address thin air.

She stood by the smokey blue centre island. Just two months previously they had had this whole section of the house modernised and redesigned. A new kitchen, otherwise white with grey marbled work surfaces, underfloor heating and an adjoining snug that could be separated off by a floor to ceiling sliding glass door. This was the old part of the house. Originally it had been a farm cottage, two up, two down. They had built the extension when they could afford it, soon after they had moved to the village thirty years previously. This was where Sam had grown up.

The landline rang. It was Sam. He sounded different. Trying not to sound worried.

"Why wouldn't you be ok?"

"There've been explosions and...I don't know, other stuff."

"I hadn't heard. Bloody electricity's down."

"That's part of it."

He cut out and again there was only silence. Henry glared at the old black phone as if it could give him some clue, but it looked dumbly, almost insolently, back at him and he returned it to its cradle. Modern technology - he expected it to go wrong. Bombs in London — what else was new? Sam was all right, there was nothing to worry about.

\*\*\*\*\*\*

Impatient for the coffee that had never quite brewed, Henry dug out an old camping-gaz stove from the garage.

"Have you got electricity?" called Isabel, their neighbour, over the hedge. "Mine's been off for nearly an hour."

"Nothing, Izzie; can't get any internet connection either," he said.

"Seems like there's been some sort of explosion in London."

"Yes, we caught that too. I can't see how that's going to affect us though."

"No," she said. "Unless it's hit a main power station or something."

"I suppose so," he muttered as he went back into the kitchen.

He transferred the lukewarm coffee from the hob to the camping-gaz ring, but when he came to drink it, it tasted bitter. He felt ill at ease, unearthed.

He went out to the garden and dug a weed-strewn section of the vegetable patch as if the very life of the planet depended on it. His clothes were bathed in sweat when he came back in. He wondered where the spider was now, where was the wren.

The March of the Valkyries suddenly burst into life on his mobile. Sam had set it up as his ring tone on his sixty-fifth birthday – they'd had an argument about Wagner or Day in the Life.

"Sam?"

"I'm going to try to get …"

Josephine looked at him almost aggressively. "What did he say?"

"He said he was going to try to get…and then it cut out. Help? Home? To the railway station? Out?" Henry called back but the number just dropped.

"I think I'll go into town and see if I can find out what's going on," he said, trying to sound calm for Josephine's sake.

"Pick up some bread if you're near Tesco."

He climbed into his Landcruiser. It was dirty bronze and twelve years old. It was a present to himself. He liked the smell of its old leather seats. He liked the manual four-wheel drive system lever and the running boards. He liked the driver's seat position - someone had called it the command position. He felt indestructible there.

High clouds obscured the early summer sun and there was a silence about the land as Henry drove in on the main road, as if the day to day run of things had been suspended. A queue stretched several hundred yards on the outskirts of town, the traffic at a standstill. For a while he sat there punching buttons on the radio, willing it to give him some sort of information. A car overtook on the wrong side of the road. He spun the wheel to the right and followed, realising the queue was for the fuel station.

Horns blared in the impatient jam of Tesco car park. People with overloaded trolleys jinked and lurched their way across, shouting and cursing other drivers. The store itself looked strange, only dimly lit. A generator must be keeping the fridges and freezers and tills going, he thought.

He went straight towards the bread shelves. On the side where the brown loaves were normally stacked, there was nothing. He walked round the bay. The white was all gone too. He fought his way through a mass of shoppers in search of the fresh bread counter. A line of people stretched up the aisle and he joined the back.

"To hell with it, I'll get some tomorrow," muttered someone in front of him, turning on their heel.

A tall, overweight man in grey track suit bottoms and a loose red t-shirt barged his way to the front. He grabbed the last French loaf from the shelf as an elderly lady reached out for it.

"Give it back," people shouted, then cowered under the man's glare.

As he strode away, a close-cut blonde woman stuck her leg out, almost casually. A flick of an arm and the big man was on the ground, the bread flying across the floor. He stood up, forehead creased and red, eyes flaring. He moved towards her.

"No!" cried people in the queue, but the woman remained impassive, her eyes focussed on her adversary. He raised his fist and in an instant she had shifted her weight, leaning into the driving arm, and the big man was on the ground again, flailing against the back of the cake counter. He slunk away, defeated, eyes down. The woman picked up the loaf and passed it to the lady.

"Good on yer, girl," someone shouted. Others clapped.

By the time Henry got to the counter, only a few loaves remained. They were all white and he knew Josephine would not be happy.

"One please," he said. It would tide them over anyway.

A scrum of people lay between him and the checkout. Water. A stack of polythene-wrapped packs was rapidly dwindling. He stretched an arm through the melee and pulled two five-litre bottles from the top. He looked at them as he waited in the queue to pay. He didn't really know why he had them – he never normally bought water. The water from the tap was fine.

"Anyone know what's happening?" he said, trying to sound cheery, trying not to sound part of the frenzy, but people just looked at him.

\*\*\*\*\*\*

"Town's a madhouse. I got one of the last loaves in the place – brown was all gone."

"The power's come on again."

5

Henry punched the TV button. He flicked through the channels. BBC was just snow. ITV was snow. Then Al Jazira. Al Jazira was working.

'We are receiving information of a terrorist incident in London. Normal communication channels seem to be down. Unverified reports indicate that some TV and mobile reception has been lost throughout the UK and many houses are without power.'

The Al Jazira pictures were broken and pixillated and the sound stuttering. Images would appear, then disappear before his brain had had a chance to process them. He caught a glimpse of crowds running up a road. It looked like the Edgware Road. That was close to where Sam lived. The TV and the lights spluttered, dimmed and went out again.

'Sod it,' thought Henry and opened a bottle of wine.

# CHAPTER II

THE NOISE woke him from a deep sleep. Behind the drumming of the rain, something was hitting the window pane. Stones. Stones were being thrown against it. Now he could make out a voice, shouting. "Parents…mother…father…wake up, it's me."

Sam was standing in the driveway, two other people behind him. In the torchlight he recognised Shani, his girlfriend, her raven black hair and city clothes drenched. The other woman he did not know. He unlocked the door and they piled in, exhausted, drained and sodden.

"Christ! Are you all right?"

"Just about."

He lit the giant green and yellow candle that stood on the kitchen table. Someone had given it to them for Christmas many years before. They'd lit it the previous evening and rivulets of wax now lay solid at its base. He took the wet clothes and Josephine appeared with an armful of old coats, sweaters and fleeces. They sat, huddling thankfully in the warmth of the house, silent for some moments.

"This is Rabiyah. We met her on the road. She doesn't have much English," said Sam.

It was only then that Henry realised that it was not a rucksack that had been on the woman's back but a baby. She was shivering uncontrollably – fear, cold and the protective instinct tied into a tidal wave of relief. Josephine grabbed a blanket. She took the baby and cradled it, while Henry put the kettle on the camping gaz stove.

"The power's down again," he said, unnecessarily. He looked at Sam. "It doesn't sound good, whatever's going on down there. What happened to you?"

"Dad, it was a nightmare. There were explosions – Westminster, Piccadilly tube, Heathrow. Those were the ones we heard about. Someone said the Piccadilly one was a dirty bomb. And then, I don't know…Chris came in to the flat. He was covered in dust. He tried to sluice himself down. He threw up – he was in agony. Natalie…the same." He held his head in his hands. "I don't know if they'll make it. We had to get out."

The scent of sandalwood now began to envelope the room as a pool of molten wax formed in the centre of the candle.

"The M40 was chaos. Cars, people walking amongst them. Everyone trying to escape London. The service stations were completely blocked. We got off eventually…managed to make it up the old A40. We ran out of fuel outside Banbury. We walked from there."

"You walked fifteen miles?"

"Felt like fifty," said Shani. "Thank you so much." Then she broke down.

"I've been trying to call my parents."

"Where are they?" asked Henry.

"Kent," she said, "Chiselhurst. I can't get through to them on my iPhone. Nor Sam's." Sam laid his arm around her shoulders.

Henry studied the face of his mobile.

"No signal on mine either, I'm afraid. You can try the landline – it just might work if they have an old-style wired-in telephone, not a cordless."

Shani dialled the number as Josephine laid out bread, cheese and fruit in the candle light. She shook her head, holding the phone out so that everyone could hear the continuous tone.

The kettle began to boil and, as Henry poured the water into a teapot, the blue flames sputtered, then died to a whisper. He wondered if they had any more canisters. He looked at Rabiyah. He held the tips of his fingers and thumb to his mouth and pointed to the baby.

"For the baby?"

She indicated a banana.

"Noor," she said. "Shukran."

# CHAPTER III

THE MORNING dawned bright and Henry felt almost a spring in his step as he went downstairs. The sound of a baby crying brought him back to reality. Rabiyah, her hijab hanging loosely around her head, was sitting on the garden bench, cradling the child. Henry needed tea. He tried the power, but there was none. He hunted for more camping gaz canisters but there were none. The only option was the barbecue. He loaded it with charcoal and firelighters and lit a match, then laid a kettle across the top.

Josephine warmed some milk and handed it to Rabiyah and only when the baby had quietened did she allow Henry to make tea. Shani sat down with them, her hair tousled, dark curls formed from the night before.

"Tell me where you have come from," said Henry, looking at Rabiyah. She looked blankly back at him.

"My father is Egyptian," said Shani. "I can translate." She spoke in Arabic.

"Syria, Homs."

"I am sorry," said Henry, waving his arm vaguely in the direction of the power lines that bordered the road and the English sky.

Rabiyah spoke.

"It is nothing," translated Shani. "Where I have been, this is…Jannah; that means 'heaven'."

"How did you get out?"

Rabiyah sighed. "It is a long story." She did not seem inclined to elaborate.

******

"I'm getting an intermittent signal," said Sam from the open door, tapping his mobile. "Noone seems to know what's going on. One report said the government had gone to ground in some emergency location in the Chilterns. The hospitals in London are overflowing and can't cope. People are still pouring out – it's awful."

At that moment, the major, as everybody called him, walked past. He was the leader of the parish council.

"We've told them the Village Hall and the playing fields can be used to house people until all this business dies down," he said heartily. "If anyone gets the message that is. So we may have some extra visitors these next few days."

Sam, pragmatic as ever, looked around.

"How much food have we got in the house, Mum?"

"I think we had better get some more," she said evenly.

"Come on Shani, let's go and stock up."

"Be careful," said Henry. "There were a lot of frayed tempers at Tesco's yesterday, to say the least."

Shani climbed into the passenger seat of the Toyota. Red blossom carpeted` the road beneath a wild cherry tree as they drove past. To Sam, everything looked normal, in its rightful place - except that he knew it wasn't.

He did not head to Tesco's but to Chiefy's. It was some twenty years ago that Ashok Naran and his wife Vajni had bought the Village Store and Post Office. The relentless good cheer of Mr Naran, who greeted every male visitor with a 'Morning Chiefy' or 'Afternoon Chiefy' meant that the shop had gradually taken on the name Chiefy's and even Vajni Naran became Mrs Chiefy. And so, although there were some mutterings when Mr Naran refurbished the building and put up a garish yellow sign with Chiefy's emblazoned across it, it had by then become such a centre of information, gossip and essentials that no one really minded.

Without light, Chiefy's looked forlorn on this morning and inside it was an unusually cheerless 'Morning Chiefy' that greeted Sam. Mr Naran was staring at food from the freezer cabinet. The packets had lost their glaze and were already well on the way to defrosting.

"I don't know what I am going to do, Sam," said Mr Naran, who had known him since he was a small boy. "The milk is going off, all the freezer food is unsaleable and we can't get any supplies."

"We're all in the same boat, Chiefy," said Sam. "No power, no internet, no one knows what's going on. But, look, we need food. We've got several mouths to feed at home. We'll take three of these big shepherd's pies – we need them defrosted anyway."

A van drew up outside. It was a mid-blue transit rusted around the lower edges. Three men got out. Two had shaven heads, a look of cold, muscular disdain on their faces, tattoos snaking up their thick necks and black, military-style boots on their feet. The third man was thin and mean-looking, like a weasel, with a long nose and lanky dark hair. They were carrying large hessian sacks of the kind builders merchants use to deliver sand.

"Morning Chiefy," said Mr Naran bravely.

But the men ignored him. They walked up the aisles sweeping the contents of the shelves and cabinets into the sacks in great armfuls. Swathes of semi-frozen food, the remaining bread, vegetables and fruit, cereals, milk, biscuits, tins of soup and rice pudding disappeared almost before Chiefy or Sam could react.

Out of the corner of his eye, Sam saw Shani slip out of the side door. He headed towards the main door himself. He was not a small man. He had played at number eight for Edinburgh University. Tall and bearded, his blonde hair turning now to brown, he blocked the doorway.

"You need to pay for those things," he said, as the men dragged the sacks towards him.

"Fuck off," sneered the weasel man .

But Sam stood his ground. Chiefy stood behind the till, a nervous smile on his face as if this was just a misunderstanding.

"The till is that way," said Sam.

"Money's no use to anyone now, mate," sneered one of the shaven men, unbuckling a knife from his belt. Almost casually, he strapped the knife to the back of his hand, its grip shaped to his knuckles. The blades like the blades of a ploughshare, only honed and serrated. Four of them.

Chiefy turned and picked up a half bottle of scotch from behind the till. He hurled it at the knife man. It caught him on the side of the head and the man fell, the bottle crashing to the ground behind him. Sam had the measure of the weasel, but the third man slipped by him with a sack. The knife man now rose from the floor, dazed and livid. Chiefy's second bottle thumped off his chest as he turned. Sam picked up a shopping basket, the only protection to hand, and fended off the first lunge. The man lunged again. The knife glanced off the wire tearing straight through his jeans and gouging his thigh. Sam roared with pain. He collapsed against an empty gondola, unable to do more as the men dragged and scraped the other sacks across the ground and into the side door of the van. They kicked the Toyota for good measure as they left.

Blood poured from Sam's furrowed leg. Chiefy rushed over, calling to his wife. Vajni Naran cut his trousers. He winced as she pulled cotton wool from a roll and laid it over the torn flesh, then wrapped a bandage tightly around.

"You were lucky, silly boy," she said. "You need to get to Casualty."

"Fat chance," said Sam. "I'm OK. It's just superficial. He missed the artery by a mile."

Shani came back in. She was shaking.

"Are you OK?" she said. "I was trying to call 999."

"And what happened?"

"Nothing - no signal."

"No, I think we're on our own now," said Sam. "Let's just see if there is anything left here that we can use. Chiefy, do you and Mrs Chiefy have what you need – enough food for yourselves?"

Chiefy nodded.

"We have food, Sam," he said.

Shani and Sam looked around the shop. The dried goods shelf had been missed, and they selected large packs of porridge oats and raisins. Shani picked up some soap and some shampoo. She turned to Chiefy.

"Do you have any tinned milk or condensed milk anywhere, Mr Naran?"

He went over to a shelf at the side. In amongst a chaos of upturned packets that had escaped the looting, he found two tins.

Sam hobbled to the till to pay.

"How much do I owe you, Chiefy?"

"Don't be ridiculous. You tried to defend me against these people."

Sam was suddenly aware that someone else had come into the shop. It was Isabel, their neighbour, a woman who had been virtually a second mother to him in his childhood when Josephine was ill. Her own husband had been killed in a car accident and she lived now on her own with two cats, increasingly frail.

Dressed in her habitual jeans, with her oversized, purple-framed spectacles and her long grey hair snaking over her shoulders, she looked aghast about the store - the blood on the floor, the broken glass and the stench of whisky.

"What's happened? Sam are you all right?"

"I'm OK Izzie. Three bastards just came and raided Chiefy's. We couldn't stop them."

"I am very sorry, Isabel," said Chiefy, as if the lack of provisions and power were somehow his fault.

She appeared almost to crumple.

"What am I going to do? I have virtually no food left at home - all my food comes from Chiefy. How long is all this going to go on, Sam? They must sort it out soon, surely?"

"Heaven knows, Izzie. But come to us tonight," he said, putting his arm around her shoulders. "We'll feed you. Want a ride back?"

He limped out to the car. He pushed the shepherd's pies across the back seat to make room for Isabel, then handed the keys to Shani.

"Think you'd better drive."

Lines from the Second Coming drifted into his head on the way back:

*Things fall apart;*
*The centre cannot hold;*
*Mere anarchy is loosed upon the world,*
*The blood-dimmed tide is loosed,*
*And everywhere*
*The ceremony of innocence is drowned.*

He'd had to learn the poem by rote at school.

.

# CHAPTER IV

HENRY was speaking on the landline when they got back, his face screwed in an effort to hear.

"Maybe we will," he shouted down the phone. "Thanks, bye."

"It was Anne-Marie," he said, putting the phone back in its cradle. "Worried about us. Said we could go up there if we want."

Anne-Marie was his younger sister. She lived on the Isle of Mull in glorious solitude and normally did not bother herself with worldly affairs. Henry looked up.

"Jesus, what happened to you? Jo!" he called.

Josephine had been a doctor until a few years back. She was a small, lean woman, with short, pepper and salt hair and a meticulous way about her. She looked, and somehow withdrew her horror before it had been expressed, as she had been taught.

"Sit down there and put your leg on that stool, darling," she said.

She moved upstairs and returned with scissors, antiseptic and more bandage. She cut Mrs Naran's dressing and gradually pulled it off. Sam winced as the scoured flesh raised with the already congealed blood.

"OK Samuel, I'm going to clean the wound with antiseptic," she said. "It's going to hurt."

Shani smiled. She had never thought of him as Samuel.

Rabiyah watched, then gesticulated, saying something in Shani's direction.

"She was a nurse," said Shani. "She will help you."

Josephine looked across at Rabiyah and held her hands out wide, inviting her to help.

Sam could see, just as they seemed to see, a large fold of flesh, scoured, almost entirely detached from its home, and weeping. Blood oozed in parallel rows behind it. He saw them look, for a brief moment, into each other's eyes. He cried out as the two women wiped the raw flesh as gently as they could with the antiseptic, then gently massaged the fold back into some semblance of its appointed place.

"Are you OK…Samuel?" asked Shani, as they finished the dressing. He pulled her down to him and hugged her.

"Never better," he said. "Dad, we couldn't get anything much at Chiefy's because of those morons. We'll have to go back in to Tesco's."

"I don't think there's a lot of point in doing that," said Henry. "The major came round again while you were out – other people have come back from town. Tesco's has been ransacked. It's just empty shelves, shopping trolleys littered across the car park and broken windows."

"Shit…OK. But still we'll go in and get fuel."

"Same story. I should have joined the queue yesterday. Now apparently there's no fuel, nothing. They've shut up shop. The only good news is that people are using the generator down at the farm to recharge their phones."

"Good news if there was a signal, I suppose."

Shani went across to Rabiyah, speaking quietly with her. She showed her the condensed milk and they moved together towards the kitchen.

\*\*\*\*\*\*

17

It was later, when they were eating the shepherd's pies, somehow successfully heated on the barbecue in the garden, that they saw the first person go past. He was a man dressed in khaki chinos and a blue tee-shirt pulling a wheelie suitcase. He was humming to himself as if he was somehow from a different and superior world and was paying only a temporary visit to this god-forsaken village in the outback. When he heard their voices, he popped his head around the hedge.

"Village Hall this way, mate?" he asked.

"Quarter of a mile down on the left," said Sam.

They all looked at each other.

"Message must have got through," said Henry. "Some fractured form of communication is still happening."

He sat back. There was something about the garden in early June that entranced the senses - the smell of the barbecue smoke, the bees buzzing about the white daisies and the purple clematis on their perennial quest, swallows perched on the telegraph wires, the feel of his bare feet on the cut grass. Nothing of this had changed; yet in the base of his gut, Henry knew that all had changed.

"You feeling better, Izzie?" he asked, turning to Isabel.

"I feel safer now, with all of you," she said. She did indeed look happier.

A couple moved past on the road, wheeling a pushchair, the man hobbling and a baby crying. Noor's little eyes lit up as she heard the sound. An old white Mercedes followed, passengers pressed hard against the windows.

Rabiyah looked over at Shani.

"I feel that I am a burden on you," Shani translated. "I am not your family. I am part of the family that walks along the road. You have been very kind to me, but I should leave you now."

Josephine glared at Henry, warning him not to speak with her gaze.

"Rabiyah," she said. "What is happening is totally new to us. To all of us. You arrived here with Sam and Shani. You are part of our family now. And whatever happens to our family happens to you."

Rabiyah's face lit up as Shani completed the translation, but already another group of people were coming down the road. It was not the pace of their walk but the steady increase in their numbers that hastened Henry's disquiet.

******

Sam lay awake. His leg throbbed at the site of the wound and he slipped out of bed to find some paracetamol.

The bathroom window was open and he did not at first understand the sound he could hear. It was as if a herd of horses were passing, shod not with metal but with something softer. He looked out. A stream of people was pouring past in the summer half light, murmuring, as if re-enacting some Salvador Dali image. He gasped and tiptoed back to bed.

Shani lazily moved her arm across him.

"Are you OK, Samuel?"

He stroked her hair. He recognised the fragrance of the almond shampoo from Chiefy's and drew her to him.

"What is that sound?" she asked.

"It is the sound of hundreds of people walking along the road towards the village hall," he said. "Hundreds. Heaven knows where they're all going to go."

"My God!"

They were silent for a few moments and then, very gently, she moved on top of him, sensitive to the slightest movement that would hurt his wound. She moved slowly and rhythmically and he pulled her down to him until he could feel her nipples against his chest.

"Wait," he whispered, but she did not seem to hear him nor want to pull away.

Somewhere in his unconscious mind, Sam asked himself why he should be worried about protection, when the order of life as he knew it seemed on the verge of collapse, and the act of love was one of the last pieces of reality that remained. He drew her even deeper into him. They lay silently, joined, wishing that these moments could last.

"Perhaps we made a baby," whispered Shani as she carefully lifted her leg away from his wounded limb and rolled back over. He laughed quietly.

# CHAPTER V

HENRY had slept through the unremitting footsteps passing his door during the night. The contemplation of his retirement, which only two days before had seemed so real, now seemed a distant ideal, a memory from some other world. He thought idly that if he could see the spider again, the spider that had woven its web outside the window before all this started, then perhaps things could return to normal. If he could unravel its web. Or did the wren have the answer?

But instead of a  spider or a wren was a sea of people, now backed up and encamped on every side - on the verges, on the pavement, on the road itself, making way only reluctantly if a car came by. The flotsam and jetsam of human life – empty drink cans, plastic bottles, crisp wrappers, lost clothes – were littered everywhere.

Immediately people saw him come out of the house, the questions started. These were people from his own country, from London and the cities and provinces of the UK. In cultured tones, in rough and ready tones, in northern accents and southern accents, they clamoured for help.

"Excuse me, could we possibly fill our water bottles."

"Could I use your toilet, mate, I'm dying for a shit."

Henry prevaricated.

"I'm just going to see what's holding everything up," he said. "I'll be back very soon."

The rain that had prevailed only two days before had been replaced by a ridge of high pressure. It was already hot. He made his way down to the village hall, stepping between the prostrate bodies and the litter. An unfamiliar stench hung in the air. With a gasp, he realised that it emanated from piles of putrid faeces. They were human faeces and they were beginning to cake on the outside, horseflies gathering about them.

The door of the village hall would not give. He peered through the windows. Every inch was filled with people. At the back, the car park and playing fields were crammed.

"Where can we get food? Is there water somewhere?" people called.

The major appeared from the opposite direction.

"This is a bloody mess. They've sent far too many," he said, as if there were some unseen authority directing the refugees.

"I'm putting a sign up at the end of the road to try and stop any more coming, but what the hell do we do with this lot?"

"We need to get them water," said Henry. "Can we rig something up?"

A helicopter flew over. It was painted in matt black, with no other visible markings. It hovered low over the playing fields. People cowered, terrified, while others raised their arms, as if expecting a food-drop as they had seen on television in some famine-stricken, war-torn African country. But the helicopter merely circled, then swooped to the west.

"Fuckin' ISIS," somebody shouted and a shiver of fear ran through the crowd.

Fragments of information had been gathered from texts, snatched telephone conversations and occasional internet connection with Al Jazira. All were jumbled together like letters of the alphabet in a Scrabble bag, mixed and regurgitated in no particular order and without authority, yet gaining credence with every telling.

"Army's been infiltrated by extremists."

"Nuclear power stations blown up."

"VX nerve gas in London."

"Water poisoned in Manchester."

"Chaos at airports."

"Massive cyber attack."

"Terrorists holding the government to ransom."

Everything was plausible individually but nothing as a whole.

Henry found a hose from the allotments and fought his way into the village hall with the major. They attached one end to a tap and fed the rest of it outside through a window. A woman on the playing field took control. Though her blue coat was torn, her boots muddy, her face scratched and her greying blonde hair wild from the rain, she had the sort of strident voice that people obeyed. She recruited others as her officers and gradually they organised first the people on the playing field and then the closest of the people on the road to fill their water bottles or any receptacle they could lay their hands on. Some had nothing and simply picked up squashed cans or plastic bottles from the ground.

Henry made his way back. He was pleased with his work.

"We've fixed something up," he called to those who'd asked for water. "That way," he pointed.

The crowd had expanded onto Isabel's lawn. She, to her credit, appeared to be carrying a tray of cold drinks and digestive biscuits back and forth as if catering for her builder or plumber. But, even as Henry watched, more and more people came towards her, like the inexorable flow of lava from an angry volcano.

An ugly commotion greeted him when he reached home.

"Bloody muslims!"

"They've got ISIS people in there."

Unwittingly, Rabiyah, wearing her hijab, had gone outside to feed Noor. Josephine had called her back in straight away, but the damage had been done. They closed the doors and waited, uncertain.

\*\*\*\*\*\*

Just an hour later Isabel appeared, drained and exhausted.

"There are too many of them," she said. "I can't do any more."

She collapsed at the kitchen table, her head in her hands. From an upstairs window, Henry watched helplessly as a man leant against her front door. He threw himself against it once, then again. This time, with a loud crack, it splintered and people poured inside.

In the corner of an old wardrobe was a twelve bore that he'd inherited from his father. He had not used it in many years and wondered now whether the cartridges would still function. He broke the gun and peered down the barrel. The oil that he had applied long ago seemed to have kept the rust at bay. He loaded two cartridges. Sam limped into the room.

"Dad, what the hell are you doing?"

Henry nodded out of the window towards Isabel's house.

"Christ!"

He was quiet for a while.

"Still, Dad, no, you can't. It's pointless. Keep it for later."

Henry looked at him.

"What do you mean – later?" he asked, but then, "You're right."

He took out the cartridges and put the gun back in its case. He saw a woman with a baby in her arms and a toddler at her feet approach the front door. She was pleading with Josephine. And then he saw his wife open the door wider, allowing them in. He shuddered. The last bastion of his freedom was being breached. Yet he could see that there was no alternative. Perhaps, this way, they could control the flow.

"How can we work this?" he said to Josephine, back downstairs.

"I've put them in the lounge," she said.

"It's got to be women and small children first, and anyone sick, and then we'll see."

"I sound like the captain of a sinking ship," he said, hearing his own words as if from some outer body.

With Sam's tall figure policing the door, Henry moved away. It did not take long for a crowd of dishevelled women and children to step gratefully inside. To the fathers, he said no.

Rabiyah tended to the sick and injured, smiling and nodding to them as they spoke to her as if she understood. The people filled the lounge, and then they filled the dining-room.

"We're full," said Josephine. "We can't take any more."

But another family pushed forward. The woman started shouting at Sam. The husband joined in, a barrel-chested man with a mane of curly hair, and pushed past. He could not stop them. Little family groups were now spread across the hallway and the stairs.

Sam closed the door and bolted it, eyeing the crowd outside. Henry turned. The carpet on the way to the bathroom was already plastered with mud but he was not expecting what he saw when he went inside. The toilet bowl was blocked, the paper, faeces and urine of a score of people swirling uselessly. Someone had thrown up and though they'd made it this far, they'd missed the bowl. Its foul smell filled the air and he wondered idly if the contents of their stomach had been bought in some other time when food was close at hand. It looked to him like pizza.

He went upstairs again, a temporary haven, then watched as a group of men marched across the garden. They leant against the wooden door of the garden shed until it gave, then began to pull out its contents. Deck chairs, the mower, paint pots, tools, old bicycles, all came tumbling out. More men appeared and a fight seemed to break out over the ownership of this new-found space.

He heard a shout from the kitchen. He found Josephine turning the cold tap one way and then the other. There was a gurgle and the sound of air passing through. A few drips appeared, and then nothing.

"Oh shit!" said Sam.

"I don't think this is tenable any longer," said Henry. "We're going to have to pull out."

Sam nodded.

"Get what we can into the Toyota. "

He took his father aside.

"Dad, put the gun in."

Then louder, "There'll still be some water in the hot water tank. Mum, do you have any big bottles?"

Josephine produced some empty lemonade bottles. Her face was set in a look of tense determination. She reached for a large briefcase.

"What's that?" said Henry.

"All the documents," she said. "Passports, laptop, driving licences, title deeds, cash."

"My God."

He took the briefcase and stowed it quickly under the driver's seat. The bread and water that he had bought in Tesco's, the porridge oats and raisins from Chiefy's, the contents of the fridge and food cupboards were thrown into the back.

"Bring matches and candles," said Sam.

"What about fuel?"

"The spare can is petrol – it's useless for the Toyota."

"Bring it anyway."

People were milling about outside, brushing against the windows. There were shouts from the hall. Someone was thumping on the kitchen door.

"We need to be really quick," said Sam.

"Can we get everyone in?"

They looked at each other, realising suddenly the enormity of the question.

"Mum and I, you and Shani," said Henry.

"We can fit one more."

# CHAPTER VI

A CALM sea cradled Anne-Marie's boat. She guided it into the mooring, as she had always done, for years now it seemed. There was no wind, and the hills encircling the bay were purple with heather. Her weekly supply trip had become a tradition almost, a connection to the outside world. Fraser would regale her with the local news and she would glance through the Highland Times and the Scotsman.

She waited for Fraser to come out and catch the rope, but there was no sign of him. There was a silence about the wooden jetty, just the creaking of the Lizzie, his fishing boat, and the Lady Ffiona, his supply boat, as he called it, stretching against their moorings nearby. No human sound, no voices or radio or clatter of machinery, disturbed the rise and fall of the sea – the endless breath of the waves.

Then Rabbie barked. He appeared from the old sheep house at the back and came hopping down the gangway on his three legs, his black and white coat and handsome, comical  face – one eye in the white half, the other in the black - scuffed and dirty. He stood on the jetty looking at Anne-Marie. 'Thank god you're here,' he seemed to be saying. He'd been caught in a snare a long time back. Fraser had come upon him and rescued him.

"He'll outlive me, that collie," he used to say. "He's more intelligent than any of us."

Anne-Marie edged the boat in more gently now. Stretching for the post, her limbs protesting - for she was no longer as agile as she had once been - she coiled the rope around it. Clinging onto the chain that ran the length of the jetty supporting a line of ancient half-tyres, she pulled alongside and stepped out.

Far enough back to escape the highest tides, yet close enough to the shore to be battered by the winds and the spray of the fiercest waves, Fraser's house stood proud and white, unbowed by the weathers. A soldier, a platoon even, refusing to give ground to the advancing enemy. With a chimney at each end and two windows in the roof, the house faced square west and many an evening she had passed with him watching the sunset.

"Och, they'll never make another like that 'un," he'd say every time.

But this day the house was empty. Anne-Marie called. Rabbie barked again. Otherwise there was only silence. She bent down and patted him.

"Where's he gone, boy?" she asked, and in the plaintiff sound that came in reply, half whine, half growl, she sensed the answer.

She looked about. The pick-up, an ancient, army-green VW, was not in the lean-to behind the house. Fraser had gone in to Fort William then – that much was clear. If he took the Lady Ffiona, he went to Oban; if he took the pick-up, he drove up to the Corran ferry and on to Fort William. He would decide at the last minute - it depended on weather and weight and what he needed to collect or repair.

She searched the house. A cup of cold coffee sat on the kitchen table. His ancient mobile that always sat beside the solid black landline telephone and played the old

Nokia ring tone, was gone too. She called the number but there was only static.

The problem was not that Fraser was away in the pick-up. The problem was not that Anne-Marie did not have her oranges, the repaired chain saw, the fuel, the case of Glen Isla. The problem was that, in his normal routine, Fraser would have been back the day before.

She knew of course of the situation on the mainland – some of it anyway. That was why she had called Henry. But that brief shouted conversation had done nothing to assuage her fears. Somehow she had not expected the breakdown of the normal day to day run of things to impinge on her own life so suddenly.

She tried to boil Fraser's electric kettle, but there was no power. She poured water into a saucepan and turned on the calor gas. The water here came from the stream that sluiced down the cliff in a white curtain of spray every day of the year. It tasted of peat.

She looked around the room. A photograph of Fraser as a young man with Ffiona stood above the dresser. They had made a handsome couple. He had been a striking man, she thought, with his red hair and craggy jaw. Ffiona was long gone now and only a hint of ginger remained amidst the grey.

The house smelt a little of the man, with a hint of damp mixed in. It was never the neat and tidy home that Rhona, his mother, had kept, but it was warm. A tartan rug was slung across a square -ended sofa, dog hairs, Rabbie's hairs, all over it. Anne-Marie had often wondered how many years it was since that rug had been washed.

Candles sat in the top of old wine bottles, a lava flow of wax cascading down the sides, frozen in time. Watercolours hung on three walls – paintings that Rhona had done. On the fourth wall hung a display of butterflies – swallowtails and fritillaries – that Fraser himself had mounted.

She sat down to think. What was the last word Henry had said at the end of the shouted, almost inaudible, conversation?

'Ill, kill, pill, 'til, will?'

'Perhaps we will?' Those were the words she hoped she'd heard. Balmanie had always been a safe haven.

# CHAPTER VII

SAM LOOKED across at Rabiyah and Noor, and at Isabel.

How could he abandon Rabiyah, with this tiny baby? He could only imagine her full story. How could he leave her at the mercy of these people in the house and outside, unthinking bigots amongst them? And yet images of Isabel walking him to school, Isabel making his tea, Isabel helping him with his homework and hugging him flashed through his mind – the woman who had been his surrogate mother for six months while Josephine lay helpless, struck down by the illness, and his father in Iraq.

He could see his mother brushing the ball of her right thumb repeatedly against the back of her left hand – a sure sign of her agitation.

Shani was watching him, her hand to her mouth.

"How did it come to this?" Henry breathed, barely audible.

"Do you have milk? We really need milk for the baby?"

"I will come in a second," called Henry. He leant against the door.

"Rabiyah, Isabel," said Sam. "We have no time, seconds. I'm going to flip a coin. The first flip, Isabel has the call, the second flip Rabiyah. We go on until someone has two correct flips. The first with two correct calls comes with us."

Shani machine-gunned her way through the words, and Sam flipped.

"Heads."

It was tails.

"Heads," Rabiyah called. It was heads.

"Tails," said Isabel this time, and it was.

They had one call each.

"Let Rabiyah and the baby go," said Isabel, holding up her hand. "I am old. I can take care of myself."

Shani spoke to Rabiyah, and listened, urgently.

"No, please. I am already a refugee, you cannot leave her here."

Sam swallowed. The banging on the door was louder and more insistent.

"Seconds," he said. "Rabiyah's call."

She stuck with heads. The coin spun on the table, then landed with the Queen's head to the sky.

Henry put his arms around Isabel, his back still braced against the door as someone tried to push it open from the other side.

"I'll be all right," she said, but there was fear in her eyes. "I'll follow in my own car."

"Do you have your keys, Izzie?" There was no time to tell her about her house.

She held up a keyring.

"We'll meet you at the end of the road then," he whispered.

"Don't think. Go, go, go; get in the Toyota," commanded Sam, pointing to the back door.

He swept up an armful of coats and hats from their pegs as he ran from the house, hurling them on top of his mother, Shani and Rabiyah in the back of the Landcruiser. They had all forgotten about his leg and only the driver's seat was empty. He raced around the front. The barrel-chested man was already charging through the kitchen. Other people were coming towards the vehicle.

Wincing, Sam jammed it into reverse and swung around, the back hitting the house as it turned throwing up a spray of gravel. He gunned the engine. Bodies leapt to their feet on the driveway. A man leant half-way over the bonnet, waving his arms. Sam heard a thud as he turned onto the road but there was no time to look back.

Suddenly, directly in front of him, was a little girl with curly blonde hair. She was carrying a doll.

"Look out," shouted Henry.

Sam could see her mouth open, her blue eyes. He dragged the wheel to the left, the Toyota climbing the kerb and the bank, veering, then skidding back onto the road with a crunch, his head hitting the roof as it came down. Shani was screaming in the back; the baby was crying.

And then he saw the doll. Somehow, as she'd leapt out of the way, the girl had thrown her doll to the side. In slow motion he took in its every feature. Its straw blonde hair, its orange gypsy smock, its purple pantaloons. And beyond all that, its warm innocent smile.

He swerved again, wrestling with the wheel, but he was too late. There was nowhere to go. He heard the sound of crushing plastic. He could picture in his mind the fragments of broken doll on the road. He wanted to stop and say sorry to the girl but he knew he could not. In a daze, his leg screaming, it was all he could do to drive out of the village.

He pulled in at the entrance to a field and buried his head in his hands. Everyone was silent for a moment, until Noor whimpered again. Sam looked up, then slammed his fist against the steering wheel.

"I just couldn't avoid it," he said,.

Shani stroked his hair from behind.

"What do you mean?" she asked.

"The doll. There was nowhere else to go…"

"But you missed all the people, darling," said Josephine gently.

She pulled a pack of paracetamol from her pocket .Sam nodded, swallowing two in one gulp.

"Dad, you'd better take over driving."

"We'll give Izzie another five minutes," said Henry as they changed places. But even as he said it, a group of ten or more youths appeared from the hedge that bordered the road.

They approached the Toyota.

"No time, Dad – GO."

# CHAPTER VIII

ANNE-MARIE looked at Fraser's landline phone again. She would pay him for the call, she thought, when he re-appeared. She punched in the numbers and could hear the ring.

"Hello." It was a hunted, gaunt, doleful voice.

"Hello – Henry, is that you? Sam?"

"There's no one here love. Nothing here. They've gone. Left us – just a few minutes ago. Where are you love? We need help. There's children, old folk, people everywhere, and no food, no water. There's a woman says she lives next door – she's been taken ill. Can you help us?"

Anne-Marie was speechless. Christ, she thought, he must be talking about Isabel. She'd met her a few times when she'd stayed with Henry – usually marriages or deaths.

"I'll do what I can," she said eventually, knowing that the situation, whatever it was, was completely beyond her control. Then, as an afterthought, she asked, "Did they leave by car?"

"Yes love. Just left us. One minute they were here, the next they were gone like greased lightning."

"How many of them?"

"Two older folk. Younger man, maybe son and probably his girlfriend. And another woman with a baby. Carload."

"I'm sorry," said Anne-Marie.

She could think of nothing else to say and put the phone down. She stared out of the window at her boat with its sea-worn white hull and black rim and matching black and white outboard. She could hear, faintly, its rhythmic tapping and rattling as it bobbed beside the jetty.

The Lady Ffiona beyond was not unlike her boat, just a little longer and navy, with a red Evinrude outboard beneath a protective cover. An irregular orange stripe ran along the sides. The Lizzie, however – the Royal Yacht, as Anne-Marie liked to call it – was a proper boat according to Fraser. Her sky blue paint faded and weather-beaten, she had an onboard Perkins engine and central wheelhouse. She was, in fact, a small fishing vessel, built for the vagaries of the Hebridean waters and as sturdy now as when she had been built forty-three years previously.

"The Lizzie would take us to Newfoundland if she had to," Fraser had said.

Anne-Marie shuddered at the thought of that journey. But she had been out on the Lizzie with Fraser often enough on fishing trips and to see the kittiwakes on Staffa. She had taken the wheel on a few occasions. She didn't understand the Garmin GPS, the depth finder, the path locator and all the other electronic gadgetry that Fraser had installed, but she could move it.

On the spur of the moment, she started writing on the back of an old envelope that lay on the dresser. She wrote for several minutes, then rummaged through Fraser's drawers until she found a plastic bag. She inserted the paper and sealed the bag. She wrote again, this time to Fraser.

'Have taken the Royal Yacht and looking after Rabbie. Call me when you get back. Will explain.

A-M.'

She left the message on the kitchen table under a red and purple mug that proclaimed 'Keep Calm and Go Fishing.' She washed up the dirty plates.

"C'mon Rabbie," she said.

She picked up a large stone and clambered back onto her own boat. She placed the plastic bag on the forward seat plank, below the prow, the stone on top. Now she released the ropes and picked up the oars. She pushed herself off and, with a few strokes, was alongside the Lizzie.

With her left hand she held her boat's rope while with the right she clung to the Lizzie, pulling her level. Rabbie leapt across without hesitation. Standing carefully, Anne-Marie climbed across, stretching for the edge of the wheelhouse for balance. She wound the rope against a cleat on the deck, then moved aft, securing the stern of the two boats. They moved together now, in harmony, like conjoined twins.

She picked up the boat hook and moved to the prow. Fishing in the water, she caught the Lizzie's small pick-up buoy and hauled it in. She unhitched the forward rope from her own boat and attached it to the buoy with a mooring hitch. Knots had never been a problem for her. From Brownies onwards, she had always understood the loops and twists of rope, while many of her peers sat shrugging and beaten.

Stumbling across a rusty chain that lay across the deck, she entered the wheelhouse. The red button beside the lever was marked 'Forward', 'Reverse', 'Neutral'. It was clear enough. She pressed and the engine coughed into life. She checked the fuel gauge. All seemed to be well. Now she released the aft of her boat from the Lizzie and then the Lizzie herself from the buoy.

She was shocked by the power she felt in her hands when she engaged the gear – the power of a wild stallion straining at unseen reins. Reversing a little way, she watched Fraser's bothie recede into the distance. No smoke curled from its chimney and the hills behind looked darker. The wind was getting up now. She had just enough time to get across.

She wondered whether Henry would remember the route to the old house, the haggis route as they used to call it when they were teenagers. She'd felt invulnerable in those days and knew Henry felt the same. They weren't of course. That was how they'd lost Emma. She had always wanted to be as strong as her older twin brother and sister. She'd tried to do it on her own, or at least that's what everyone thought. Though now - when she remembered Emma's dark days when she would not come out of her room, and her bright days when she was like the shimmering coloured swirl of a dancer, so beautiful and uncatchable - she wondered.

Her father had found the remains of the boat washed up on the north side of the island, but they never found Em's body. Though she was in London at the time, Anne-Marie had always felt guilty that she had not been with her little sister.

Emma could have taken the conventional route, of course, the ferry to Craignure or Fishnish, or even Tobermory, and Mum or Dad would have picked her up. But all three of them preferred the haggis route – the descent through the pines down the narrow track to the bothie where Fraser now lived; the smell of the sea, the assessment of the waves, the wind and the tide, the view of the island. Was it shrouded in mist or fog? Would they be able to make the crossing (forty minutes on a good day) before the weather turned, before darkness fell, before their landmark, the chimneys of Balmanie, disappeared from sight? The decision to go or no-go.

Their destination was the big rambling stone house that had been built by their great grandfather. It stood above the bay, looking East across the Sound towards the old castle. To the North lay Morvern on the mainland. Loch Linnhe stretched inland to the North-East and, on a clear day, Ben Nevis could be seen, towering above the land. Douglas firs protected the house from the coldest winds from the North, and wide lawns encircled it on three sides. They'd played endlessly on those lawns as children.

The front door of the house was guarded by two stone pillars. Inside, the wooden floor boards, uneven in places, were worn to a deep and creaking patina. The rooms were large, with huge sash windows looking out over the sea or across the island, but always they seemed a little dark, as though the light was spent before it could reach their farthest corners. Four tall chimneys stood proud of the house peaking in places above the trees, giving away its location. The garden was filled with rhododendrons and azaleas and in spring they would create a palette of colour – orange, white, pink and mauve.

The bedrooms had come to be known by the name of their occupant – Henry's room, Anne-Marie's room, Em's room, Mum and Dad's room, the spare room, the green room. And when friends or cousins came to stay in the summer, they would cram into whichever room was most appropriate. That was the case until they were teenagers, when girlfriends or boyfriends who had been lodged in spare rooms might be heard creeping down the corridor in the night.

Balmanie House was its official name, though everyone just referred to it as Balmanie, and, after their grandparents, who had lived on the island, died, it became a holiday home for the family and a haven for anyone needing a respite from the demands of life.

Rhona McBride, Fraser's mother, had looked after the house in those days. She had watched the three children grow up. She would ask no questions when they appeared

– sometimes by car by the ferry route, sometimes on foot through the trees with only a rucksack, but maybe also a friend. She had cried with everyone else at the funeral but somehow Emma's death had broken a spell. Henry became busy with his own work and family, and was increasingly abroad and it was Anne-Marie who eventually became the guardian of Balmanie.

For a while, in the '70's, she'd turned it into a retreat centre for Tibetan Buddhists. The drawing room became a meditation room, a shrine at the centre. Some people would spend three months there on silent retreats, others would simply come for a week or two and would help out chopping vegetables or wood, gardening or sweeping up. A few times Tengpa Rinpoche would come to stay and other attendant monks. They would cut quite a sight wandering through the gardens and the pine woods in their burgundy and saffron robes, the sounds of their chanting and the resonance of the Tibetan gong, the deep note of OM that quietly called to the people and the birds and the trees, mesmerising all who heard it.

But gradually, as harsh realities hit and the '70's became the '80's, people left and Anne-Marie was on her own again. As a sixties child, she had had her fair share of boyfriends, but none had lasted. She had had no great desire to have children and so, when the last man left, she simply carried on, quite happy to live a secluded life with her books, her garden and the island.

She would wander down to the shore sometimes and sit on the grass above the rocks and listen to the sea. She knew its every mood – its dalliance with the wind and the clouds, its quiet silent moments and its sudden furies. She would feel, sitting there, that there was nothing else, that she had reached the end of the world.

# CHAPTER IX

"I'M GOING to head for Balmanie," said Henry, glancing back. "It shouldn't take us more than a couple of days if we can get through."

He knew, and he knew that Sam knew, that they did not have enough fuel to get to Carlisle in the Landcruiser, let alone the Highlands. But he was not going to worry everyone with this information just now – it was hard enough negotiating the next moment.

"God, I hope Izzie makes it out," said Sam.

Black crows arced and wheeled over the silent roads waiting for their moment of roadkill. They reminded Henry of a book he'd read way back when he was at university. The black crows spelled out a man's fate in Carlos Castaneda's world – a world based on mescalin - and Henry, who had sampled the delights of hallucinogens in his day, felt now a sort of clarity. Everything was etched in outline, the trees, the crows, the road, the hedges - as if photo-shopped to a more perfect clarity than that presented by the human eye – and he knew what he must do.

A few other cars passed, and he eyed them with suspicion, taut and aware. A tractor moved slowly in the opposite direction, the trailer behind it filled with children. The children were playing in the back like puppy dogs, oblivious, seemingly, to the plight of the world outside them. Henry wondered where they had come from and where on earth they could be going.

Sam clicked on the satnav. The screen fired up, then froze. 'There is a system error. Reboot your device,' said the voice accusingly.

"Stupid woman," he said.

He tried the radio. On Five Live there was a hint of the SOS signal behind a blizzard of white noise. 'En Angleterre, la grande crise continue. La gouvernement ...' he could hear on some European station, before the broadcast became unintelligible.

"Are you going to try the motorway, Dad?" he asked, stretching his leg out now against the passenger glovebox and massaging his thigh vigorously.

Henry looked across. He was so proud of his son and so helpless in the face of his injury. He wished he could take him to a hospital, or conjure some antibiotics to his aid.

"What do you think?"

"It's the devil and the deep blue sea. If we try the motorway, it might be completely blocked somewhere. If we go on the main roads, we have to keep going through towns, and who knows what we'll find?"

"I think I'll go up to the M5. See how it looks. It's safer...I think. The further north we can get with as little fuel as possible, then maybe the craziness will be less."

"Makes sense," said Sam, wincing

At that moment, Noor started crying and a wet, squelching sound came from the back seat.

"Ohhhh," cried Rabiyah.

"Don't worry," said Josephine. "That was going to happen sooner or later."

Shani translated, stroking the baby's head.

"Poo," she said, pointing at the baby's bottom.

Rabiyah held her nose and everyone laughed. But it was a kind of manic laughter, thought Henry as he drove on.

"Pfoof, open your window, Sam," said Shani after several minutes.

"The baby needs to be changed," said Josephine, "Can we stop before we get on the motorway?"

They drove down a side road and pulled in by a field. Rabiyah got out with Noor.

"No nappies," said Shani.

Josephine pulled a box of Kleenex from the passenger seat. They cleaned Noor and she looked around for somewhere to put the soiled tissues. There was nowhere. Josephine, who in normal times would stop the car and pick up litter from the road leading to the village, held her hands up to the sky in imprecation, then dumped them beside the road. She took the dirty nappy into the field and wiped it again and again against the long grass as best she could. Lining it with more tissues, she handed it back to Rabiyah.

"It's all we can do," she said grimly "…Unless we can get hold of a pack of pampers."

They circled the roundabout above the motorway. The road looked clear.

"Go?" said Henry, raising his eyebrows towards his son, wanting complicity in the decision.

"Go," said Sam, and they headed down the slip road.

# CHAPTER X

ANNE-MARIE eased the Lizzie along the channel
that wound between the rocks and glided into calm
waters. From the sea, the two overlapping promontories
appeared to be continuous shoreline. It was only when you
sailed in close that the secret harbour, as they called it,
became visible. It had been a safe haven for Anne-Marie
and Henry in real terms, keeping successive boats safe; and
in metaphorical terms, welcoming them home. Even when
the seas were at their wildest, the waters here would merely
shiver with the slightest swell.

Anne-Marie cut the engine some way out, allowing
Fraser's boat to drift in slowly towards the orange buoy
where her dinghy bobbed. Though the buoy had been set
for her own boat, she judged that the water here would be
just deep enough, even at low tide, to accommodate the
Lizzie.

It was, however, an old style buoy with a ring at the
top. It was easy enough to pick this up from her boat, but
the deck of the Lizzie was covered at the prow and higher.
She collected the coiled mooring rope and grabbed the
boat hook again. Allowing the bow of the Lizzie to slip

past, she hooked the ring and pulled the buoy alongside. Now, from the aft deck, she could just reach it.

She threaded the rope through and made it fast, then, using the boat-hook once more, drew the dinghy alongside. She took a deep breath – this would be hard enough on her own, let alone with a dog. Gripping the side of the Lizzie, she leant forward. She swung her left leg down into the centre of the dinghy. She waited for it to settle, then brought her right leg over. The dinghy began to move away but she still held the side of Fraser's boat and, by shifting her weight, steadied it. Rabbie was now barking furiously, standing on his three legs on the aft seat.

"Come on, Rabbie," she called. She pointed to the dinghy. "Come on, boy."

For a moment, she thought he would jump, but he froze, glaring at the water. She patted the seat of the dinghy and tried one more time.

"Come on, boy."

It was no use. She manoeuvred the dinghy round. Releasing her grip on the bigger boat and praying that there was no sudden swell or gust of wind, she stood up, sweeping him into her arms. The collie yelped and writhed, and momentarily she was unbalanced. She fell backwards, casting him into the water as she caught herself.

"No! Rabbie!" she shouted, terrified that the dog would be unable to swim. "Shit!"

She picked up the oars and began to row towards him, but Rabbie was already paddling towards the shore, now apparently unconcerned.   He shook himself wildly, spraying her with water, as she beached.  She stowed the oars and dragged the fibreglass dinghy across the stones and up to its home above the highest tideline, securing it to a tree.

They climbed together, woman and dog, back up through the pines and rhododendrons towards the house. Rabbie  ran amongst the bushes, excited to be back here, remembering, apparently, old trails. They could have taken the path that skirted the shoreline, but Anne-Marie preferred the track through the middle. These days it was so overgrown that it was only she that knew it. She could recognise it from the trees that lined the route, the angle of the hill, the occasional glimpses of the sea.

A long meadow stretched from the wood to the back of the house. It was bordered, on the inland side, by an area of rough ground, almost moorland, strewn with bracken and lichen-covered boulders. Anne-Marie's own Jack Russell, Aragorn, came rushing up to meet them as they emerged into the open, barking excitedly. He looked at her askance, then dashed off into the undergrowth with Rabbie, determined to show his old friend who was boss.

Anne-Marie pushed the back door open - she never bothered to lock it - and pulled off her boots. She opened a tin of dog food. She was going to fill two bowls, but then she stopped. They're going to have to deal with this too, she thought. She only half-filled the bowls and called for them. They ate as if they'd never eaten before, then looked at her, pleadingly.

'What, is that it?' they seemed to be asking. She nodded at them.

"Yes, that's it," she said out loud. "There's strange stuff going on."

The dogs lapped up some water and ambled off, seeming to accept the situation. Something made Anne-Marie stop and listen – a slight change in the sounds that rumbled and echoed around the old house. The generator had kicked in.

"Dammit," she muttered.

The central power supply on the island had cut out. It happened in mid-winter sometimes when the snow was thick, never in summer. She went to the generator settings and turned them to manual and off.

She dreamt that night of a great eagle sweeping Henry off the sea and bringing him back to Balmanie. But then the seas became rough and the boats were being thrown around and Fraser appeared. He was bloodied. His beard was cut to one side and his eyes, though kind, were wild. He said, there, there, that one and seemed to be pointing. But when she asked him who, who he was pointing at, it was too vague. It washed away and she could not fathom his words and it was all gone.

# CHAPTER XI

HENRY was frightened, but, for the sake of Josephine especially, he was trying not to show it. He could remember, vaguely, and without definition, hitch-hiking as a student back in the late sixties with no food in his rucksack and no clear idea of where he was going. He remembered once being so hungry that he had eaten the young leaves of a stinging nettle in a stale roll. He would carry a sleeping bag and a tent on his back and just pitch it where he ended up. Usually, that would be with other 'heads' and the evening would pass. Stoned, by a fire.

Those carefree days were long gone. He had not camped for twenty-five years or more, when Sam was very small. A secure roof over his head was no longer sufficient. A glass of wine, an air-conditioned room, were his minimum requirements now – or had been. Yet here he was, just four days into his retirement, embarking on a journey the outcome of which he had absolutely no idea. Not, he thought, that it would have made any difference whether he had retired the day he did or not. If, in theory, he had still been working for Sirios Oil, he would still today have been driving up the M5 in a dirty bronze-coloured Toyota Landcruiser with his wife, his son, his son's girlfriend and a refugee from Syria and her baby, through a world of uncertainty.

He could almost touch Josephine's anxiety as she scratched at her wrist and gnawed her lower lip. He wondered how long she could last without her medication. He could guess the thoughts that must be burrowing like worms in her mind, eating away at her – what would those people do to their house, would they see their house again, how were they going to get to Anne Marie, how were they going to eat, how could they look after this baby?

"What's that?" said Sam, suddenly.

Ahead of them, the cars that were on the road seemed to be bunching to the right, their brake lights on or flashing on and off.

"Careful, Dad. We don't want to get caught with nowhere to go."

As they got closer, they could see cars stopped and slewed across the outside and central lanes, people standing or leaning against their vehicles. Henry felt a hidden momentum to just follow the flow of traffic, to move to the outside lane. An image rose in his mind of the murdered of Srebrenica - he had always wondered why they hadn't risen up en masse when they were told to walk to the freshly-dug graves, to kneel in them and lower their heads. Was it exhaustion, hunger, fear? Or just a kind of herd instinct to do as instructed?

"Drive onto the emergency lane," said Sam. "Don't go right."

Henry had to force himself to swing the steering wheel to the left.

They made ground for a quarter of a mile until in front of them loomed a truck, stationary and wide. There was no space on the right, and even on the left, the grass verge was blocked by a white van. The motorway here was flanked by a bank on either side, a cutting through some ancient hill country and woodland. Sam looked around, then pointed. It took a moment for Henry to understand what he meant. He shoved the vehicle into four-wheel drive.

"Hold tight!"

The Toyota responded valiantly, forging up the grassy bank like a racehorse. From the top, they could see a maelstrom of stationary vehicles on the northbound carriageway. Southbound was clear. Behind them, a bright red Ford Fiesta seemed to be trying to follow their path, but stalled in its efforts, its wheels spinning, flailing in the grass like a giant ladybird. To the left a patchwork of fields, woods and farmland passed as Henry sought an exit.

"There," said Shani. "That gate."

Henry turned the wheel.

"Lean right," he shouted as the Toyota hung precariously downhill, but they were already doing so.

"Careful!" cried Josephine.

Saplings brushed the windows on either side and thickets of bramble reared in front of them as the Toyota lurched down the slope . There was a thud as the undercarriage grounded against some unseen branch or rock. At the bottom, a rivulet lay between them and the dry land beyond.

Henry accelerated gradually, purring the wheels into submission. For a moment they spun, then grabbed the bank on the other side. He stopped in front of the gate. Sam looked pleadingly towards the back. Shani got out and struggled with a chain for a while, then threw up her hands in despair.

"It's locked," she cried, holding up a large padlock. "It won't open."

Henry reversed the Landcruiser along the narrow space between the bank and the fence bordering the fields.

"OK," he said decisively and took a deep breath.

"What on earth are you doing?" asked Josephine.

"It's OK, Dad, go for it," said Sam, ignoring his mother.

Henry slammed the vehicle into first, his foot on the accelerator. They picked up speed - there was no time to think. He spun the wheel towards the gate. A crash and the old wood gave in without a struggle. Splintered timbers scraped along the side, but they were through.

They found themselves on ground that was neither track nor ploughed field – a strip of land that had been left untouched. They followed the line of a hedge until, rounding a small copse, they could see farm buildings in a fold in the hills below them. Henry drove steadily, negotiating the ruts, wary of movement from the farm. He stopped a few hundred yards from the buildings.

"I think we need to check this place out before we drive in," he said.

"I'll go," said Shani, but Sam heaved himself out and, with the aid of a stick, limped towards the buildings with her.

Henry, Josephine and Rabiyah watched. They saw them move forward, then stop and look at each other and clutch hands.

"There's someone lying in the yard," said Sam when he got back. "It's all quiet."

They drove in in silence. The body of a woman was on the concrete, green bile, congealed, tracking from the corner of her mouth and down her chin. Her trousers were torn and soiled where her bowels had released and bare, stippled flesh peered from her waist. Horseflies filled the foul air around her.

"Dear God," said Josephine. "These people too. What have we done? What has happened to them?"

Circumspectly, they moved towards the farm house. Sam lifted the latch of a claret door, flakes of thick paint peeling away from its face. It led into a small scullery. The bare brick walls might once have been whitewashed, but now carried the colour of dust and cobwebs and years of neglect. On the floor were scores of jam jars, along with a random collection of wellington boots. Old paint pots sat on makeshift shelves and a long-handled broom lay against them.

To the right, a door opened into the farmhouse kitchen. It was dark and silent. The oak chairs and table and cupboards wore an expression of careworn toil. No hint of modern design had touched this place. A musty smell – of age, of generations, of no sunlight – lingered in the air and the same faecal stench as outside. A coffee filter pot, still tepid, sat on the table and white and orange chrysanthemums, only just beginning to wilt, lay beside a vase.

"It's almost like she was trying to cheer the place up," murmured Henry, moving across the kitchen to an archway that opened to a narrow hall beyond. In the dim light he saw the boot first. And then the rest of the body, half-concealed in the mess of coats and hats and waterproofs and walking sticks. This time it was a man, his blue dungarees smeared in the same green bile, his face etched in pain.

"Christ!" said Sam.

A sound came from the kitchen. He spun. Rabiyah had turned on the tap, a tumbler poised in her hand.

"Noooo!" he shouted. Half-hopping, half-stumbling, he dived towards her and swatted the glass away before it touched the baby's lips. He crashed to the floor, the glass in smithereens around him; Rabiyah backed against a dresser, her wide brown eyes shocked and accusatory, Noor screaming.

"What the hell did you do that for?" said Henry angrily.

"The water's poisoned," Sam said. "I knew there was something when I saw the woman in the yard. God, it's only about four days ago, but Chris and Natalie in London. It was the same…green. Green shit, Dad."

Still on the floor and grimacing in pain, he looked over at Rabiyah. He touched his chest with his palm, then opened both hands to her in apology

"I'm sorry but…"

He pointed to the taps and made a slitting throat gesture with his right hand, leaving Shani to explain.

# CHAPTER XII

"THERE'S got to be a tank for the tractors," said Sam. "What's that over there?"

"We can't just help ourselves," said Josephine.

"Mother, it's about four hundred miles to Balmanie from here, and we've got fuel for another hundred and fifty. Do you want to get there or not?"

There could be no argument with this logic. Josephine did not respond and looked down. Henry manoeuvred the Toyota to the fuel tank, filling up with the red tractor diesel. They hunted around for spare cans or anything that would carry the fuel. Some plastic containers that bore the name FieldClear on the label lay on the floor of the nearby barn. Sam emptied them on the edge of the yard, pumped in a little diesel, swilled it around to rinse them, then poured it out and filled them too.

"Let's see what we can get from the house."

"We're not common looters," said Josephine. "They may have family."

"Mum, for Christ's sake," said Sam, suddenly angry. "We don't have much food. The baby doesn't have nappies; I don't have antibiotics; the people who live here are dead."

"Don't speak to your mother like that," said Henry curtly.

"I'm sorry," said Sam. "It's just…" He threw up his arms.

Henry looked at Josephine, nodding.

"Darling, I know we would not normally even dream of it. They may have family and they may not – if they don't, someone else will no doubt find anything useful, or edible, in the house. For the moment, I think we just have to look at it like your robin in the garden foraging for food. When you put out the bird seed, he doesn't say 'after you' to the sparrows."

Josephine's upper lip trembled but she followed Sam back into the kitchen. He opened a plastic sack and handed it to her. He grabbed everything he could – anything that had not touched the water – and passed it across. Tins of fruit and soup, bottles of milk and beer, a wedge of cheddar cheese, an unopened salami wrapped in netted plastic, a cut loaf of brown bread and a torch. Upstairs, they found soap, toilet paper, towels and paracetamol .No antibiotics.

There was a shout from Shani in the yard below.

"There's a van coming across the fields."

Sam hopped and limped downstairs. As he turned at the bottom, where the mess of coats hung and the man's body lay, something orange caught his eye. ELEY, it said in white. 50 Rounds. A box of bullets. Behind it, intermingled with the walking sticks and umbrellas, an old .22 bolt action rifle stood against the wall. He swept up the box and the rifle and in an instant was outside.

"Everyone into the Landcruiser," he shouted.

******

Henry had already loaded the twelve bore and waited, holding the gun in front of him. He felt a little self-conscious, like some latter-day movie gangster, but at the same time ready to protect his family. He wondered idly what effect the pellets of a 12-bore cartridge would have on a toughened windscreen. It wasn't a van, it was a motorhome, he realised. It lurched and careened over the ruts and tracks on the edge of the field towards them. As it drew closer and stopped in front of him, he could see two women through the windscreen. They were barely women, girls.

The driver half-opened the door, raising her right arm in a gesture of surrender, a cigarette clenched between her fingers. The smoke rose in little eddies through the warm air. Henry could taste the smoke. For some reason it took him back to his room at Exeter all those years ago. A hint of coffee and Led Zeppelin and discarded clothes.

"Is anyone else in the back?"

"No, it's all right, it's just me and Lou, here."

The girl was trembling. Her thin body was covered by a pair of tight jeans and a slate green half top. A pair of shades was pushed up on her head.

"Show me," he said.

She went round to the side of the vehicle, stumbling in her navy pumps on the farmyard concrete, and opened the door. Henry glanced quickly left and right inside. There was no one else. He slowly lowered the gun, embarrassed now, guilty almost, to have so threatened two young women.

"Do you live here?" he asked.

"No… we've got nothing," she said, looking away. "Nothing except the motorhome and a pack of cigarettes. They took everything. We just managed to escape."

Henry realised that their own experience was being repeated all over the country – people fleeing their homes, escaping, with no base of their own, perhaps a vehicle but for how long, and now, like themselves, on the run, needing food and water, criss-crossing the country like ants, seeking sanctuary.

The other girl, named as Lou, had been looking on impassively, but poised, it seemed, like a leopard. Now she got out. She had short blonde hair and an athletic build. Her trainers were a lurid shade of green.

"Oh… my… god," she said, suddenly seeing the body lying in the yard.

"Can you help us? Is it safe here? Are you going somewhere? Do you know what's happening? Have you heard anything? Have you got any food?"

The questions tumbled out of her mouth in a frenzy and an accent that Henry pinpointed to somewhere south of Manchester. Probably not that far from where they were, he thought.

"Why should we help you? We have enough problems of our own," said Sam.

In normal times, Henry knew, Sam would not have hesitated to help, but two more people was two more mouths to feed, another vehicle was another problem. Josephine looked at Henry and then at Sam, pleading.

"Sam," said Henry, beckoning to his son, "Just come over here a second. I just had a thought."

He turned back towards the girls.

"Don't touch the water. Don't drink it or touch it. Not here or anywhere. Whatever's going on, they've poisoned it."

The girls looked around them. They sat down on the edge of the yard, hugging their knees. Lou pulled out her mobile and started scrolling through the screen.

"I can't get a signal, there should be a signal here," she said, turning to Shani. "Why isn't there a signal? Do you have a signal?"

Shani shook her head.

"They're all down as far as we can see. EE's down, O2's down, Vodafone's down; there's no internet, no electric."

"No electric?" said the driver as if electricity was as much a part of nature as the blue sky and the brown earth.

58

Sam and Henry came back.

"Can we have a proper look in the back?" said Henry courteously.

The girl waved her arm. The side door still hung open and Henry went inside. This time he took in the detail.

"Good God," he muttered to himself.

A kitchen area lay to the right and in front of him a table between two bench seats. A small door led to a toilet cubicle. Beyond, a sofa curved around a corner, a bunkbed above it. It was not the practicalities of the interior that surprised him, but its opulence – grey suede upholstery on the sofas, stone tiles around the kitchen area, a burled walnut folding table and flooring that looked for all the world like boards of oak.

He opened the doors beneath the hob – a gas cylinder sat there. He turned on the gas and lit it briefly, then nodded. He looked around in the cupboards and drawers beneath the beds. There were some blankets, a few bottles of cleaning materials and some cutlery and plates.

"Whose is this?" he asked.

"It's my Dad's," said the driver. "Or was, I guess." She looked down at the ground.

Josephine went over to her and put her arms around her shoulder.

"What happened?"

"I…I just got back from uni. Slung down my rucksack and the phone rang. It was Dad. He was coughing. He sounded exhausted. He just said, 'Take Mum, take the motorhome, and get as far north as you can. NOW.' And then he coughed forever and there was a shout, and the phone went dead."

"I'm so sorry… But your Mum isn't with you."

"She wasn't there. She left a message saying 'Back in 5, gone to the church'. I tried to call her but there was no signal and people were coming into the house. They were crying and begging for help and some of them were just taking our stuff. What could I do? We had to get out of there."

"Stef shouted and screamed for her Mum," said Lou. "We drove past the church and I ran in. She wasn't there. People were clambering to get into the motorhome, trying to open the side door. We had to keep driving."

"Presumably this thing's diesel?" said Sam.

"I don't know, I think so," said Stef.

Sam looked at the fuel point.

"OK," he said. "I don't know how the hell you managed to drive it cross-country, but you can come with us for as long as you have fuel. You can fill up from that tank there – it's farm diesel, tractor diesel. It'll probably wreck the engine but who cares?"

A jet flew low overhead. It was black, its engines screaming as it contoured the farmland, like a carrion crow. There was a distant boom and the aircraft banked to the left and turned back.

"Hide behind the motorhome and stay still," shouted Sam.

The aircraft loomed large above the yard and something seemed to fall from it, but there was no explosion.

"What do you want? What do you want? What are you trying to do?" shouted Josephine, her arms held out to the sky. Then she slumped onto an old tractor tyre and wept uncontrollably, her face in her hands.

Shani sat down beside her and hugged her.

"It's going to be OK, Jo. We're going to make it. We're going to make it to Balmanie."

\*\*\*\*\*\*

"I'm exhausted," said Henry. "Maybe we should have something to eat and spend the night here. Set off first thing in the morning."

Everyone nodded. They pulled some bales of hay from the barn and made a makeshift table out of an overturned cardboard box. Shani laid out bread, cheese, salami – anything simple she could find from the food they had plundered. Some bananas that had come from their own house had already gone brown. Stef produced some plates and knives from the motor home.

A silence and a sort of sadness seemed to settle on the group as they ate. Sam opened a packet of granola he'd rescued from Chiefy's just the day before.

"Mmmm, dry granola for supper…delicious," he said, trying to raise their spirits.

"Think of the fresh fish on Mull," said Henry. "Sea trout, mackerel… a big knob of butter in the pan, some black pepper, a touch of sea salt, lemon juice. Maybe some parsley. We'll be there tomorrow or the next day."

"I'm going to sleep," said Josephine, sighing. "But nowhere near this house."

Sam felt the same. They could not sleep, uninvited, in this strange house, on another's bed, quite apart from the implicit dangers all about them. Stef and Lou retired to their motorhome. The rest of them clambered back into the Landcruiser. Rabiyah said something quietly to Shani and slipped away into the hay barn with Noor.

"She's quite used to sleeping in the open," said Shani. "She says this way the baby won't keep us awake."

"One of us needs to be on look-out all the time," said Sam. "Mum, you sleep – Dad and I and Shani will take one hour shifts. That OK with you?"

He looked into Shani's coral eyes. She smiled and reached a hand across to cup his cheek.

"Of course. How is your leg?"

"Shit," he said. "But it's fine. We'll make it. I'll take the first shift, then you, then Dad. Quarter past the hour. OK?"

The clock on the dashboard glowed green and Sam sat back. He was aware of the others closing their eyes, letting go to an exhaustion not just of the body but of the spirit too, that such a situation should come to pass.

The moon was nearly full. He looked out through the windscreen across the concrete yard – the body lying there, prostrate, the farmhouse looming beyond. The body no longer worried him. He had been here two hours now - he was used to it, he thought, no different to a badger or a pheasant killed on the road.

He could feel his eyes closing. He jumped as an owl called, very close. A barn owl glided slowly across the yard, luminous in the darkness, then dived swiftly and suddenly into the rough grass to the right. He could hear squealing and the sounds of a fight…and then silence until it flew back, something held in its talons.

He thought of a time in his childhood when he had been intrigued by birds. Where had that interest gone? And why had it gone? Here was life at the sharp edge. The owl needs food. The vole is in the field. The owl must hunt, the vole must flee, and only one will win. He saw the bird fly again, its honey-coloured body and long, long wings clearly visible in the blue light. He'd flown, sometimes, in his dreams.

'These birds are free,' he thought. 'If we could all just fly now, we could be in Balmanie in no time; but we are grounded, limited.'

He looked at the clock. The second hand was flashing slowly towards 12.15 and he counted the seconds down, slapping his face, until it hit the quarter hour.

"Darling," he said, touching Shani's soft cheek, feeling the longing for her. "It's your turn."

She woke, looked at him with wide eyes as if in a trance. It took her a moment.

"Yes, yes. I'm awake. Anything happening?"

"It's quiet," he whispered. "And I love you."

She touched her hand to his.

"You sleep."

He woke again to his father's voice.

"Sam, Sam…"

"It's your turn to watch."

Sam shook himself.

He looked at his father as he lay back and closed his eyes again, and knew that he loved him too, whatever way this whole thing turned out.

The clock showed 2.16.

The turn of each second seemed to take an hour and the thought of hanging on for three thousand six hundred of them horrified him. Very gently, he opened the door of the Toyota and crept out, moving behind a tractor to urinate. The sound of his stream hitting the ground seemed to disturb the silence. He hobbled around the yard, glancing up at the moon now hanging over the barn, a spotlight on the scene of their plight. At least everyone was sleeping, he thought.

His foot suddenly slithered from under him. He crashed to the ground, banging his head against hard metal. He must have been out for several minutes, he judged later. When he came to, the bandage on his leg was partially dislodged below his shorts. Blood oozed from the wound. He felt around him gingerly. He seemed to have slipped on a pile of manure, dry on top and wet below. Within it and around it were pieces of broken glass, rusted farm machinery and brambles.

He brushed off the worst of the dirt. With an old tissue, he wiped away any blood he could see. He pressed the bandage back against his leg and climbed into the passenger seat. His father was snoring loudly, but Shani and Josephine seemed immune to the racket, breathing rhythmically.

There was movement on the edge of the yard. Sam sat up, ready to shout. Two eyes glimmered in the moonlight. A fox stole across the concrete and stopped in front of the woman's body. It seemed to study the filthy bile, now dried, beside her mouth and pulled away; then moved to the bare skin at her waist. Sam watched, mesmerised, as it sniffed and nibbled, then pulled at her shirt and trousers, exposing her left buttock. It tried to drag her away, but the weight was too much.

It bit into her, gnawing and pulling at the flesh. Blood dripped from its jaws as it wrestled with the body. Finally, a large piece came free. The fox dropped it on the ground and adjusted its grip, then grabbed it again and ate. It seemed in no hurry.

It moved forwards again, ready for another course. But now Sam felt a kind of guilt. This woman had been killed by the poisoned water. They had come and taken advantage of the situation, taken her food and her fuel, and she was not even allowed a decent burial, left to rot on the concrete, torn and violated by a scavenger.

He opened the door of the Landcruiser clapping his hands, and the fox ran for cover. At least he had done something.

He felt so tired.

It was only 2.47.

He stared at the green seconds flashing slowly forwards. He wondered at the slowness of time, fighting the heaviness of his eyelids and the sleep behind them, so inviting. Just a murmuring, the merest hint of sound, came to him. He looked around, wondering whether one of the others was sleep talking or humming. But no, the sound came from outside the truck.

Again, stealthily, he opened the door and, careful with his footing, crept out. He stood still for a few moments, orienting himself to the sound. It was coming from the hay barn. There was a murmuring, and then a brushing, as if of a long breath exhaling. He slipped around the back of the Landcruiser but could see nothing; then, behind the motorhome, he saw her.

From somewhere, Rabiyah had found a piece of carpet and upon it, towards the moon and, perhaps, Mecca, she was prostrating herself on the dirt floor of the barn, praying.

Sam was astonished. Astonished and respectful and humbled. Mixed responses came to him. As a photographer, he wanted to capture the image of this wonderful woman in a barn in some far corner of a foreign land and in some far corner of existence there. And as a fellow-traveller, a fellow refugee now, he wanted to make space for her.

He slipped back out of sight and waited until the sounds of her prayers had finished.

It was 3.24.

This time he opened the passenger door and touched his lips to Shani's as he woke her. She opened her mouth and they gloried in a silent embrace before he lapsed back into his seat and the warmth of sleep.

Henry woke him again at 5.18. The land was strangely silent and Sam struggled to let go of his dreams.

"What did you see on your watch?" he asked Henry. "What did you hear?"

But Henry and Shani just shrugged.

"Nothing."

Sam shook himself. He looked up at the sky. He looked up at the barn roof. Where was the owl now, where was the fox? He looked over at the woman lying prostrate on the concrete and he was thankful in a strange sort of way that the remains of her left buttock still stared bloodily to the sky, a gaggle of rooks and jackdaws pecking at it.

# CHAPTER XIII

ANNE-MARIE woke to an apricot sunrise.

"This is my land, my wonderful land," she thought as she looked out of her window to the east.

It took a few moments to remember the realities. Fraser – where was Fraser? Henry – were he and the family on their way back to Balmanie? If Henry made it to Ardgour, would he remember the haggis route, would he find the note on the boat?

She did not know. What she did know was that the Sound of Mull was strangely empty. The Caledonian MacBrayne ferries - Cal-Mac as people affectionately called them - with their black, ageing hulls, white decks and red funnels, were part of the landscape of the Inner Hebrides, plying between the islands. Normally Anne-Marie could set her clock by the comings and goings of the Isle of Mull into and out of Craignure, disgorging and engorging another load of trucks and cars and motorhomes bound for or from Oban. But today, though the sea was calm and innocent, the ferries were absent.

A clanking in the pipes heralded the day's first news. She turned a tap and her fears were confirmed – no mains water. The well provided back-up but there was not an endless supply. The noose had tightened another notch.

She went down to feed the dogs. She looked at them as they bounced hungrily towards her. Again she gave them only half a tin, and filled the water tray with just a brief splash from the jug on the side table. She let them out. Perhaps they'd better get used to fending for themselves.

She decided to go into Tobermory. She would pick up the provisions that she was missing from Fraser's drop and try to find out more of what was going on. She would see if Findlay was at the hotel.

She normally timed her run to leave just as the ferry was passing the old castle. She could then be assured she would be ahead of the crowd, many of whom had no clue how to drive on the single track roads. She would time her departure from Tobermory to bring her back to Craignure close to the departure time of the ferry – that way, all of the traffic heading in that direction would have run its course.

But today a long line of cars, three deep, stretched back from the ferry departure point. People were standing outside smoking and gesticulating. Someone waved her down.

"What do ya know, love? We're stuck here. They haven't told us nuffing, and I've gotta get back to work. Got a bloody mortgage to pay."

Anne-Marie tried to remain civil.

"I'm afraid I don't know anything," she said, "Except that there are reports of bad things happening on the mainland."

"Well, there's bad things happening bloody here. No ferries, and this shop has nearly run out of food. The toilets are overflowing. Shit everywhere. They need to get something sorted."

A silver Police Scotland vehicle appeared. It was Donnan McLaghan. He nodded to Anne-Marie.

"Trouble?" he asked.

"Not yet," she said. "But they have no information from Cal-Mac and they're very  frustrated."

People were gathering around the policeman now.

"We don't know much more than you, but we have been told that the ferries will not be running until further notice. Their fuel has not come up from the south and there are problems at Oban. A notice will be posted on these boards and around the island as soon as any further information is available. In the meantime, I suggest that you leave here and find somewhere to stay or camp on the island."

There was a muttering. People shouted a thousand questions. Anne-Marie fired the accelerator of the old pick up before the horde of cars headed for Tobermory, a sinking feeling in the pit of her stomach. The pick-up was an old Ford that had served her through many winters. It was twenty-three miles to Tobermory, and today the road seemed long. Signs that she would not normally have noticed took on new meaning. 'The Isle of Mull Rugby Club Sevens,' 'The Mull and Iona Abattoir'. More cars spilled out of the side road that led to the small Fishnish - Lochaline ferry.

'They could almost swim it,' thought Anne-Marie. 'The Sound is so narrow there.'

She drove on. She could see two small boats moving back and forth across the Sound.  Had someone decided to provide their own ferry service, she wondered, their own Dunkirk?  Did they think it would be safer on Mull? A RIB*, was moving fast towards the island, building a huge bow wave. She reached Salen. Old Mrs Maclean was standing outside the Spar, staring down the road. Anne-Marie slowed.

"Watch out for the invasion, they'll be on the way back from the ferry. Donnan has told them they're not running till further notice."

*RIB (*Rigid Inflatable Boat*)

"Well, I won't be running until further notice soon, if we don't get the truck in," she said.

"I'm going to try my luck in town," said Anne-Marie and headed north onto the long section of single track road.

Though her mind was racing, she drove with a high degree of caution. She hugged the left-hand side, ready at any moment to swerve onto the moorland. There were too many gruesome tales of tourists killed, unprepared for trucks roaring through the narrow corners. But today there were no trucks on the road.

She drove down the hill into the colourful centre of town on the sea front. A woman on a bicycle laboured up the hill, her saddle bags filled to the brim. The Co-op was dimly lit and the shelves were emptying. Disgusted with herself, Anne-Marie joined the scrimmage, her trolley clanging against others, blocking the aisles. She looked at the list she'd brought and stopped.

'What do I really need now?' she asked herself.

She remembered the old days when you could buy one hundredweight of brown rice in a sack. A 10kg bag was all she could get now – Akash Basmati, it said. Boxes of Quaker porridge oats, olive oil, onions, apples went into the trolley, a couple of bottles of Tobermory malt. She pulled the last pack of Pedigree Chicken and Liver with Gravy from the shelf, but there were no batteries left. A horde of people began to enter the shop as she reached the till.

"Where's all the food? There's nothing on these shelves."

"Oi, share it out mate."

She paid and made her way guiltily to the pick-up. She felt like a thief. She drove up to the Western Isles Hotel. Only natural light penetrated the narrow windows of the bar. A few guests nursed their drinks, their brows furrowed. Findlay Geddes greeted her.

"Good morning, Anne-Marie, how are you? What can I get you today?"

Anne-Marie felt a sense of relief to hear him say this yet again, as he had done for years, in his Edinburgh Morningside accent. It was an accent totally different to that of the West coast, yet probably, to a visiting tourist, would have sounded the same. His calm, measured tones told her that somehow, somewhere, normal life would be restored, that those who had disappeared or could not be contacted would appear again, that wrongs would be righted and problems solved.

"I am well, Findlay, though these times are worrying. Do you know - I'll have a Ledaig Eighteen today," she said. "Though I shouldn't."

He poured the whisky, and passed her a small jug of water with the tumbler.

"A measure will do you no harm, and you'll be needing it," he said. "Aye, worrying times indeed."

She noticed now that there was a hint of anxiety in his voice.

Findlay was no more a son of Mull than she was a daughter. He had spent five years with the SAS before leaving the army and managing one of the Henderson Law Investment Trusts in Edinburgh. Back in the 90's, he resigned from the company and moved to the island with his wife, Morag. Her parents hailed from Mull and, in their old age, needed care. Findlay had liked the idea of throwing off the responsibilities of his position, however well paid, to come to Tobermory. He had always been, for Anne-Marie, granite. She could confide in him, discuss with him, laugh with him.

"No power, Anne-Marie, and no mains water," he said. "We're on the generator and guests are complaining. Many of the staff have not come in. We're low on food and bottled water too. We're not going to be able to keep the freezers going much longer."

Anne-Marie nodded.

"But it is nothing compared to the mainland," he went on. "Have you heard anything? There are rumours of law breaking down, people scouring the countryside for food, people looting shops. It is a worry – not having internet or TV or these mobile telephones, we have no idea what is going on."

"I managed to speak to my brother in England a couple of days ago. I told him it would be safer here. Henry – you know Henry."

"Of course. And is he coming?"

"I don't know. I think so, I hope so. The line was faint," she said. "Yesterday I sailed across to see Fraser. He wasn't there. He seemed to have left in a hurry."

"I am sorry. Are you all right out there in Balmanie, Anne-Marie?"

"I'm fine," she said. "I have my own generator, plenty of wood and we have a spring. I'd be more worried about you, Findlay. If you want to come down with Morag..."

"Och, Anne-Marie, we could not impose ourselves on you so. Anyway, we have guests to look after."

A storm of voices and the brush of swing doors interrupted them. Many of the people who had been waiting for the ferry were now barging into the hotel.

# CHAPTER XIV

RABIYAH emerged from the barn, the baby in her arms. Noor was crying again, hungry no doubt. It was time to leave this place. Henry hammered on the door of the motorhome.

"We're going in about twenty minutes," he said. "Can we save some time and use your gas for a kettle?"

Stef and Lou appeared tousle-haired at the door, nodding. Rain had started to fall and they all huddled inside.

"Do you know how much water you have on board?" asked Henry.

Stef shook her head. Sam looked for a gauge. There was none. He asked her to turn on the ignition, then played through some screens.

"About a quarter. ..two gallons."

"So between us we have what, nine litres, in your tank, plus the two five litre bottles that we have and what's left of another one. That's it, that's all we have till we get to Balmanie. So...no washing-up, no showers – only drinking."

"How am I going to wash my face?" asked Stef.

Henry pointed to the rain sheeting down outside the window.

"That's safe enough."

The girls seemed glad of the leadership and acquiesced.

"Do you have a map?" he asked.

Stef looked blank.

"To find your way, you know, a map."

"We just use the satnav."

"Well, that's not going to work now. Isn't there one in the front of this thing."

They searched in the cab and the front pockets, but there was nothing. It was entirely electronic. Henry was glad of the dog-eared AA map that he kept in the Landcruiser. It might have been nearly as old as the vehicle, but it could get him from A to B.

"You're going to have to follow close behind us then."

He glanced down at the corpse one last time. The woman's clothes were saturated, a bedraggled, lifeless heap on the concrete.

They left the farm, taking the side roads, heading north. The girls seemed comfortable enough behind. They responded with a thumbs up when Henry checked with them every so often. There were fewer cars now. Those people that remained had retreated into themselves, he thought. They did not know which way to run and so, frozen in their shells, ran nowhere. At least he knew a safe place to run to.

He stopped at a junction at the top of a hill. To the right, the road wound down into the town of Comberwich. The field below them was scattered with black and white and Henry's eyes could not adjust, at first, to the sight that lay before him.

"Friesians," said Sam, his voice strangled.

And then Henry understood. The cattle were upended, as if a child had found a toy farm and knocked all the animals over. Their legs were splayed in the air, their bodies bloated. Some had rolled down in their final agonies and a pile had gathered at the bottom of the fall line. The offending water trough sat innocently at the top of the rise.

To the left, a narrow lane headed out between banks. It would mean miles of precious diesel thrown at the countryside. He looked right again towards the town and glanced across at Sam.

"What do you think?"

"It's a gamble, Dad, but I think we have to go for it."

Henry told the girls what they were going to do.

"Lock the doors," said Sam. "All the doors. Follow right behind us, close. Don't stop."

A pall of black smoke hung away to the right. A smell that hinted of a barbecue permeated the air.

"Mmmm…" murmured Shani, trying to lighten the tension.

Henry looked around. He could see Rabiyah pulling a face, her palm over her mouth, hugging Noor very tight. He knew that she knew.

"I don't think so," said Henry.

He had arrived at the scene of a car bomb in Baghdad many years back, the flames still licking at the scorched metal. It was a smell, people said, that never leaves those who have smelt it.

"They're burning bodies."

It made sense, of course. The corpses would soon have brought disease. Someone must have been brave enough to take the lead. There would have been no fine words or eulogy for these people; no soft tears, no wake. Just piled up one upon another, like pallets on Guy Fawkes night - a gentle silence and bowed head from the onlookers, before the flames took them.

They rounded the last bend past a church and drove into the town. In the centre, where the road forked either side of the Tudor-style market building, people were slumped against the crumbling red sandstone of a fountain.

"Left or right?"

Sam shrugged.

Henry noticed, as if in slow motion, the Barclays Bank eagle logo and an ancient pram that sat in the bay window of an antique shop. A discordant yellow sign on the opposite side of the street proclaimed 'Tattoo You'.

'Not much use now, any of that stuff,' he thought.

A group of people surged across the street. Perhaps they believed the vehicles were some sort of relief convoy, the motorhome carrying food and water.

"Speed up."

Sam's face was set. The people separated into a V, some throwing themselves to the left, some to the right, but one man stood defiantly in the middle of the road.

"Don't stop, Dad."

Henry saw his face. He was bearded. He wore a lime green t-shirt with a circular logo emblazoned on its front that read 'Doctors of Madness'. One of his front teeth was missing. His arms were raised and he was still shouting something as the muscular silver of the bumper slammed square into his knees. Henry shielded his face as the body glanced against the windscreen in its somersault curve over the Toyota. He thought that he could hear the sound of the man's skull crashing against the tarmac behind him, though he knew it was impossible.

He drove on, breathing in short bursts. Josephine was quivering in the back, cradling her face. He saw the lights of the motorhome flashing on and off behind him but still he drove on. It was not until he was well out of the town that he pulled onto the verge. Stef leapt out behind him. She was screaming.

"I ran over the man, I couldn't avoid him, I think I killed him. We should go back."

Sam looked at her almost coldly.

"Stef, he stood in the way. If Dad had stopped, all those people would have been clambering over the motor home and you'd have ended up outside it."

"But I killed someone."

"He was already dead when you went over him," said Lou. "You saw what happened. He killed himself by standing there. He had time to move. Sam's right – we wouldn't be here now if we'd stopped. We can't go back Stef."

Stef was quiet for a moment, balling her fists either side of her forehead..

"He just landed there …I didn't have time. I think I went over his neck."

Henry sighed deeply.

"I know…everything inside me was telling me to brake."

He brushed his hands through the strands of his greying hair.

"But we have to protect ourselves. This is kind of war… and in war you have to try to survive. Still, somehow we have to keep some norms, to retain a level of decency. If we're alive when this is all over, we want to be able to hold our heads high, not regret what we've done – not end up as some sort of monsters. It's difficult, really difficult."

They looked at him. Noone seemed willing or able to say anything in response. No blame and no alternative course of action was offered.

"What's that?" said Sam. He cupped his ear.

A faint whirring bled from the south. The sound grew louder and louder, whining now, until a black drone emerged from the clouds. It loomed overhead, like a mocking witch, circling them.

"What do you want?" shouted Josephine. "WHAT DO YOU WANT?"

She addressed it as she might an errant child, imprecating a response. But the drone just whirred and whined, and she crumpled again. Henry looked for the lorazepam. Long ago they had agreed that he would keep it. He hated the drug; he knew that it was short-term and that his supply would soon run out; but for the moment, it was his only choice. Shani glanced questioningly at Sam, who nodded silently.

"That leg is really hurting him," murmured Henry, as he handed her the little white pill, so innocent-looking, and poured a thumb of water into a mug. He picked up the map.

"We need to plot a route," he said. "We're here, at Comberwich…"

"Comberwich? Yeah, you're right," said Lou, looking around.

"My mum lives near here. Picksford. I know the way there."

"Does that mean…Is that what you want to do, Lou, go home?"

She looked about her. Henry could see her calculating - this band of people that she had barely met, this fleeing few who had some sort of a plan, or the pull of home.

"I don't know. Fuck – I don't know. I need to know that Mum's OK. Can we go and see?"

Henry hesitated. He thought of Shani, so far from her family; he remembered Stef's account of her search for her mother. He studied the map, buying time, thinking. It was not just the route. It was the mother too. Could they bring her with them? Was there enough food, enough water? Could they safely stop even? Eventually he nodded. If it had been his own mother, he realised, there would have been no question.

"We're going to have to go on the M6 past Manchester, and, beyond, it's the only road that can get us north. Picksford is more or less on the way – we can get onto the motorway not far from there, so OK."

Stef pulled the last cigarette from the packet, her hands shaking. Hungrily, she lit it and drew a long lungful of smoke. She held the keys out to Lou.

"You drive," she said.

They set off, this time the motorhome in front. The rain had stopped but it had not cleared the air. It was stiflingly hot, dulling the midday senses. An occasional rumble of thunder threatened a far greater storm.

Lou pulled in at the top of a terraced street. Picksford was no more than a large village and there were no fires here. Flies infested the corpses and a dark stench infested the air. All seemed quiet. She pointed to a red door half way down.

"That's where my mum lives."

"How are we going to know if you are OK?" asked Stef.

"I'll wave."

"And what if it's not OK? No, I'll come with you."

"Leave us the keys," said Sam.

Stef looked at him.

"What?"

"You have to trust me, Stef."

She passed the keys over hesitantly.

"If your mother has any antibiotics, Lou… " Josephine's voice trailed off.

They watched the girls walk down the street, the diminutive figure of Stef, her unkempt curls dancing on her shoulders, and Lou moving with muscular, blonde purpose. There was a hint of movement in some of the houses, an adjustment of the curtains, a shadow in an upstairs window. Henry had the sensation of things happening beyond his control. He looked across at Sam.

"I don't feel good about this."

Sam nodded in agreement. He felt to the floor beneath his seat. He picked up the twelve bore and quietly loaded the two chambers, checking again that he knew where the cartridges were for a reload.

Rabiyah held Noor close, nuzzling her into her breast. Sam caught Shani's eye, holding out the keys to the motorhome.

"You OK to drive it?"

"I'll figure it out."

She slipped over to the other vehicle. Stef looked back. She faltered as she saw Shani in the driver's seat of her father's pride and joy, then walked on. Shani started the engine.

Lou knocked on the red door. It stayed closed. She knocked more firmly. They could hear her calling 'Mum, Mum', but still the door stayed closed. Stef kept glancing back up the street. Lou pulled out a key. She turned the lock and the girls disappeared inside.

In the two vehicles, they waited. They waited, it seemed to Henry, for an age. He was sweating. The air was thick and close and stale. The baby's makeshift nappy needed changing.

\*\*\*\*\*\*

*It were so hot in there. And it stank. It stank of beer and bodyshit and there must have been some old fish or something in the fridge. There was no sign of Mum, but he was sitting there on his fat arse, his legs splayed out on the sofa in his torn grey trackies. He wasn't moving. I thought he were dead at first until a rumbling lungfart came from some part of his stinking body. His eyes were closed, fluttering, and beer cans were all over. Either side of him on the sofa, on the carpet and on his bulging stomach. A newspaper was open at the football page and he was just sat there in front of the tellie. It was just a blank dark screen of course, but he didn't know how to do owt else, so that's what he was doing. Waiting to see a match.*

*Other than him, it were completely silent in the house, except a bee was caught behind a curtain. It was buzzing frantically. It wanted out.*

*'Where's Mum?' I asked. 'Where's Jodie?'*
*He just grunted.*
*'Who is he?' asked Stef*
*'It's my sister Jodie's husband. He's a cunt.'*
*'MUM!'*

*We went in the kitchen but it was empty, except the foul fridge. There were empty water bottles on the table, and tins of baked beans that looked like they'd been opened and eaten with a spoon. We went upstairs, but Mum wasn't there either.*

*'WHERE'S MUM?' I shouted, trying to penetrate his stupor. This time he stirred. I don't know whether he ever expected to speak to another human being again. Perhaps he had decided to die there in front of the stupid television, waiting for a football match. 'Hello, Mister God — Man City were supposed to be playing today and then something happened, we had no power, no Sky, and all kinds of stuff was going down. And then I got a bit pissed and well, here I am…have mercy on me.'*

*We went to my room. I gathered up a jacket and another for Stef though it was way too big. I found my sack and my boots. I looked in the bathroom. There were no antibiotics but there was a bottle of TCP.*

*I slapped him. I slapped him across the cheeks. I know, that was silly but…*

*'Where is Mum?' I shouted. 'Why are you here in Mum's house?'*

*This time he woke up. He seemed to collect himself.*

*'What are you doing here?' he slurred. 'They said everyone's dead.'*

*'What are you doing here, more to the point? Where's Mum, where's Jodie?'*

*'Gone.'*

*'Where have they gone?'*

*He moved towards us. There was an iron look in his eye. His legs were unsteady, but slow and purposeful, like an elephant's. We edged towards the door.*

*'Where do you think you're going with that stuff?'*

*I tried to stay reasonable, to keep him calm. I was fuckin' shaking inside.*

*'Stef's got a motorhome. We're trying to head north. I want to see if Mum wants to come. See whether we can escape this shit.'*

*'I'm coming with you.'*

*I realised what an idiot thing I'd said.*

'No, you'll be fine here. It'll be over soon.'

He lunged forward. He's a big bugger and he had both of us, one in either arm. He swung us round, blocking the door, squeezing the breath out of me.

'Let me go, you bastard,' Stef shouted. 'Get off me.'

I squirmed and shoved and elbowed him until I could wriggle free of the jacket. Then I kicked him in the balls and lunged for the door.

# CHAPTER XV

THE RED door opened again. Lou stumbled out –
backwards, almost falling. Only Lou.

"Jesus!"

"Bastard brother-in-law's got Stef," she shouted. "We
have to get her out."

A large bag was slung across her shoulder. It was khaki
and appeared to be made of military-style webbing. Sam
picked up the gun. He half ran, half hobbled down the
pavement. A few people were coming out onto the street.
A woman with purple hair brandished a large butcher's
knife. She was running towards Lou.

"You cannot control us, you motherfuckers," she
shouted. "You can keep your ideologies and your guns.
You try and come all disguised as one of us. Well, guess
what, I can tell one of you bastards when I see one."

Lou held her ground. Clutching the buckle end of the
long strap, she whirled the bag round her head like a
lassoo. It caught the woman on her left cheek and
momentarily she backed off. Sam reached Lou. He held
the gun firm in his grasp. A girl and two youths began
hurling stones and debris  from the other side of the street.

"Get the fuckers," the woman shouted, moving forwards again.

Sam ducked as a splintered plank brushed past his face. Lou held her arms high but could not shield herself. It caught her on the forehead and she staggered sideways. The woman was nearly on them, strands of purple flailing behind her, the vicious blade raised.

Sam fired. It was virtually point blank. He did not even raise the gun to his shoulder, his arms recoiling behind him with the blast. Henry watched, mesmerised, as the woman's midriff seemed to disintegrate, implode, a bloodied mist filling the air around her.

Lou brushed her forearm across her mouth, wiping blood from her face and lips. As she spat, a man appeared at the red door. He was dragging Stef in a neck lock, her arms pinned to her sides by his other arm.

"Take me with you, shitface, or she stays with me."

Sam did not hesitate. He swung the twelve bore round.

"Get behind me, Lou."

He raised the gun again, this time to his shoulder. Stef screamed. That Sam fired way to the left was irrelevant. The shot, so close, was enough. The man reeled back as the air crashed about him, and for a second slackened his arm.

Stef spun like a dervish. She jammed her index and middle fingers, their long nails still painted in a hectic pattern of mauve and yellow, deep into his face.

Henry saw the motorhome beside him lurch forwards, then stop. He looked across at Shani. She was peering at the controls, a look of frustration on her face, but the motorhome wasn't moving. He could not wait. He let out the clutch.

Stef's fingers landed in a mess of nose and eyes. As the man's head jerked back, she freed herself and sprinted for the Toyota. She dived in head first, sprawling across Josephine's lap.

Henry caught his breath. Sam had fired both barrels and needed to reload. He could see his son fumbling in his pockets for the cartridges. Perhaps a man used to shooting pheasants, like his own father, would know how to clasp two cartridges expertly between his fingers and slot them into the twin barrels of a twelve bore in one fluid movement. An image came to him of Legolas firing an arrow, drawing another from the quiver on his back, fitting it to the bow and firing again in a glorious, fluid sweep. But Sam was no Legolas. It seemed to take an age for him to load even one cartridge, the gun useless in his hands.

The youths and the girl were closing on him, enraged. For them, Henry could see, he was the enemy, the cause of all their thirst and hunger, the cause of their useless iPhones, their blank televisions, their deadly water. The purple woman had ensured that.

Lou reached for a side pocket in her bag. In one swift motion she pulled out a knife. Its blade was wide and tapered, yet not long. Its handle was of polished wood. It seemed to fit her like a glove. It was a weapon, Henry thought, yet not a weapon.

She held it in front of her with both hands, like a lethal pixie. Blood still poured from the wound above her left eye. One of the youths came close. He was wearing green and pink checked shorts that reached his calves, a premature belly dangling over his waistline. He was holding a piece of copper piping, jagged at one end as if ripped from a building site. Perhaps he wanted to impress the girl. He thrust at Lou and she danced around his thrust, taunting him almost, until he made another move, coming in on her. She leant a leg one way, it seemed, leaned her body weight the other. To the naked eye, it was not clear what happened. But the man was on the ground, at her mercy, her foot on his throat, the copper pipe clattering on the empty road.

She wielded the knife over him, daring the others to come closer, giving Sam precious time, the twenty seconds he needed to complete the reloading. The man from the red door was lumbering forward now.

"Go, go, go," Sam shouted, covering Lou as they edged backwards towards the Toyota.

Stef held the door open. She grabbed Lou's arm, hauling her inside, the man's grasping, fleeting arm catching only bare metal. He punched the side of the vehicle as it passed.

"Fucking shitface arsehole cunts," he screamed, kicking at the vacant air.

"He shows a fine command of the English language," said Henry as they veered out of the village.

Sam looked around anxiously.

"Where's Shani? This isn't a fucking joke, Dad!"

"The motorhome stalled…it was looking really bad. I had to come for you and the girls. She'll be behind us."

"But she isn't! I was fine. I had the fucking gun. I had cartridges. WHERE IS SHANI?"

# CHAPTER XVI

"I'M SURE we'll find her, darling," said Josephine plaintively, but Sam ignored her.

"Dad, we have to go back. It's my fault she's in that motorhome – I gave her the keys. It was stupid, STUPID. We have to get her. She's alone in that thing."

Henry stopped beside a copse. He summoned everything he had left in him.

"How can we go back? You saw those people. You just told Stef in that last place that we can't go back."

"For Christ's sake, Dad, this is completely different. It's one of us, I can't leave her…I love her. You wouldn't leave Mum behind. Dad, now! We need to go NOW!"

Henry looked behind at Josephine, her shoulders hunched, her face drawn and anxious. He looked at Rabiyah, nestling the baby. And he looked at the two girls.

"If I ever see my Dad again," said Stef, "he'll kill me if I told him I lost the motorhome."

"If you don't want to drive back," said Lou, forcefully, "I'll go back with you, Sam. Of course we have to get Shani. And we need the motorhome. It's got our food and water in it. We can't all fit in this Land-Rover or whatever it is anyway."

Loading his pockets with cartridges, Sam opened the front passenger door. Lou and Stef were ready to follow suit from the back. From nowhere, church bells rang out across the fields. They all stopped, their hands poised on the door handles. The bells sounded pure and clear against the summer air. Henry tried to picture the bellringers. Were they in hope or despair, or were they in prayer? Were they sending a warning? Who were they? Did they have food, water? Were they old or young? Did they have sons and daughters?

The wheat, still green and unharvested, swayed in the fields around them and the song of the bells carried him to his childhood and an innocent place where bravery and impulse and uncharted waters were the norm, a diver swooping from a high cliff into the depths of a still pool below.

He heaved a deep and resigned sigh. He did not have the luxury of time. He did not have the luxury of time to discover why the bells pealed and he did not have the luxury of time to mull over a decision.

"OK, we'll go back," he said. "Lou, you know this place. The map doesn't show enough detail. Is there any way we can get back to the top of that street without retracing our steps or driving all the way out to the next village?"

Lou closed her eyes.

She slapped her head with the side of her hand.

"Think…

"There's a footpath. It comes out over there. It goes up to the wood, and then across. If we can get through the gates…"

"Go Dad, go. Which way Lou? Tell him."

"There's a stile. That opening there. Can you get into that field? Then follow the track."

Henry could not think any longer about the discomfort of his wife or the baby. It was not that he did not care. He cared more than anything, but competing cares had to win this time. He did not back down on the accelerator as they lurched across the field and joined a furrowed track, fit only for tractors and 4 x 4's, that wound up to the edge of a wood.

From here they could see the houses nestled below them. Henry drove on fast, circling the village. They passed a large oak and the white, burgundy and blue of the motorhome came into view. It was reversing. Someone was beside it and with a sinking feeling Henry realised that it was the big man, Lou's brother-in-law. He was hammering on the vehicle pulling at the side door. Suddenly it opened, swinging free. Another man, the younger man in check shorts, appeared.

As Shani pulled the motorhome forward on another turn, the two of them hauled themselves inside.

"Jesus!" said Sam. He looked at Stef.

"Is the front open to the back?"

"It's closed. There's a bulkhead – just a small window in it."

"Thank God."

Henry raced along the last of the track, bumping and bouncing at every dip. Rabiyah held onto the baby with one arm, the other supporting herself against the seat in front. Josephine, Lou and Stef were hanging onto the coat hangers and doors, desperate to protect the baby and, crammed as they were on the back seat, trying not to crush each other.

"For heaven's sake, Henry," Josephine cried out, but there was no time to be worried about bruises.

At the point where the track met the road a metal gate blocked their way.

"Shit!"

Sam leapt out on his good leg and hopped across. A chain held the gate around a solid wooden post, but there was no padlock. He lifted it easily and flung it to the side with a clatter. He barely had time to remount before Henry accelerated towards the motorhome.

*\*\*\*\*\*\**

I could see everything that happened through that huge windscreen. The purple-haired woman coming at you. That blade. I was so scared. I saw the big man coming out of the red door. Stef looked so small, all wrapped in his arms. I was trying to make the bloody thing go and every time it stalled.

'Come on you stupid woman,' I told myself. 'You can fly a helicopter. You must be able to drive a motorhome.'

You fired at that woman before she got you and then at the man. The other ones, the two younger guys and the girl, were coming for Lou. It was like some movie was being played out in front of me and at the same time I was trying to make the thing move.

And then you both leaped into the Toyota and disappeared into the distance. 'You're on your own now baby,' I thought.

That was when the man started lumbering towards me. My mind froze - he was so, like, inevitable. Time seemed to stop and I just watched as he came on like some ugly, frigging giant.

The other one, the one in shorts, was right behind him, shouting and screaming. They were getting very close. I don't know what they wanted. Did they think that shouting at me, killing me, would solve their problems?

Something kicked in. 'Come on Shani, get yourself into gear. You can deal with this.'

I leant across to the passenger door and locked it. And as I leant across, I saw the button - whatever it is that counts for a handbrake in that thing - it was on. By now, they were battering the sides. I felt like I was outside my body...I thought this was it.

I pushed and pulled at the button – I was trying to stay calm, not to rush it. And then, with just a flick, it released.

The younger guy had a knife. He was trying to slash at the tyre. I could see him in the mirrors with his knife raised. I accelerated backwards. He screamed as he dived sideways. I accelerated the other way... and then there was a crash and the side door swung open.

'Shit,' I thought. I was sure it had been locked.

*I felt the motorhome lurch as the big guy stepped in. I felt so alone. He was in there behind me. He couldn't get to me for the moment, but he was there, just a few centimetres behind me. I could almost smell his fetid breath. I could feel his movement. I could feel the weight shift as he moved around. When I glanced back, I could see his sneering face through the glass in the bulkhead.*

*And then I saw you guys in the Toyota across the field.*

\*\*\*\*\*\*

Shani was driving the motorhome fast, swerving from one side to the other back out of the village. She slammed the brakes on hard as the two vehicles drew level. Sam had the gun. Stef and Lou leapt out with him.

"There are two of them in the back," he shouted, as Shani opened the window.

"I know. It's the big man, the one from the house."

She climbed gingerly out of the cab. She was shaking. Lou opened the side door, knife in hand. Sam stood outside with the twelve bore.

"Come out of there, Dave."

The man's mouth was stuffed with bread. He held a wedge of cheddar in his hand. A great bite had been taken from it as if by some giant rat. But it was not the sound of his ravenous gorging that shocked them. It was the sound of running water. He had turned on the tap. As she spoke, he dunked his face to the flow, sucking in parched mouthfuls.

The water was still running.

"The tap – turn the tap off!" shouted Lou.

The man just looked at her sneering, turning it on faster. The younger man was on the floor with a can of lager, his legs splayed in front of him.

"I don't want to have to do to them what I did to that woman," said Sam. "But they've got about fifteen seconds."

Lou turned towards her brother-in-law.

"Dave, you heard him. You saw what happened before. Sam here has the gun. It's loaded. You have nowhere to go. Turn the tap off NOW! I'm going to count to ten. One, two, three, four…"

The man began to whimper, cowering against the table.

"Five, six, seven…"

He moved towards the sink, sidling sideways like a crab, his eyes on Lou's knife. He turned off the tap. Lou glanced back at Sam, mouthing a message.

"Right, now, I'm going to move back. You can walk out of here and I won't touch you, and Sam won't fire. Take your friend with you. Or…"

There was a moment of silence. The man jerked his head in the direction of the youth.

"Fuckin' terrorists," said the younger man pointlessly.

Lou stepped backwards out of the motorhome and stood beside Sam, waiting. The youth came first. His head was bowed. He moved a few yards away cautiously, his hands in the air. Dave lumbered forward. He looked at Lou. He looked at Sam.

"Fucking …"

He belched. And then he spat. A great gob of spit landed at her feet. She did not blink. She stared impassively at him, still leaving him the space to move. And he moved now, sheepishly, back towards the houses like a hunted dog, his shoulders hunched again, his head bent. His friend shrank, mutantly, at his side – broken.

# CHAPTER XVII

HENRY pulled off the road down a rough track. He stopped beside a pond. An oak, on its knees with age, grew horizontally along the far bank.

"Let's regroup here for a few minutes before the motorway," he said.

Sam took Shani's hand. They moved away a little and lay in the rough grass in the shade of the tree. Two dragonflies flew across the surface of the water, their blue so luminous it seemed some source of electrical power must be harboured in their bodies – a colour that no man-made palette could replicate.

"How is it?" asked Shani, gently stroking the wounded leg. Sam recoiled.

"Sorry, it feels really inflamed. Probably need some antibiotics, but that's not going to happen unless Lou found any. I'll survive."

She lay back and closed her eyes.

"I'm so sorry Shani. I should never have given you the keys. I never imagined…"

"What do you mean? Do you think I didn't handle the situation?"

"Of course I don't. I just never intended to put you in that situation in the first place. I didn't think. Will you forgive me?"

Her wide brown eyes stared at him.

"You'd be surprised what we girls can handle. We can handle a pack of wild people out for our blood - that's no problem. We can learn how to reverse a bloody great motor home while a lumbering oaf is trying to attack it – that's no problem. We can handle a bunch of idiots slashing its tyres, breaking into the back door and breathing their stinking breath just an inch from our nose - that's no problem. We learn all that in finishing school. Didn't you know?"

For a moment he looked at her uncertainly, but her eyes were playful and he leaned over, tracing her jawline with the back of his hand. He bent to kiss her. Her lips were soft and parted warmly. Then she stopped.

"Tell me about your mother," she said gently.

"Yes."

He sighed.

"She's suffered from depression for a long time. Clinical depression. People talk about being depressed and they are not talking about anything close to the real illness. They've just had a bad day. Clinical depression is… it's a really, really shitty condition. Dad said she's probably had it in some way since her teens, maybe earlier. It seems like it got worse after I was born. She struggled through it, she was a doctor, prescribed her own medication. But I think they just masked the symptoms.

She tried to hide how bad it was from Dad, but he found her one day just weeping uncontrollably. She'd kind of broken down. I was just a little kid at the time – five or six, but I can still remember it. That was when Isabel looked after me for six months. Dad got her treatment. I don't think even psychiatrists really understand mental illness, let alone GP's, but she's been on a different medication since then. It keeps her on the level most of the time but in reality she's on a knife edge. Big things, sudden changes in routine, can throw her. She has panic attacks. That's what happened back there. Those pills Dad has, the lorazepam, are for that….but that was the last one."

"Your poor Mum. Has she ever said – what it's like?"

"Depression? I asked her once," he said. "I can remember every word she said, as if it was a poem I'd had to learn by heart at school. She was kind of in remission at the time, in nearly a good place."

******

*It's very difficult to explain darling…unless you've had it. But I'll try. Imagine you're in the garden on a beautiful summer's day. You're lying on the lawn beside a flower bed and all sorts of beautiful flowers - white michaelmas daisies, purple fuschias and orange petunias - are there. And from this angle, little insects are moving around on the leaves and beetles on the soil. Bees are flying from flower to flower and you can smell the sweet dampness of the earth. There is a whole little world down there, different to our world. And yet you recognize none of its beauty, you look at it as if it is second-hand. As if someone drew an invisible veil between you and that beauty and you feel nothing. Worse than nothing, you feel such a pain inside. You can't move, you can't decide. You may look fine on the outside – that's the trouble, it's invisible – but there are voices hammering away inside your head telling you you are worthless, nothing. And you just want to end it.*

*I shouldn't have said all of that. The last bit, I mean.*

******

"I'm so sorry." They did not speak for some minutes.

Shani stood up and held out her arms, hauling Sam up on his good leg.

94

"Come on, we should be getting back. How long is it going to take us to get to Balmanie from here do you think?"

"We could be there tomorrow with a following wind."

Henry had laid the farmer's .22 out on the bonnet of the Landcruiser. He was peering down the barrel and inspecting the trigger mechanism.

"There's a bit of rust on it. I'm going to test it."

He scrambled around in the boxes of food until he found a bottle of olive oil that had come from the farm kitchen. Pouring some of it onto an old rag, he rubbed the trigger and trigger guard. He peered down the barrel and poured some drops of the oil down it. He located the orange boxes that housed the farmer's bullets. He loaded one and looked at Sam.

"You ever used one of these?"

"Nope."

"Me neither." He held it to his shoulder. He was about to take aim at a wood pigeon, perched on the top branch of the oak, when Rabiyah spoke. She was gesturing with her hands.

"What did she say?" he asked Shani.

Shani held out her hands for the baby.

"She knows these guns. Her husband taught her how to use them. She will show you. She wants to be useful."

Henry nodded. He passed the loaded gun to Rabiyah, the stock first, barrel to the sky. She held the rifle to her shoulder and closed her right eye.

Her long green jilbab was scuffed and dusty at the bottom and her coral hijab torn at one side. A rifle might have seemed out of place in the hands of such a woman, yet Rabiyah looked born to the weapon, like a dancer to her music or a rider to her horse.

The pigeon sat motionless and unsuspecting. Rabiyah's index finger closed on the trigger. She held the pressure, eyeing the target. She looked around at Noor, in Shani's arms. A huge sadness hung in her eyes. 'This is for you and for all that we have lost,' she seemed to be saying. She eyed the target one more time.

There was a whiplash crack. Grey feathers burst into the hot air. Crashing and thudding through the branches, the pigeon toppled through the tree to the ground. Henry walked over. He held it up by its severed neck. The bird was not just dead. She had blown its head off.

This woman was no longer simply the devout mother, fleeing with an unknown family in an unknown country from an uncertain past to an uncertain future. She had become a warrior, fighting for her own country and her husband and her religion and, above all, her baby. A hard edge, an intelligence, a statement of womanhood, a survival fighter was now present amongst them.

"That's good," said Sam. Good that the rifle could shoot, good that they had a marksman in their midst, good that he and Henry had material support.

"How did you learn to shoot like that?"

"It is a long story," she said, her eyes roaming to another corner of the world and another time.

# CHAPTER XVIII

*WE LIVED in Homs. My father was a schoolteacher. My husband, Hassan, had a shop — he sold food, and... all useful things, safe things. We lived above the shop.*

*The war started. Rebels came, different groups came — we did not know who was our friend and who our enemy. Hassan said I must learn to shoot. He bought two guns like this one. He took me to a place he knew, a valley, where we practised. I learnt well.*

*When the bombs came, they hit the school. Children died in the classroom. They found my father, his arms spread out above them, protecting them, a huge piece of concrete slammed across his back.*

*Hassan vowed revenge, he vowed to fight, but I said no, think of our children, they need a father. We have...we had, I don't know, two children — Noor here, and Abdul who is four.*

*A man came. His name was Kareem. He was my brother-in-law. My husband's eldest brother. But he was not like Hassan or their younger brother Tariq. He wore jeans and plimsolls and an old curved sword hung from his belt. I knew it. It was their father's sword. It was engraved with beautiful patterns and verses. Their father had shown it to me. The handle was made of woven rope, like gold braid.*

*He told me to leave the room. I heard shouting. After a little while I went back in. Kareem's face was contorted with rage.*

"If you do not …" he screamed. He did not finish the sentence. He raised the sword above the canary's cage. The bird squawked and cried.  He brought it crashing down cleaving the cage in two. Two halves of severed metal bars.

The canary fluttered about the living room - it made a mess everywhere. It was unsure it wanted this freedom. I think it wanted its cage back - it felt safer there. But then it found an open window and flew out into the evening.

"You next," my brother-in-law sneered, and walked out.

That was when Hassan said we have to leave.  He gathered my mother and some friends together. I don't know how he did it but in the middle of the night two trucks picked us up. I had my gun with me.

We drove for a long time. Finally they dropped us in the mountains and a man led us over. We reached a lemon grove.  At any other time it would have been a beautiful place with the sweet scent of the lemons and the hills in the distance, but we were terrified. Terrified and exhausted. We had some bread and lay down to sleep in the shade and when night came we moved along a path by the blue light of the moon.

We stopped when we were close to the border. We could see the sentries moving along it from side to side. We were hidden deep in the bushes and the trees. It was then that little Noor decided to cry out. I held my hand across her mouth, but it was already too late. Hassan looked over at me. I could see the anguish in his face. I could see Abdul next to him. Thirty other people relied on him to get out and his own baby was giving them away.

"You have to move away with her," he mouthed, pushing the air with his hands.

I saw Tariq, my brother-in-law, crawl towards him. I could almost hear their shouted whispers. Then Tariq came towards me. I turned to wave to Abdul, but already he was torn from my sight. We moved back and to the left, crawling behind the scrub, Noor crying occasionally before I could raise my palm to her.

When we were some distance away, I stopped, tears streaming down my face. Tariq was beside me, his gun slung over his shoulder.

"I promised I would look after you and Noor," he said. "Hassan will look after Abdul and your mother and the rest of the group."

We lay beneath a bush, trying not even to breathe, our heads buried in the parched earth. We heard movement - footsteps on the old turf of the lemon grove, twigs breaking and the crackle of dry leaves. A man passed within a few metres of us. Suddenly there were shouts and we could hear people running. There were shots, so many shots. There were screams and cries and echoes that haunt me at night. I thought I could hear Abdul calling for me. And then there was silence.

We lay still for an eternity, unknowing and praying. Somehow the baby was sleeping. Eventually, Tariq said, "It's just over there, the border. I think we can make it. Leave your rifle — you'll be safer without it."

We ran. Suddenly in front of us there was a soldier. He looked young, almost frightened himself. He raised his gun, then, perhaps seeing the baby, lowered it, nodding his head in the direction of safety.

I do not know what happened next. One moment I could hear Tariq behind me, the next there was a shot. I ran on. I ran and ran...

# CHAPTER XIX

AT LAST they made good headway. Lancaster, Kendal, Penrith, the endless white dashes on the tarmac ahead of them. Henry had learnt his lesson. When people straddled the road, trying to guide him into Southwaite service station, he did not falter from a straight line. If some of them felt the wrath of the Toyota's bumper, that had been their choice. The Land Cruiser was not, under any circumstances, going to be any spider's fly.

He felt a tired elation when the motorway name changed to A74(M) and he read the words 'Failte gu Alba' on the blue sign. They'd crossed into Scotland. Alba – just the name excited him, a wild land. He conjured a vision of Balmanie, of Anne-Marie welcoming them - a roaring fire, gulls screaming over the roof, trout sizzling in butter in a pan, dogs lapping around them and a bottle of whisky on the sideboard.

"I'm hallucinating," he thought.

The brightest of the light was fading and he was exhausted. The Toyota stank – it stank of the baby's makeshift nappies and the sweat and unwashed breath of all of them. It stank of something else too – he did not want to think about it. He slapped his cheeks to keep himself awake but a weight of sleep was overpowering him. His eyes, his shoulders were leaden. He slapped again but it was no use. He turned off at Junction 20 after Gretna Green and pulled into a field.

"Do you want to drive for a bit, Sam?"

Sam stepped out of the passenger door, but his injured leg could not hold him. He fell forward onto green, unharvested oats, clutching at his thigh.

\*\*\*\*\*\*

Shani knelt beside him. Holding her shoulder, he hauled himself upright.

She looked at Stef. "Can we lay him down in there? We need to look at the wound."

They moved gingerly towards the motorhome.

"Let me undo your belt," said Shani, easing off his shorts as he subsided onto the lower bunk. "Look away girls."

She could smell it before she saw it. Putrid, rotten flesh, the stench of no medical intervention - of decay and infection. Sam himself sniffed the air.

"Urgh," he groaned.

Shani looked down at the bandage. It was stained in parts to a dirty, wet pink and in other areas grey-brown and dried. It clung like a limpet to the serrated flesh.

"We need to change it," said Josephine bleakly. She was scratching, clawing almost, at her wrist. Sam glanced across at his father.

"It's OK, Mum. It's just a bad cut."

A tense smile appeared on her lips.

"Do we have scissors?"

Noone could offer any. Josephine hovered over the leg again, indecisive. Rabiyah handed the baby to Stef and moved forward. She held either side of the dressing and gently began to pull. The edges of the wound were an angry, strained purple. She pulled more firmly.

"Owwww!" shouted Sam.

He squeezed Shani's hand, grimacing, as another few centimetres came loose. To the left, a section had turned almost black, forming a crater, but Shani's eyes were drawn to the centre. A broiling sea of puss seemed to be rising and falling and weaving, writhing on the surface. Something fell from the wound.

"What's that? Jesus!"

Her shout was drowned amidst the cries of the other women. A small white maggot was squirming now on the faux-oak flooring of the motorhome. She could see the segments of its body, two little eyes staring piggishly into space, searching for more flesh, the point of its tail quivering.

Shani stamped on it with the full force of her boot. Rabiyah yanked now at the bandage, ignoring Sam's pain. On its inside, in a mess of rotten flesh , a crowd of maggots seethed, crawling up the sides to escape, some falling to the floor.

"Get it out of here," screamed Josephine, as the bandage released.

Rabiyah carried it quickly to the door. She threw it as far as she could across the field. Shani slammed her foot down left and right, then bent over the leg, oblivious, it seemed, to the stench. More, many more, maggots heaved and squirmed in an ever-changing pattern across the wound. Under a flap of skin, a yellow puss had formed. They seemed to move towards it like starved men to a barbecue.

"Shit."

Josephine started slashing at them manically with a tissue, the maggots falling onto the bed and the floor. Rabiyah brushed her hand away.

"No," she said.

She made a sign for water, but Sam shook his head.

"We can't use the water. We don't have enough."

Rabiyah held her hands out in despair.

"A can of beer from the farm house," said Sam. "No, there was a bottle of whisky. Get the whisky."

Shani raced out to the Toyota and rummaged in the back. It was a bottle of Johnnie Walker.

"Give me a slug," he said. "And then use the rest."

He drank from the bottle, a thin line of spirit running down his chin and onto his chest. He paused for a moment, swallowing, then took another gulp. He handed the bottle back to her.

"Go for it," he said.

Her eyes searched quickly for cotton wool or something to ease her task. A blue jiffy cloth hung by the sink and she grabbed it. Sam drew in his breath. She poured the whisky onto the wound.

"Jeeeesus," he screamed as fire raged in his raw flesh.

He sat up, grabbing his thigh, his eyes weeping, face contorted, breath coming in short gasps. The maggots writhed in their death throes as she filled the cloth and flung out its revolting cargo. With Rabiyah she pushed him back.

"Deep breaths, we have to get them out."

"Noooooo!" he shouted, but she poured again.

He tried to twist, still clutching his leg, but they pinned his shoulders. Maggots seemed to appear from every fold, burning with the spirit, trying to escape. Shani threw another clutch out into the dusk. The leg seemed to clear. She dabbed a small amount of whisky this time, an anaesthetic. For a moment the muscle relaxed and Sam subsided on the bed. From the dark crater, a head appeared, the head of a deep mining maggot, now desperately seeking air and relief from the flames. Shani waited.

Josephine looked on, silent, her fingers still clawing.

******

*She was on the edge.*

*I knew that Sam could see it too, the way he'd looked over at me. Over the years we'd learnt the signs.*

*Maggots had collected now in the dip in the bunk where his buttocks lay. They coursed about on the sheet beneath his scrotum like lost sheep. Josephine began to thrash and slap at them again but as soon as one was killed another appeared.*

*"Mum, Mum, it's OK, leave them," said Sam dreamily.*

*But it was too much for her and she ran screaming from the motorhome, past me, her arms clamping her head as if to drown out the sound of their silent hunger.*

*She was breaking. I wanted to hug her, to comfort her, but I knew that, at that moment, she would not speak to me, I could not help her.*

\*\*\*\*\*\*

Still Shani waited. She waited till the maggot was out, wriggling free, then grasped it. She dripped more of the whisky over Sam's refusing flesh. Sweat poured from his skin. He clenched his teeth, moaning sometimes, as she dripped it into every crater, every suppurating crevice of the septic swamp that was his thigh. Finally she turned back to him.

"Brave boy."

She took a towel from Rabiyah and kissed him. A hint of a smile passed his closed lips.

"I'm going to get rid of these ones under your bum."

She rolled him on his side. The sheet was a mess of squashed maggots and whisky.

"Sorry," she cried in the direction of Lou and Stef as she yanked it out from under him and hurled it far into the green oats for the crows and gulls to feast on. Outside, she spoke with Rabiyah, her arms whirling in helpless urgency.

"Have another swig," she said, coming back into the motorhome, a forced cheerfulness in her voice. "I'm going to give a dab all around the wound. It's the best we can do until we get to Balmanie. I'm sure your aunt will have some antibiotics there."

Sam drank and slumped back, asleep or at least, for the moment, unconscious. Stef wandered into the motorhome.

"I need a cigarette."

Manically she hunted in the cupboards and dressers. At the back of a drawer, she found a pack of Silk Cut.

'Yes!' she cried.

But it was empty.

\*\*\*\*\*\*

*Bloody baby were wailing. Stef had been good with it – all cuddly and rocking it. She'd be a good mum. But she went in to try and find a fag and gave it to me. Soon as she did it started crying. I couldn't handle it. I didn't know what to do with it and gave it back to its mum.*

*The motorhome stank. Stank of bloody whisky. Reminded me of my old man before he left. All those fights with mum, when I was a kid. Coming out of me bedroom at night, creeping across the landing, and watching them. They'd fight like cats and dogs. But Mum would win. He'd crawl across the floor in the end. Dis-bloody-gusting it were to see yer dad crawling like that, asking her to forgive him.*

*And Sam were lying there, stark fuckin' bollock naked from his waist down, fast asleep. It weren't his willie, lying there on me bed, just fuckin' lying there, limp, that shocked me though, it were this great hole in his thigh. Shani had turned him half over on his bum - that were a good looking bum - but there were this white part in the crater. I looked again and realised – it were his fuckin' thigh bone. Shit. Shit, shit, shit. My thoughts were all over the fuckin' place. He's completely wounded, I thought. There's fuckin' maggots, I thought. That's my bed, I thought. I know he saved my life but where am I supposed to sleep, I thought. It were not like that oaf of a brother-in-law had taken over, but this were Stef and my home - the remains of our world.*

*My feet slipped on something on the floor and I looked down. It were white and mashie. That shook me into my senses as you might say.*

\*\*\*\*\*\*

Lou pulled a bandage from her webbed shoulder bag and handed it to Shani. Next, she took a roll of gaffer tape and unsheathed the knife. Expertly she cut a length of the tape and secured the bandage around the thigh.

"What *is* that bag?" asked Henry.

"Survival kit," she said brusquely.

Sam was snoring now. Shani laid a coat over him. She looked at Stef and Lou.

"I'm sorry … can we just let him sleep here."

They moved the vehicles away from the road and it was the girls who stood sentry duty that night.

# CHAPTER XX

SOUND carried long across the water on this coastline. The ears became attuned to the songs of the sea and the shore and the islands – oyster catchers piping across the beach, the ferry's horn as it came into Craignure, a shout from a boat, the cry of the gulls, the drive of the wind. But today the sound was somehow out of tune. An uneasiness filled Anne-Marie.

To calm herself, she walked to the top of the hill above the secret harbour. She trained her binoculars on Fraser's bothie. There was no smoke coming from the chimney. She could just make out her own boat in the water. With a jolt, she saw that the Lady Ffiona, his other boat, was gone.

She looked to the right, south. There was a glimmer of movement in the water. She thought at first it was two fishing boats but, as she focussed, she saw that they were not fishing but were loaded with people. They were heading towards the island, pitching and rolling in the growing swell.

A shiver ran through her. She had always felt safe enough in Balmanie on her own, though she was two miles or more from the nearest habitation. She figured that, if she fell ill, or something else occurred, she knew the hospital, and the police knew how to find the house; and, if, in the end, she were to die there, then what better place to die. But just for the moment she had no means of contact.

She felt an almost overwhelming urge to escape, but she knew it was pointless. There was nowhere to run to. She would have to face whatever would happen. And she owed it to Henry to be there for him when he got there - if he got there - and to provide him with some sort of shelter, though that shelter did, in fact, rightly belong to him too. She raised the binoculars to the point where she expected the two boats to have been but there was nothing.

'They're on their own,' she thought.

There was a chill in the evening air, though it was June. She filled the log basket from the woodshed and laid a fire. For some minutes she stayed on her knees, watching the unscripted rhythm of the flames. Rain began to fall. It tapped against the window panes, politely and timidly at first. She pulled a bottle of whisky from her store in the cellar and curled up in the womb of her favourite armchair. She opened 'The Narrow Road to the Deep North' and began to read, cherishing the snug warmth of her home.

The book was, she thought, appropriate to the times. For months, these men had been forced to work with barely any food, their clothes shredded, their feet bare, their bodies contorted in starvation…and yet some had pulled through.

She let the Glen Moray envelop her and closed her eyes. It was from this cocoon that she woke to a knock at the door. The rain was pelting down now. She picked up an old golf club from her father's bag that still sat in the hallway, the metal rusting quietly. She laid it against the wall, within reach, and opened the door.

There were perhaps fifteen of them. She was used to seeing walkers passing from time to time in two's and three's, but not normally this many. And these people, on closer inspection, did not look like walkers. They carried no walking poles and were not wearing walking boots. It was certainly not a time, anyway, nor a time of day, for holidays or walking. They looked tired and bedraggled, their clothes unkempt, rucksacks sagging from weary backs. All but one of them.

At the back, slightly apart, a woman stood, poised and upright like a model. On either side of her, two of the group held a groundsheet over her head, protecting her from the weathers. She reminded Anne-Marie of some rock goddess whose name she could not remember. Her olive skin hinted at Spain or South America. Dark hair hung in waves down her back and, unlike the others, she looked almost dry and clean. Her cobalt green smock sat perfectly over white cotton trousers that were wet only at the bottom.

A youngish man at the front was clearly the spokesman. A beard was already beginning to form on his unshaven face.

"I'm sorry to disturb you. We… we're asking for some help," he said. She could detect an element of nervousness in his voice.

"We've come from the mainland. From Oban. The police have lost control…nothing is working…people are fighting for food. I'm sure you've heard."

"I have," said Anne-Marie. "It is awful. I'm…"

She was going to say that she was hoping her brother and his family would make it to Mull, but something told her to hold her tongue. A sinking feeling had begun to envelop her.

"We could not stay. We took a fishing boat and came across."

"You took a fishing boat? Did you have permission? Whose was it?"

The woman stepped forward. She spoke in an American accent with a hint of another country, more exotic. Elegant hand gestures danced around her words.

"Please – I am Mira. You have to understand – life over there has fallen apart. People are fighting for food. Everyone is making use of what they can. Property doesn't mean anything at the moment."

Anne-Marie knew, of course, from Fraser's absence, from the phone call to Henry's house and from everything that had happened in Tobermory, that things were bad, yet somehow she had not expected the chaos to arrive here on her doorstep. She thought about her own boat across at Fraser's bothie, and his boat down in the secret harbour.

"We have nowhere to stay on the island," resumed the spokesman. "We are tired and wet and hungry. This is a big house. We know that once it was a Tibetan Buddhist centre. We wondered if you would consider allowing us to stay here. We would not cause any trouble. In fact we could help ensure that no one else caused you any trouble."

"I see," said Anne-Marie, the foundations of her castle beginning to crumble around her. "But who are you? Why should I let you into my house? How do you expect to eat?"

"I'm sure that Ba… the Lord will provide," said the spokesperson. "We are just normal people from the mainland."

"You're all one family?"

"Errh no, well, yes – in a way."

Anne-Marie frowned.

"Let me think about it. If you come back tomorrow, I will let you know."

She knew already that this tide of men was beyond her control, would come and run roughshod over her life, but she needed time to get used to the idea.

"Of course," said the spokesperson, turning. "We will come back tomorrow."

"You said Baba Ji would provide shelter for us, I'm starving," she heard a young woman mutter to the spokesman. But he just nodded and smiled.

Anne-Marie watched their backs until they were out of sight, disturbed. She walked from room to room in the house, remembering how it was when it was a Buddhist centre. She understood that the contingencies of the time meant that she could not expect to live in this big house on her own. But the expectancy of sharing it with Henry and his family again, an expectancy which, in itself, she had to get used to, was now being supplanted, without warning, by the thought of sharing it with many others, and complete strangers. Her life was being invaded.

She decided that she would take the top floor, the bedroom and bathroom and ante room. She would set Henry's own room aside for Henry and Josephine, and the green room for Sam and whoever else was coming with them - the man on the phone had said there was a car load. The remaining rooms these people could use.

She moved around the house selecting books and favourite pictures. She picked up a painting of a little boy in shorts holding a purple balloon outside a French café. It was one of which her grandmother, an accomplished artist, had always been very proud.

Outside, the storm had taken hold. It flailed against the windows and chased angrily about the stones of the old house, rattling over the roof. Again there was a knock on the door, louder and more insistent this time.

"I know you said tomorrow," the spokesperson shouted against the wind. "But this weather is awful. Our people are cold and wet, we have nowhere to go and we would like to know your decision."

She looked at them. She neither pitied them nor feared them. She knew that they would be coming in, and whether it would be this evening that she had hoped to have to herself for one last time, or tomorrow, she now could not worry about. She commanded herself, against the will of the whisky, to remain calm and concentrate. She opened the door wide and ushered them into the house, a brick at the base of her feelings. The ground sheet that was still held over Mira's head was lowered.

"Jai Guru Dev," she heard a voice whisper.

The dogs raced around, greeting the new arrivals as they moved in, shaking the rain from their clothes. Some of them bent to stroke the dogs while others completely ignored them, treating them as if they were unwanted distractions. Already the tiles in the hallway were wet and the coat hooks overloaded. A pile of shoes and boots formed at the bottom of the stairs - Anne-Marie was not expecting such respect for her carpets.

"Let me show you where you can sleep. You can use the lounge and the dining-room downstairs."

The people followed her around, nodding, in bare feet or socks.

"This is the kitchen," Anne-Marie went on. "I don't know what food you have brought, but you can use these shelves."

She led them upstairs.

"You can use these two bedrooms also. There is a bathroom here."

"Where will Mira sleep?" someone asked as they milled about, trying to decide who was going where.

Mira, still barely touched by the weather, flashed a smile.

"Thank you so much."

'Who are you Mira?' thought Anne-Marie.

# CHAPTER XXI

ANNE-MARIE was dreaming. She was dreaming of a choir singing in a cathedral or some great place of worship. A mighty organ sounded and Keith Moon was playing drums manically by the altar. For a few moments, as she stirred, she could still picture the music. But the dream was over, she was wide awake, and the music went on.

She thought at first she had left the television on, until she remembered there was no power. She went downstairs. The dogs came racing around her, hungry and excited, and when she bent to greet them, she understood. The sound was coming from the lounge, and it was a choir. A choir of chanting followers. One of them played a lonely beat against a leather cushion.

The lounge door had never closed in her memory. It was far larger than its frame and, disfigured by years of damp and cold and layers of paint, the aperture now afforded her a narrow view. The room had been laid out in a different way. It reminded Anne-Marie of the shrine room when they had had the Buddhist centre there. At one end, a single upright chair had been placed, the chair that her grandfather used to sit in, and on it a large photograph of an Indian man, with long curling hair and a benign smile. He was wearing saffron robes.

She could see Mira holding a metal tray, one of her own trays that they must have found in the kitchen. On it were a number of nightlights, lit. She was swaying the tray around, moving it in time with the chanting and the drumbeat of the leather. Anne-Marie was surprised how much music could be conjured from that cushion. The group were chanting in unison, their hands folded in prayer or devotion in front of them. Some of them had their eyes closed, as if they had consumed some sort of heavenly pill.

"Jai Guru Dev, Shri Bhagwan Ji…"

The chanting was in Hindi but she understood the words. Something along the lines of 'Hail, great guru, great master, your glory fills the world, you are the protector of the weary and the weak.'

'Oh for God's sake,' she thought.

She had traversed the guru world even before Balmanie was a Tibetan Buddhist centre. It was not, now, that she did not seek, or at least accept, that there may be some higher truth – it was just that she was done with following some guru or teacher who claimed to have the answer to everything, who demanded her exclusive devotion. If others were happy with such an arrangement, that was fine with her.

Suddenly the dogs raced in to the room. Mira looked around disapprovingly as they nosed around. She was still upright, tall and regal but she looked a little irritated this morning. Anne-Marie watched her closely as the chanting finished, the tray was put down, and everyone knelt on the floor and bowed their heads towards the photograph, Mira spearheading the prostrations. She sat up and turned to face the rest of the group, cross-legged on the carpet. The others looked towards her, wide-eyed and eager for her words.

"By Baba Ji's grace, we have been looked after so far," she said. "If we follow His path of puja, service and meditation, He will continue to look after us. Puja – what is puja? It is devotion, in the presence of Truth and His…"

Anne-Marie could almost recite the rest herself and she wandered off to the kitchen. She needed a cup of tea. She guessed that Mira's address would go on for half an hour or so. The old aga, fuelled by wood, was always hot and she was onto her second cup when they came through. Some looked high, some tired, while one girl looked positively pissed off - it was the one who had said she was starving the night before. She came into the kitchen. Anne-Marie recognised the symptoms.

"Hug? Cup of tea?"

"Both please," said the girl.

Anne-Marie embraced her. She had never thought of herself as a mother figure, that her hug would be received as warm. She turned to the stove. The cup of tea that she extended carried a second embrace.

"I'm Anne-Marie," she said, holding up her palm.

The girl did not respond at first. She clenched her fist, then opened it.

"Leah," she said, slapping her hand against Anne-Marie's.

"Like in Princess?" said Anne-Marie, thinking immediately how uncool a question this was. But the girl seemed unfazed, nodding.

"So what's going on here? Who's this Baba Ji?"

"Baba Ji is the guru…our guru. That's his sort of nickname. His real name is Bhagwan Shri Vrijaya, I think that's right."

"But you seem to treat Mira like a guru herself."

"Well…she's kind of his representative over here. That's what they say."

Anne-Marie detected an opening, a break.

"And how long have you been into this?"

"Just a month really. My boyfriend, Daniel – he was the one who knocked on your door – got me into it. I think Mira's got him under her spell. No, I shouldn't have said that. She's very beautiful, but it's not about beauty, she says, it's about Truth. Baba Ji is Truth."

Anne-Marie bit her lip, keeping her silence.

"And what is this Truth?"

"I don't know yet," said Leah. "I'm just a neophyte. I haven't been revealed it."

"Revealed it?"

"Yes. Baba Ji reveals it to you on something they call a Truth Day."

"Oh," said Anne-Marie. "And does Mira show you this Truth too?"

"I don't know. I don't think so," said Leah. "But Daniel is so infatuated by her."

"Well, I think I'd be infatuated by her if I were a young man."

Leah sighed.

"I suppose…" she said. She ran her hands back through her blonde hair.

"We were in a place near Oban when all this happened, on a kind of retreat. I don't…I don't really understand it all. We're not allowed to sleep together. She keeps talking about celibacy."

Two other devotees appeared. They looked stressed.

"Mira wants her breakfast."

"What does she want?"

"Muesli and a mango."

Anne-Marie laughed out loud.

"She can sing for the mango," she said.

The others looked at her as if she had uttered some kind of blasphemy, as if it was a sin to question Mira's requests.

"What can we give her then?"

"Whatever you've got. There's nothing else. The blackberries in the brambles won't be ripe for another two or three months."

Mira walked into the kitchen.

"Morning!" said Anne-Marie breezily.

The others stood silently, their hands folded in front of them.

"It is a beautiful morning."

"Ain't no mangoes on Mull, though." Anne-Marie's take on an American accent lightened the tension. She looked at Mira directly.

"Where is your boat?"

# CHAPTER XXII

HENRY had slept only fitfully and his neck ached. He sat in the long grass, nursing a cup of tea that Lou had conjured from the motorhome. It was black and bitter. The old road map lay open in front of him. He turned from one page, the approach to Glasgow, to another, Argyll and Bute and north.

As an oil industry executive for thirty years, he understood geology. It was the baseline of the industry - research, explore, test, drill. He knew well the effects of the Ice Age two million years ago. He knew what happened in the Pleistocene and the Holocene periods. But when it came to the Highlands of Scotland, he threw that knowledge aside, he stepped out of those dry scientific clothes. Instead he stepped into another world where warring gods had formed the land.

They had come upon this place of greens and browns and mighty purples and, desperate to take possession, had fought over it like eagles over the carcase of a fox. In a bitter, jealous frenzy, they had slashed at the carcase again and again, casting pieces of torn flesh far and wide. Then, in some form of penitence or regret, they had poured gallons and gallons of water onto the wounds.

Scotland was gashed. This was its beauty and its problem. Water. Water everywhere. To get anywhere you needed to go over the water or round the water. If there wasn't a bridge, you needed a ferry. If there was no ferry – and there were going to be no ferries now – then it was the long road around.

These were the thoughts that formed in his mind as he studied their route and waited for his son to wake. Glasgow was little more than an hour away. Whatever else they might come across, they had to get to the Erskine Bridge. From there they could follow Loch Lomond or Loch Long north. Any other road led way off east and would mean at the very least that a lot of water would have to be skirted before they got back on track. If they could get through. If they had enough fuel. If food and water lasted.

******

"How are you feeling?" asked Shani when Sam eventually stirred, stroking the hair from his eyes. He paused for a moment.

"Mmmm ... so far so good. Head clear – check. Thigh..." He lifted the blanket that lay over his bare legs and backside and studied the bandage. A stain from the weeping flesh had formed a tide mark. A hint of stale whisky and putrescence still hung in the air. He looked up.

"... only dull pain – check.

"Beautiful woman – still stonkingly beautiful – check."

He pulled her to him and hugged her, nuzzling hungrily into her neck and her hair.

"Stop," she cried, "Cool down! Your stubble's like a hedgehog!"

He manoeuvred his legs off the bunk and fought his way back into his shorts, then yawned and stretched his arms.

119

"Sorry about that," he announced to the world in general, leaning against the door of the motorhome. He wanted to shake off the maggot-strewn trauma of the night before but the image of their crawling was stamped on his mind.

He looked about him. Lou was whittling some wood and Rabiyah was changing the baby on the grass. She was using giant dandelion leaves to clean her. His father was studying a map splayed out in front of him and Stef was swiping her mobile strenuously, as if a more powerful swipe would somehow bring her a signal, another candidate on Tinder or Hinge.

Sam shook his head loosely from side to side to ensure he was awake. An everyday image of a family camping, he thought. Almost.

"There are no more men out there," he called to Stef. "I'd save your battery."

Lou held up a branch of ash, forked at the top, to his shoulder, measuring his height. She cut a few centimetres from the bottom. One fork was higher than the other, and this she scored part way down. She bent the wood across, slotting it into a notch that she had made in the opposite side. She handed Sam the crutch.

"That's amazing, Lou," he said, testing it with an exaggerated limp. "Better than the NHS."

If his cheer was forced, it was not evident.

"Where's Mum?" he asked, his tone suddenly serious.

"Jo," shouted Henry, "Sam's up. We need to leave."

They looked around the vehicles. There was no sign of her.

"Jo," shouted Henry again.

She appeared from behind a hedge, her face blank.

"I needed the loo."

******

The monolithic pillars of the Erskine Bridge strode majestically across the Clyde, oblivious to the affairs of men. The river ran brown and silent beneath them. Henry slowed as they approached. The carriageway was clear to the centre section where the road rose higher. He had no view further. He had no choice either.

He accelerated. Beyond, he thought, is the final run. The spans of the bridge looped grey and giddy above them. The sides were netted and closed off to fifteen feet and he wondered, idly, how many people had jumped to their death from there to make that necessary. It didn't really matter now.

They reached the mid-point. A silver car came slowly towards them on the opposite carriageway. Fear and uncertainty were etched in the driver's eyes. Nothing else was on the bridge. No car, no person, nothing.

Henry breathed a sigh of relief as they made it to the north side. He selected the A82, Loch Lomond. Plan A was to get to Oban. That was the direct route, the main route. It was the way they had always come in his childhood, although later, when he would drive his old green Morris Minor up there on the epic journey from his university in Exeter, he would often go on to Lochaline and take the haggis route, as he and Anne-Marie called it.

"Watch out," he murmured as they approached Alexandria.

The name might have sounded romantic, but this was no place for the timid, its junctions and buildings ambush country. He glanced at Sam, next to him, cradling the twelve bore, alert. Trucks and cars littered the road. He could see the motorhome in the rear view mirror and drove faster, weaving between the abandoned vehicles. His mind conjured images of hooded men at road blocks and guns poking from upper storey windows in Dallas. But he'd thrown a double six, and the dice took them clear through to land on Go. Safety…for the moment.

It began to rain. Soon he could not tell the waters of the loch to his right from the thick grey mist that descended. North of Tarbet, the road became single lane. In places it was cut so close to the rock that he thought the top of the motorhome in his rear view mirror would scrape against it. He veered tight to the left as a truck came the other way. The driver was flashing his lights.

"What was that about?" said Sam

"What?"

"He was waving his hands sideways as well as flashing."

They soon found out. Splayed across the road a quarter of a mile ahead was an artic. To its front, a rag-tag series of vehicles lay empty, frozen in mid-manoeuvre – some facing forward, some back, some in mid-turn. The doors of a red VW van hung open and Henry caught a glimpse of clothing. The clothing did not move. The signwriting on the van read 'KW Painting and Decorating.'

The flotsam and jetsam of the vehicles lay discarded on the road - the manuals, the frost scrapers, the road maps, the CD's, the empty Costa cups and sweet wrappers. Cans of paint lay behind the van and a pool of blue emulsion had formed.

"Give me the gun," said Henry recklessly. He dragged on a rain jacket, pulled up the hood and jumped out.

Very cautiously, using one vehicle after another for cover, he crept forward. There was a crash behind him. He spun around. It was just a branch from a pine, brought down by the weight of water.

But above the steady beat of the rain he could hear a humming, almost a siren call, now louder, moaning like a swarm of bees, now fading, now louder again. He glimpsed movement in the grey dreich and slowly his eyes made out a black drone, circling. He raised the twelve bore.

"What do you want?" he shouted angrily.

The drone spun and looped. An image came into his mind of the operator – perhaps close at hand, perhaps miles away - watching him in black and white and laughing at him. He lowered the gun. There was no point. He'd just be wasting a cartridge. He could only deal with what he knew.

He hauled himself up to the cab window of the artic. There was no one inside and he clambered in. He slid across the seat, his head low to the worn plastic, and peered out the other side.

A man's body lay face down, straddling muddy tyre marks on the verge. Aside from that, there was nothing. Nothing except rain and thick mist and a black drone. Of the ambushers, and those who had been ambushed, of the drivers and passengers, there was no sign. A chill filtered through Henry's spine.

He studied the dashboard. He'd never driven an artic and did not intend to learn now. But if he could just start this one and back it up a few yards…otherwise, there was no choice and the gods would claim more fuel. The keyhole was in the centre console but there was no key in it. He searched the seats and the floor. He searched the glove pockets. The sleeping section, behind the seats, reeked of scotch and aftershave. He searched there too.

There was one more possibility, one that he had unconsciously recognised but hoped he would not have to explore. He leant out of the window towards Sam and gave a thumbs-up; then, hugging the rain jacket around him, he climbed down to the body on the other side. The drone moved in an arc in front of him.

Leaning back, as if touching something foul and diseased, he placed his toe under the dead man's hip and tipped him onto his back. The man's face was blotched and unshaven. Henry felt in the coat pockets. A sodden packet of cigarettes, a lighter. On the other side, coins and tissues.

Gingerly, he put his hand in the right-hand trouser pocket. Something in his upbringing told him that this was sacrilege, that he was defiling the dead; but something more present and more urgent told him that this was no more than roadkill and he must take what he could.

His fingers touched the dead man's scrotum and, in revulsion, jerked back. And, in jerking back, they alighted on the key. Moving back round, he held it up to the others.

"We need to move this thing before anyone else comes," he said urgently.

Rabiyah took up position at the rear, marking point.

Henry walked quickly to the back of the trailer with Shani. It was at an angle to the tractor and a silver-coloured Volvo was slewed behind it as if the driver, in a desperate bid to escape, had tried to squeeze between the trees and the loch.

There was probably enough space, he judged, to back the truck up about three metres. They just needed to clear one carriageway. He climbed back into the cab. He was surprised how quickly the engine started. He felt a deep throb beneath him, the power of five thousand horses. He released the handbrake and moved the lever to reverse.

With his right foot, he applied power gently, he thought, but, like an angry gorilla wakened from its sleep, the tractor lurched backwards. In a fraction of a second he glimpsed Shani in the side mirror leaping out of the way and heard the sickening crunch of metal surrendering to hard steel, and glass breaking irrevocably. He was thrown against the seat back as the trailer stopped, wheels spinning, straining against some immoveable object.

He pushed the lever into neutral and stepped out. Shani was surveying the situation. The trailer had skewed at a greater angle than they had expected. It had torn through the silver car like a chain saw through tissue and come to rest against the trunk of a broad pine. They went round to the front. The tractor was still more than half way across the road.

"I think we can get through there," said Sam. "If we can move the van and that green car."

He limped across to the van. He pushed the owner of the unmoving clothes to the floor without ceremony, a young woman. The back of her head was matted in blood, misshapen. Grimacing, he released the handbrake and pulled the wheel around.

"If we push from the front, it should just free wheel down when we get to that slope."

Gradually the van picked up momentum and in slow motion crashed into the stone wall that bordered the road fifty metres further down. The green car still blocked their path.

"We'll have to roll it," said Sam.

They all lined up along the side.

"One-two-three," shouted Henry, but the car would not move.

Sam hobbled between them.

"Rock it," he said and they began to rock it from side to side.

"Now," he said, in time with the rocking and, with a final push, the car went over on its back.

There was a sudden crack. Everyone froze. A car was coming up the road behind them. Another crack. A bullet ripped into the side of the red van. Rabiyah had done enough with this second warning shot. The car swerved and skidded into a U-turn and retreated, its engine screaming.

The rain still teemed down. The air was heavy with the scent of the sodden loam that the downpour had lifted. Stef's hair hung matted and dripping and Shani's left side was spattered in mud and pine needles. They ran back to the cover of the vehicles.

Henry inched the Toyota forward. Making contact in the middle of the green car with the full width of the mudguard, he nudged it forwards on its roof until, slowly at first, it slipped and scraped across the tarmac towards the bank. Then, in an instant, it tumbled down into the ditch and lay there like a beached insect, its legs flailing helplessly in the air.

Now, turning the wheel left and right, he could weave past the truck and through onto the open road. The motorhome followed, scouring a deep and grating silver line along the blue paintwork of its right side in the effort to bend between the truck's bumper and the muddy verge.

Henry scanned the sky. At last the drone had gone. He glanced at Josephine. She sat looking straight ahead, unblinking and expressionless. He laid his hand over hers, but she did not respond. He looked at the fuel gauge.

"We need to fill up from the cans," he said. "It's a long road ahead."

"Yeah, but this is crazy," said Sam. "They're going to be refuelling the motorhome. We're going to be filling this thing up. We're wasting fucking fuel. We could abandon the motorhome. Take the girls in this. Or all go in that."

"Yes, I know. But we don't have the space for them...let's wait. Just for the moment. See what happens. It has its uses that motorhome. You saw that."

Sam grunted as his father pulled into a rhododendron-strewn drive. The sign outside read 'Glen Torraig Country House Hotel'.

# CHAPTER XXIII

MIRA WAVED her hand dismissively at Anne-Marie's question.

"We don't need our boat. It has served its purpose."

"Do you think so? A boat on this island is more than a taxi, you know. Farmers don't come home from the fields with their tractor in the evening and just abandon them. They park them up for the night and the next day they plough with them or carry with them or harvest with them."

"What do you mean?"

"A boat gets you from A to B but you can fetch supplies in a boat or you can go fishing in a boat too. The sea is a wonderful place if you treat it with respect. When you have eaten the fish you caught yesterday, it will yield up more fish today. More than ever we need a boat at the moment."

"We don't eat fish."

"What do you propose to eat then?"

"Baba Ji says we should not eat meat, fish or eggs."

Anne-Marie sighed.

"I say again, what will you eat? There are no restaurants functioning on the island now, let alone vegetarian ones.

All the food shops have sold out or been ransacked. We're on our own here, Mira."

A look, a shadow that might have been concern, passed across the sculpted contours of her face, but she remained adamant.

"Baba Ji will provide."

Anne-Marie gave up.

"OK. If you don't want your boat, I will look after it. I may need it. Someone may need it. Tell me where you landed."

"It was nearly dark."

"Was it rocky, sandy?"

"It was muddy," piped in Leah. "My shoe came off when we climbed out and I felt this mud oozing through my toes. And then there was seaweed, you could hear it popping and you could smell it. And slippery stones. Not big rocks, stones."

Anne-Marie nodded. She could picture where they had landed. They must have come in, she calculated, at the top of the high tide.

"Did you secure it?"

Mira looked at her haughtily, declining to respond.

"Right, I need two people to help me. Leah, will you come? Who else? We need to move – NOW!"

"I'll come," said Daniel, casting half a glance at Mira. But Mira shook her head.

"I need you here," she said without explanation. "Mehau can go."

Mehau was a tall man, rugged. He posed no threat, Anne-Marie thought, to Leah's chastity.

Daniel nodded obediently and, folding his hands in front of him, waited with Mira as they left.

"Have you got walking boots, something strong. We're not strolling down a city street."

"Only what I have on."

Anne-Marie glanced at the trainers on her feet and the tight turquoise jeans, smeared in places with dried mud.

Mehau wore clumpy black town shoes and brown slacks. If he'd added a tie to his blue-striped shirt, he might, at first glance, have been an office boy. She rousted around in a pile of old wellington boots in the hallway, then handed them each a pair.

"Here," she said as they struggled into them. "Quick. We don't have much time."

She led them across the front lawn and down a narrow path through thick scrub at a fast pace, the dogs racing along with them.

"I don't know how we - how you say? - scramble through this last night," said Mehau, looking around at the chest-high gorse, ferns and brambles. He spoke with an East European accent.

"Why is rush?"

"The tide. Everything works on the tide. The tide rules our lives here."

"How you mean?"

"If the boat is where I think it is, you caught the shore pretty much at high tide. With luck it will still be there, grounded as the tide went out. It'll be high tide again very soon, more or less twelve hours later. If we're too late, it could just float out to sea, or else be dashed against the stones and break up."

She half ran across a section of grassy shoreline. A rocky outcrop blocked their path. Anne-Marie had been brought up on climbing the hills and rocks of these islands. Negotiating them was in her DNA and, despite her years, she moved swiftly, if not gracefully, over them.

Leah swore as she slipped, her jeans tearing. Mehau caught her and helped her onto the next rock. He was proving to be more interesting – more of a gentleman and more athletic – than Anne-Marie had expected.

A rhythmic drumming, sometimes irregular, greeted them as they cornered the headland. Anne-Marie gasped. It was a navy boat with an unusual orange stripe. It was

Fraser's, the Lady Ffiona. She would ask later how they came upon this boat and what had become of Fraser.

She knew what had become of Ffiona. She had been so unlucky. When they pieced it together, the coroner decided that their collie, the one before Rabbie, had leapt into the cab of Fraser's tractor and unknowingly released the handbrake. The tractor had slid back into her, pinning her against a stack of hay bales before she knew what was happening, crushing the life from her.

The Lady Ffiona, however, had been lucky. The boat was slewed at a diagonal across the beach. Waves were lapping at her stern, lifting her off the sand and setting her down again, rocking in the new swell, but she was not yet afloat and she was intact.

She was perhaps thirty years old, the timbers painted and repainted, the old navy clearly visible where the weathers had faded the most recent layer. A wide orange stripe that ran around the side of the boat, a foot below the top, dipped suddenly downwards in the centre, port and starboard, like a blip on a heart monitor, before resuming its regular course. She was unusually long for a boat with no wheelhouse.

"Come on," said Anne-Marie, quickening her pace again. Mira and the devotees must have just jumped out of the boat and abandoned it, she thought. No rope was attached or anchor and the propeller of the outboard was snagging in the muddy sand. Now, without intervention, the boat would have set out on a new journey, drifting aimlessly until it was smashed against the rocks of some outer island, unwanted.

Anne-Marie waded into the rising water. She reached into the bow until she found a rope. She handed it to Mehau.

"Hold onto this," she said as she climbed in.

She went straight to the stern and rotated the outboard forwards and out of the water.

"Damn," she cursed.

A tangle of orange fishing net curled around the propeller, throttling it. She leant over and pulled at the mesh, but it was tightly wound and immoveable. It would need a large knife, at least, or shears, and there was not time.

"Hopefully it's just fouled up and not damaged. How on earth did you make it to shore?"

"I think it stopped just before we landed," said Leah. "We couldn't really see what was happening."

Anne-Marie looked in the bottom of the boat. She was relieved to see the oars still in place on either side. She wondered how these people had survived, who had manned the outboard, how they had navigated.

"Jump in with me, Leah. Mehau, you're going to have to get wet. I need you to push the boat out. Keep a hold of the rope. We're going to row round the point. When I give you the signal, climb in."

A large wave broke. Mehau leant against the bow and the boat floated free.

"We need to get further out," said Anne-Marie. "The shore is very flat here."

Mehau did not complain as the water rose above his knees. He was waist deep when Anne-Marie said, "OK, climb in now."

He clasped the side, but his weight tipped the boat almost to the water.

"Woah! Wait!"

Anne-Marie and Leah moved to the opposite side leaning out over the sea. This time Mehau leant his chest over the side first and rolled in, his body slumping across one of the bench slats, his wellingtons draining into the bottom of the boat.

"Oars," said Anne-Marie. "Have you ever rowed Leah?"

She shook her head.

"Mehau?"

"At home, when I was child…I think I can. I try."

Anne-Marie moved to the seat in the centre, her back to the bow. She pulled an oar from the bottom and placed it in the rowlock. Mehau watched her and followed suit.

"Leah, you sit here by the outboard. You are our cox, our pilot. We need to aim first for that lighthouse on the island opposite. Just raise your arm in the direction we need to go in, and if we're on target, just keep your hands on your knees."

Mehau dipped his oar in the water and pulled. The boat spun alarmingly.

"We need to work together," said Anne-Marie. "We pull at the same time. If Leah raises her left hand, you pull and I don't, and if she raises her right hand, I pull and you raise your oar out of the water."

For some moments, Leah was motionless, then suddenly she raised her left arm.

"You," said Anne-Marie, lifting her oar out of the water.

But the strength of Mehau's stroke brought the boat too far round. Leah raised her other arm.

"Lift your oar Mehau, no stroke."

He did not seem to understand and pulled again himself, his natural power turning the boat almost in a circle. The tide was coming in fast now, and they were dangerously close to the old pier. Anne-Marie was not concerned for their lives – the water was shallow and there was not far to land – but for the boat. She knew how much Fraser had valued it, and, now, she wanted to preserve it for the sake of what it might give them. Leah raised her arm urgently on the other side.

"Mehau," said Anne-Marie, "You are not rowing for a gold medal. A gentle pull is fine. Watch."

Apparently effortlessly, she leant against her oar and he watched the prow ease around. He tried himself, pulling only gradually, glancing behind him to check the effect of his stroke, and nodded in understanding.

"Right, we just have to get past the old pier and round the next headland."

The pier stretched thirty metres out into the bay, encrusted with barnacles and seaweed. The old mooring rings were still there, rusty now, but parts of the upper concrete section had worn away with the tides and the storms. In her grandparents' day, before the proper road was built, most people who came to Balmanie, friends or builders or plumbers, or old Gillespie with the groceries, came by boat.

The scent of pine and rhododendron, and bladderwrack on the shoreline, carried across the water in the breeze to mingle with the tang of the salt sea and the fish-soaked timbers of the boat. Like a thief that cannot hold onto her booty, Anne-Marie drew in deep lungfuls of this air, then returned them, unwillingly, to the atmosphere.

"When we clear the pier," she said, "we need to turn to the North, left, towards that stone cross on the headland. You see it?"

"Yes," shouted Leah above the splash of the boat through the water and the piping of oyster catchers skimming across the tips of the waves. She was embracing her new job with relish. She raised an arm suddenly to the left, then dropped it again.

"No, sorry," she said. "It was just a big bird. What is that?"

"A heron," said Anne-Marie, laughing as the heron flapped its long grey wings languidly back to the shore.

"Imagine the length of half a football pitch. That's the deepest channel. We need to go round the headland about that distance away."

The stone cross was clearer now. Leah shivered and wrapped her arms around herself. It was chillier out here in the open Sound where the wind coursed more strongly. The water was choppy, making headway more strenuous, and the rhythmic creak of the oars in the rowlocks lulled them into a stern concentration.

Slowly, turning into the wind, they slipped past the point, and, as they did so, Fraser's cottage came into view on the mainland, a white dot across the water. Something made Anne-Marie look more closely, but for once she had not brought her binoculars. She gestured back towards the shore.

"Aim to the right of that grey rock."

Through a narrow channel, a little bay opened up in front of them. It was protected from view, and from the vicious waves and winds, by a ring of rocks. In its centre, bobbing serenely against a buoy, was Fraser's other boat, the Lizzie.

"Wow!" said Leah

"Don't worry about the rocks. The channel is deep. Just aim for the middle."

The Lady Ffiona crunched against the stones of the shoreline and Anne-Marie climbed out into the shallow water. Securing the rope temporarily around a rock, she led Mehau to the dinghy. Together, they carried it to the water.

"I'm going to take the Lady Ffiona out again. The other boat is on the buoy so I'm going to have to anchor her," said Anne-Marie. "Can you row out and bring me back?"

Mehau nodded and, with Leah's help, pushed off.

The Lady Ffiona was safely moored when an insistent hum came from the south. They looked up, trying to interpret the sound. Like the dentist's drill in a bad dream, the noise built. It was coming from the sky or the mountains, echoing across the water.

Louder and louder the sound came. Louder until, like Lucifer, they appeared – a line of five black helicopters, two hundred metres apart, soaring low over the water, their blades cutting and juddering through the unwilling air.

"Quick," said Anne-Marie.

They dived behind a thick clump of bushes. They could see the black uniforms, the pale skin and staring eyes of the pilots as the helicopters passed close in front of them, then folded into the distance again, the thudding fading.

"Whatever the hell they were, they did not look friendly," said Anne-Marie. "I don't think they would have seen us though."

"By Baba Ji's grace," said Mehau.

"By Baba Ji's grace, or the Lord's grace, or Buddha's grace, or Allah's grace – or just plain bloody good luck," said Anne- Marie.

Leah was white, her lips quivering. Mehau put his arm around her.

"Is OK. We look after you."

Anne-Marie led them up into the woods at the head of the beach. A steep path climbed to a clearing. From here they had a birds-eye view of the little bay that was home now to the two boats. An otter had slipped into the water. It hunted amongst the rocks, the sun glistening off its wet back as it curved about the wavelets.

Anne-Marie looked at them both.

"So what did happen to Fraser, the owner of the boat?"

Mehau coughed.

"Dead," he said. "Dead. She told - throw overboard. She did not look, she turned her back."

# CHAPTER XXIV

IT WAS a warm day now and the rain of the night before lingered only on the deepest leaves as they walked back. In the house, some devotees were wandering around aimlessly, while others lay on the lawn. Mira was nowhere to be seen. Daniel ran up to them.

"Are you OK - we heard helicopters?" he asked breathlessly.

Leah nodded, but she was shaking, staring at the ground. His hug seemed to hold no embrace for her. Anne-Marie went upstairs. From her bedroom window she could see, on the far side of the Sound, a tiny black speck moving low over the water.

'What do they want?' she thought.

She picked up her binoculars. She trained them on Fraser's bothie. All appeared quiet. She could see her boat tied securely still to the buoy. She wondered if the note was still in place .There was a shout.

"There are people in the trees!"

She looked out from the landing. In the trees that skirted the drive below the road, figures were moving. There was no time to find Mira.

"Mehau, Daniel,!" Anne-Marie called. "Quickly. Get everyone you can. Make it clear to these people that they are not welcome here."

The intruders had broken cover and were heading for the house. There were about eight of them. Anne-Marie heard shuffling and muffled voices below her. Then a group of devotees trooped out, a dishevelled but willing crew. Mehau led them, his tall muscular frame forming the arrowhead. He seemed to Anne-Marie unafraid.

"We are just looking for some water." A female voice.

"This is private property, please leave now," shouted Daniel, as they fanned out across the long lawn at the side of the house. Mehau waved them forward.

"We live on the mainland; we can't get back. We have children desperately thirsty."

Daniel shook his head. "There is no water available here. Please leave."

A man bent to the ground. Anne-Marie recognized him as one of the car drivers who had been waiting in vain for the ferry just twenty-four hours previously.

"Bastards! Children, our children need food, water," he shouted, hurling a stone in the direction of Mehau.

He dodged it easily, but soon a hail of stones and debris was raining down on them. One of the devotees was hit. He screamed, falling to the ground, but they left him and closed the line.

"Faster," said Daniel and they began to jog.

They seemed to carry with them a shield of invincibility, some driving faith. It was enough for the intruders and they turned and faded back into the woods and hills to look for easier prey. Leah was shivering still when the wounded devotee was carried back in, his face bloodied. They laid him on the floor. Noone seemed to know what to do next.

"Why us?" Leah asked. "Why are people…?"

Daniel pulled her to him and held her.

"It's OK. We got rid of them. They won't come back," he said. "But they're not what is really going on – they're not the real problem. They're just collateral damage."

Mira appeared in the hallway like a stern saint; she carried the cold perfection of a mannequin. Her coral green smock, though torn now in places, still hung immaculately from her shoulders. She stared at Daniel. He dropped his arms and folded his hands in front of him. She turned her gaze on Anne-Marie, but whatever spell she held over the devotees held no sway with her and it was Mira who lowered her eyes first.

"Look, Mira, I think we need to talk."

She nodded and they moved into the lounge, the de facto shrine room. The photograph of Baba Ji, its edges curling, rested against her grandfather's upright chair in front of the old stone fireplace. Mira prostrated herself in front of it, then sat cross-legged on one of the cushions that lay haphazardly across a threadbare Turkish rug. Anne-Marie lowered herself into her favourite armchair.

"I don't know what is going on," she said. "I don't think you know what is going on. But for the moment we are on our own here.

"It seems to me that you are responsible for these people. I don't know what gives you that right, but, whatever it is, you have taken that role. They have accepted that somehow you will look after them in the name of your Baba Ji. I can help, but, if we all want to survive, we need to work together."

Mira looked a little annoyed and brushed a stray hair from her forehead.

"If we practise meditation, and service and devotion to Baba Ji, He will look after us."

Anne-Marie wanted to shake her. Her commitment to Baba Ji's edicts had a kind of stubborn inflexibility about them. She was like a cold glass vase. She wanted to hurl the vase against a wall; to see it smash in myriad pieces; she wanted to find the life inside.

"You can practise all the devotion and meditation you want. I'm not going to stop you or stand in your way – in fact I rather admire it; but, if you want to see Baba Ji again, perhaps the service means doing something more."

"What are you suggesting?"

"For a start, we need to keep this place safe. We need to defend it. You saw the helicopters, or heard them anyway; you saw what just happened at the front of the house. Those were just tourists. Just tourists I say, but they are human beings like us. Did you hear them? They have children who haven't eaten, they're desperate for water and they have nowhere to stay. In just two days they have become bandits.

"We can be nearly self-sufficient here, but only for so many people. Up to this point we have been lucky. Perhaps you are right - your Baba Ji has looked after us. Or perhaps it was just our good sense. Either way, in case Baba Ji has not received the full message - of the difficulty you are in, we are all in -  I will show you around the land and the point, the area that we need to defend.

"Baba Ji does not allow violence."

"I am sure your Baba Ji does not allow violence," said Anne-Marie. "And no one needs to fight. We have no weapons except garden forks and spades and an axe or two, anyway. But we can use our brains; we can convince people by our numbers to stay away, as we did just now."

Mira nodded.

"While we are talking of violence, tell me what happened in Oban. I know the owner of that boat. Or I knew him."

"It is not your business."

"It *is* my business. If I am going to trust you in my house, to work with me, I need to know what happened. I need to know that you practise what you preach in terms of violence."

Mira looked away. She seemed to wrestle with her thoughts for several moments, then took a deep breath. A rush of words poured from her lips as if she was trying to relate a dream before the dream faded.

"We were on a five-day retreat in a big house on the edge of Oban. It is owned by the BSV Foundation, Baba Ji's organisation. These people with me have come from all over the country. The caretaker came – he was panicked. He said 'Go, go, you have to leave, don't drink the water, they have poisoned the water.' The power was not working. My cell phone was not working…

"I promised Baba Ji that I would look after his devotees. It was my first vow."

She seemed on the point of tears and Anne-Marie felt a glimmer of hope. She listened quietly.

"We went to the train station. People were lying on the platform. I thought they were sleeping until I tripped on one. The body was rigid. A man growled at us. 'There are no trains; there is nothing,' he said.

"We walked into the town and saw the mayhem. I said, 'Stay together and close.' The bodies were everywhere, contorted. The shops were being looted, the windows smashed. I was terrified, but I could not show it. I kept saying to myself that Baba Ji will protect us. People didn't approach us – I suppose we were too big a group.

"We went down to the harbour. A ferry was tied up there but there was no life on it and it was going nowhere. 'Find a vehicle, or a boat,' I said. 'We have to get out of here.' It was already late.

"At the bottom of a little jetty on the south end, a man had started the engine on the boat – our boat. He was releasing the mooring rope when a woman appeared. She was much younger than him. She was wearing yellow shorts and walking boots and a wax jacket that was way too big for her. I don't know why I remember that. They were shouting at each other and I wondered if he knew her. The boat man stood up. He had an oar in his hand and swiped at her. She ducked. 'You can't hurt me,' she yelled and pulled out a knife. It looked like a kitchen knife.

"She thrust it towards the boat man. I thought, in the confusion, that she had missed, but I suppose that she wounded him. He swung the oar again. Her head jerked sideways and, seeing us approaching too, she ran.

"I said to the boat man, 'Can we come on your boat. We will pay you. Can you take us to the island over there?' He was weak but he nodded.

"The boat rested lower and lower in the water as everyone climbed aboard. He looked surprised, as if he was being visited by every member of his family on a special birthday. I think he tried to smile. Finally he released the rope and steered towards the entrance to the harbour.

"I noticed a lick of blood edging from his lips. I saw the water in the bottom of the boat, beneath the floor boards, turning red. We were only just out into the open sea when his head fell. 'Left of the lighthouse, then right past the old castle and turn into the bay,' he breathed, then toppled forwards.

"Daniel took the tiller. The light was dying but a white lighthouse lay straight ahead, the outline of the mountains of the island just visible behind it. The directions were clear but the body of the boatman lay there. My eyes kept returning to it – I think everybody's eyes did. It was only a few minutes. 'Tip him overboard', I said to Mehau. 'Forgive me, Guru Ji.' There were already more than enough of us on that boat."

"What did he look like, this boat man?"

"He had a great mop of greying hair, it might have been red once. An earring in his left ear. He wore a bright orange sou'wester."

Anne-Marie needed no more confirmation that this was Fraser. He had gone down at the hands of some desperate woman, defending the Lady Ffiona to the end.

# CHAPTER XXV

A LARGE baronial building loomed ahead of them, its turrets peering from the pine woods that bordered the loch. The car park was empty save for a rusting green Landrover behind the kitchen area, and a white Mercedes with a number plate that indicated a vintage of the 90's. They parked out of sight of the road. A wooden signpost pointed towards a 'Sunken Garden' in the woods, to 'Tennis Courts' across the lawn and to 'Loch Lomond'.

Rabiyah climbed out of the Toyota and sat in the shade to feed Noor. Josephine stood for a while studying the signpost, scratching at her wrist. Eventually she seemed to make a decision and followed the path to the Sunken Garden.

Henry looked at Lou.

"Let's see if we can find anything."

"Looks like there's someone here. Go carefully," said Sam.

They moved circumspectly, brushing aside a sweep of crimson rhododendrons and peering through the mullioned windows. Nothing moved.

Stone steps led up to a front door of solid oak. It opened heavily, creaking on its hinges. Henry could imagine this place as a family home in happier times, children playing on the lawn and parents laughing. But now ... in the dining-room, jugs of water sat half-full on a long polished table, bottles of wine half- poured, plates of food half-eaten. The thin veneer of civilization had been torn from the gilded chairs. The room stank. It was not just the food.

Sunlight glinted off the waters of the loch through the tall windows of the bar. Stags' heads and old fishing rods adorned the walls above the dark oak panelling. Wing-back chairs, upholstered in burgundy leather, faded in places, were further testament to an era that was gone. A few nuts lay forlornly in bowls. Empty champagne flutes clung to the mantelpiece and the windowsills and the plant pots. On a carved coffee table, as if unaffected by the tsunami all around, lay a copy of The Times. It was dated the day before the chaos had started. To one side, a man's body lay thrown back in one of the chairs, his mouth open as if snoring; to the other a tweeded woman was slumped on the patterned carpet.

It was not the bodies but the headline that caught Henry's eye:

'THINK TANK FEARS CRIPPLING RUSSIAN ATTACK ON UNDERWATER WEB CABLES'

*The IRP (International Relations Policy) think tank this week published a report detailing the importance of the UK's internet infrastructure to trade and communications. The report highlighted the country's vulnerability as an island nation…*

He handed it to Sam.

"Do you think this is it?"

He waited while Sam scanned the article.

"Doesn't explain the water. Doesn't explain the mobile signal."

"No, and doesn't have to be Russia. Could be anyone, I suppose," Henry sighed.

"Doesn't explain no government, no police, no army…"

"I think that's different," said Henry. "They only exist, and are obeyed, because most people accept their rule. But if they can't communicate, if many of them are dead, if people have no food or water and are doing what they can to get it, then…there is no law. There is just us. We're just fish swimming around looking for smaller fish to eat, and above us sharks."

"And will it be any different on Mull?"

They did not have time to speculate.

Someone had been through this place before them. The shelves of the bar were empty, the bottles pulled from their holders. They pushed through a green baize door to the kitchen. The stench of rotting fish and stale milk greeted them from a row of refrigerators.

They opened every cupboard but there was nothing – just some salt and herbs. Discarded nylon sacks and empty drums of olive oil stood outside a stone outbuilding - clearly the food storage area. The shelves inside were empty. Whoever had been here had been very thorough.

There was the sound of a latch opening behind them and then a tap-tapping, coming closer. Lou spun, her knife ready. An old woman shuffled towards them, one hand on a stout wooden stick. She wore a long tartan skirt and deep red lipstick. Her hair was carefully brushed and carried a perfume that reminded Henry of his mother. The perfume seemed to mask some other, less fragrant, scent.

"It's all right my love," she said. "I'm not going to hurt you. There's nothing left. They came with a big truck two days ago, took everything. I locked myself in my rooms and they didn't find me."

"Who were they?"

"I don't know, my love. I don't have much to do with the running of the place any more. I'm too old. I let the manager do it. I never wanted to let it become a hotel – we used to have such fun here as children. But my husband insisted on it, it was the only way to keep it going he said. And then of course he died. He liked to keep the car clean.

'It's a clean machine,' he would say. The Beatles you know. Is it dirty now? I expect it's dirty. White. Never a good colour for a car, wouldn't you say, darling? Do you know, one time, that group came up here. What were they called? Jagged. Richard Jagged. We had a wonderful time. He was such a naughty man."

She rambled on for a while, reminiscing. She looked at Stef.

"Hello Ailsa darling, how good of you to come back and find your old Gran. Did you bring Tommy?"

Stef looked at her and smiled uncertainly.

"Do you have food for yourself?" asked Henry.

Sam and Lou glanced over at him sharply.

"No, Dad, we can't…"

"I have some bread and some tins of spam and my bottles of mineral water. That's all I drink these days. That's what the doctor said."

Henry looked down at his feet.

"Is that Mercedes your car, the clean machine?"

"Yes, my dear, but old Charles has gone away, went with the rest of them, so I can't get anywhere in it. Heaven knows where he's gone. He always drove me. I don't know what scared them all off. My TV went off at the same time, and the water. Oh, it is such a nuisance. Where are the police?"

"I'm afraid the police aren't working very well at the moment."

He had a thought.

"Do the guest bedrooms have fridges?"

"What do you mean my love?"

"Do they have little bars, minibars, with wine and …"

"I think so, my love. Go and have a look."

Stairs now were a problem for Sam and he stayed with the woman, as did Stef. Henry, Shani and Lou moved back towards the main building.

"And what have you been doing with yourself, Ailsa darling?" they could hear as they entered the reception area.

"If the doors are locked with key cards, we're going to have a problem."

But it turned out to be the old-fashioned system - two rows of keys hung on hooks behind the ornate desk. Some were missing. A wooden tag on each identified the room number.

The hallway carried the cocktail scent of age – of furniture polish, of fresh flowers, of cognac and leather and the perfume of a thousand women. In a split second, Henry took in the Axminster carpet, intricately patterned in gold diamonds over burgundy, and the huge oak finials that stood proudly on the staircase balustrade.

They raced up the steps, opening the first door they came to, Room 102. Vast windows filled one side of the room, musky damask curtains, elaborate affairs of red lilies and midnight blue, gathered either side with a golden cord. Henry's eyes barely registered the four poster bed that lay unmade opposite, focusing instead on the minibar that sat in the corner of the room. He opened it but there was nothing. Nothing except an empty wine bottle.

"Perhaps the people with the truck have been through the rooms," he thought aloud.

"But they can't have been, they wouldn't have left the keys all neat."

They tried the next room and this time struck gold – a full house. Two bottles of water, two quarter bottles of wine, a Glenfiddich miniature and a bag of peanuts.

It was not long after that Henry could show Sam their haul - twenty quarter bottles of wine, twenty-three bottles of water, nine Glenfiddich miniatures and an assortment of peanuts and chocolate.

"Do we give any to her?"

Sam grimaced.

"It's only four small bottles of water each. Not even that. It's not going to last us long…so no."

"Yup."

Lou beckoned to Stef who was still listening politely to the woman.

"I have to go now," Stef smiled. She gave the woman a hug and moved away.

"Are they taking you away my darling? Will you stay with your Gran tonight?"

But Stef turned swiftly and waved.

"If you have a master key," said Henry, "there may be water and chocolate in Rooms 7, 11 and 16."

"Ooh, water and chocolate!"

And the woman tap-tapped off again through a door that seemed to lead to an upper floor.

Outside, the light was fading. The beds and pillows and duvets of the hotel rooms were inviting.

"Shall we just sleep here and start early in the morning?" said Henry.

"I'm knackered," said Sam. "So, yes. But the showers and baths and basins - don't touch them, don't turn them on, don't even dream of it. She said the water's off - but not even a drop. Let your body stink, your teeth stink - use the bottled water if you have to."

They agreed the sentry roster. Henry led Josephine up the stairs to Room 15. Her feet seemed leaden and she would not hold his hand. He pulled back the duvet and laid her down, then covered her again. He took the bed closest to the door, hoping not to wake her when his turn on guard duty came; but the presence of the old woman above them and the sound of Josephine's turning and wakefulness filled his night and it was only in the early hours of the morning that he slept.

# CHAPTER XXVI

ANNE-MARIE walked with Mira across the hallway. A foul smell littered the air. In the downstairs toilet the bowl was full, sodden toilet paper and faeces dribbling onto the tiles.

"Urggh! We need to fix that," she said.

She led Mira outside to an outbuilding. Puddles of oil lay across an uneven concrete floor. The corrugated iron roof was rusted and bent, the tracks of leaks clearly visible on the walls. An oil drum sat on a wooden platform that looked as if, in days gone by, it had been a dining table. Now, the polish gone and smears of paint across its legs, it stood sturdy and defiant against the years. At the base of the drum was a tap, a black pool beneath it. Opposite, supported on piles of loose bricks at the four corners, was a large machine.

"What is this?" asked Mira, treading on tiptoe between the oily puddles.

"A generator," said Anne-Marie.

She pushed a red button. Nothing happened for a moment. She pushed it again and this time the machine stuttered and burst into life. Its repetitive hammering drowned every other sound. Mira held the palms of her hands to her ears. If, in normal times, this place would have been considered tranquil, its tranquillity now was shattered.

"What is it for?" she shouted.

Anne-Marie cut the power.

"Electricity when the mains are down, like now. And we can use it to pump water from the well; but we only have what diesel is left in that drum. After that, there is nothing."

"But they'll fix it, won't they?"

"They? Mira, *they* are people – people and computers. They the electricity people, they the water people, they the police, they the army, they the government. They are probably dead, a lot of them – their computers will be dead, anyway, and their phones dead. If they are still alive, they will be fighting to survive like you and me. There is no they. For the moment, we are they."

"Baba Ji will help us."

"That's good… I hope you are right. But we can help ourselves too. Let me show you the well."

She led her to a round brick wall, a metre in diameter, that rose to waist height on the edge of the meadow. Anne-Marie leant over.

"You see," she said. "Way down there – fresh water, though we're very close to the sea. The water comes down from the hills in underground streams. That's our lifeline. But it's limited. In the old days when the whole family was here, it would run out in the summer. It's filled up over the winter and with only me until you came there should be plenty in it for the moment, but we need to preserve it. So, do you agree, for drinking only?"

Mira nodded, frowning.

"But how will we wash?"

"Swim in the sea, stand in the rain, go down to the burn – whatever you want."

She looked uncomfortable.

"There are private places, sheltered places."

"I…I'm sorry to ask – do you have any tampax?"

The years of menstrual pain came back to Anne-Marie; the sudden rush for a folded hand towel, anything to escape the embarrassment.

"I haven't needed them for twenty years, but I'll have a look when we get back. There may be some buried in the bathroom," she said kindly.

Inwardly she raised an arm in jubilation – the door had opened another inch on the real Mira. She led her on around the property, guiding her up the long drive that wound to the road inland, then through the trees, across the meadow and down through woods again to the secret bay where the two boats floated.

"Fuck," she heard as Mira's foot slipped into a seaweed-strewn rock pool. And then, "Sorry."

They clambered back round to the house and entered through the kitchen door.

"So there you have it," said Anne-Marie. "We have to protect this place, otherwise we will be overrun and no one will survive. People may come from the sea, like you did, or from inland, like those people earlier. I am asking you to deploy your group – to secure the perimeter in military terms. We cannot let anyone else in - except some of my family who are on their way."

Mira sat at the table. She stared out of the window at the gulls wheeling and screeching above the trees. A Cedar of Lebanon stood in a corner of the lawn, its branches snaking black green across the sky.

"What about the helicopter people?"

Anne-Marie took a deep breath, putting the kettle on the aga.

"I don't know, Mira. I don't know what they want or what they're trying to do… we have no defence against them."

"Baba Ji will protect us."

"I hope so."

She pulled two mugs from a cupboard. They were striped red and green. She placed tea bags in them from a box labelled Yorkshire Tea. The house on the Yorkshire Moors looked solid and peaceful on the design. She wondered if the people who lived there were solid and peaceful now.

"Do you have herbal tea?"

"I do. Camomile?"

Mira nodded.

"There is another problem – food. I have a few bags, big bags, of rice and oats and other bits and pieces. I can share them with you and your group. There are a few vegetables in the ground, and we can grow more, but that will take time. With fifteen of you, none of this will last long, however sparsely you eat. People are going to get very hungry very soon, if you stay vegetarian. Or...you have seen the two boats. I can teach your people to fish. There are deer on the hills, and we might be able to find a way to kill one. A whole deer would last even fifteen people a long time. What do you think Baba Ji would want?"

Mira stayed silent. She seemed to be pondering the question in a private torment.

"We're caged," she said eventually. "In the open air. Baba Ji will provide."

"Well, I suppose he will provide rice tonight, yes," said Anne-Marie. "I will not speak about food – that is your decision – but will you allow me to talk to your people about everything else?"

Mira frowned, then stood up and moved out into the garden. She raised both arms in a gathering motion. When all the devotees were seated cross-legged in front of her on the lawn, she spoke:

"By Baba Ji's grace we have come to this place. All the things that are going on, the people attacking the house, the black helicopters in the sky, the dark clouds hanging over us, other things that might happen that we cannot yet envisage – these are all His lila. The eternal game between the Guru and His devotees. We must not lose sight of this. We are protected by Baba Ji's shield and He will guide us. But there are some practical things that you should know and do and these things will be your service here."

She inclined her head towards the older woman.

It seemed to Anne-Marie that the devotees welcomed the clear orders she gave to them. She explained about the protection of the perimeter and the coastline. She explained that use of the generator would only be on an absolute need basis, that the water from the well was for drinking only. She explained that the clogged-up downstairs toilet needed to be emptied by hand and latrines dug; that wood needed to be cut for the aga and cooking that night; that the vegetable garden needed to be hoed and planted.

The devotees moved to begin their tasks until suddenly, at 6 pm, Mira struck the gong that had hung in the hallway since the Tibetan Buddhist days and the group, with equal obedience, dropped what they were doing and moved to the shrine room.

"It's evening puja time," Leah winked to Anne-Marie as she passed.

# CHAPTER XXVII

A GREY desert lay before Henry, the ash still hot to the touch of his shredded boots. Dust hung uncomprehendingly in the occasional shaft of sunlight. Broken concrete drooped in furls and crazy webs from blown-out rooves and windows.

A single jagged wall, enclosing nothing, stood defiantly, old stone exposed behind paintwork that once might have been yellow. Towards the top was an opening, circular, hands of brick radiating from the centre like an empty clock. Once it had been a stained glass window, but now he could see through it. It looked neither out nor in. All he could see, from either side, was the grey desert, the crumpled buildings, the lost streets that no longer held a place on the map.

He heard a baby cry...and woke up. He shook his head, struggling to separate his war-torn dream from his present reality. An image of the wall lingered and in the image the stained-glass window was back in place. Balmanie, he thought, before the dream faded and he could no longer remember its patterns or its logic.

He stumbled downstairs yawning. He felt ragged and unrested and an uneasiness filled him. He came upon Sam outside and they studied the map again.

"I think Oban is going to be a nightmare," said Henry. "Chaos from what we've seen. No ferries and every boat in the place will have gone. How are we going to get to Balmanie from there? I think we should go to Fraser's – the way we used to call the haggis route. We can get across from there somehow - in his boat if he'll take us. If he's still there...or signal to Anne-Marie."

He began to pour from the last of the spare fuel cans into the Toyota.

"Dad, that means going way on up through Fort William and round Loch Eil. We'll just be pissing away that fuel you're pouring."

"We'd be pissing it away anyway if we went to Oban and couldn't get a boat. There's a ferry south of Fort William. It's only about three hundred yards of water...if we could get across there," Henry mused.

"Yeah, on a magic carpet. See those pigs in the sky, Dad."

"You're probably right. But we can have a look. What choice do we have? Somehow we have to get to Fraser's."

The prize, he felt, was tantalisingly close, almost within their grasp. He walked over to the white Mercedes and opened the fuel cap. It might, one day, have been a clean machine but it was petrol-driven, no use to them.

******

"Where's Mum?" asked Sam.

They looked in the hotel and around the vehicles. There was no sign of her.

"Jo," shouted Henry, "We need to leave."

There was no response.

"Damn, she must have gone off into the garden and lost her way."

"I'll go and look for her," said Sam, suddenly serious.

"Don't be silly," said Shani. "You can't go hobbling off with that leg. I'll go."

Sam looked at her and looked at his father.

"If you think you can make it with that crutch…"

"I'll go on my own," he said softly.

He knew where he was headed. It was not easy negotiating the broken stumps and branches that lay across the ground, but when he saw the sign that said 'Sunken Garden' in front of him, he was sure he had come to the right place. In slow motion he noticed a heap of vodka bottles, all proclaiming the red label of Luksusowa, in the bottom of the hedge. Someone, he thought in a frozen moment, came here and drank a bottle, in secret, night after night or week after week, before returning to their unwanted life.

He made his final approach down the slope gingerly, his heart in his mouth. It was not a surprise to see her slumped against the trunk of a Japanese cherry, its blossom now spent; rather it was the strength of the stream of blood rising in a fountain from her wrist, then faltering, rising again and subsiding, that shook him. His old penknife, the one with the red case, lay on her chest, abandoned. The blade looked bright, the parts not covered in blood way brighter than in his schooldays – as if it had been recently sharpened.

In so far as he was able to run, he ran over to her, the crutch allowing him only to move in great leaps. His feet sunk into blood-wet leaves. He grabbed her, desperately trying to stem the flow. The cut was along the line of her arm and with a gulp he remembered something he had read in some student magazine - that it is not easy to sever the artery when cutting across the wrist; the tendons and sinews protect it. To reach it you have to cut lengthwise and deep. Four minutes. Four minutes to bleed to death, that's all it took. She would know that.

For a split second he looked around for a tourniquet. There was nothing. Throwing aside the crutch, he ripped off his shirt and with a sleeve began to bind her arm above the cut.

"Leave me darling, let me go. I am no use to you or Dad. I'm just ... holding you back."

His mother's eyes were wide, glistening with love and calm now. He could barely hear the whispered words carried on her remaining breath.

"Tell Dad ... thank you."

She held a hand out to touch him but it fell away before it reached his face. His grip slackened on the bandage, then tightened as he began to twist again. He watched in horror the blood just dribbling now from her wrist. His mind was a maelstrom: 'I can't let her die here...I have to get Dad...she wants to die here...I have to help her...I can't leave her...she needs a hospital...there are no hospitals.'

"Dad," he shouted.

"Dad," he shouted louder, but there was no response.

The blood was too far gone, the fountain too far exhausted, the leaves too far soaked and Josephine slid back across the bark and down into the soft arms of the ground below. Sam fell on her, hugging her desperately, thumping the earth with his fists.

Great waves of tears engulfed him. He did not know how long he wept, but when he got back to the vehicles, his face set, the others were eating ravenously. Two plates lay untouched on the bonnet of the Toyota.

"Jesus, what happened Sam?" Shani cried out, running over to him.

Sam looked down at the remains of his shirt, and his knees and arms smeared with blood.

"It's Mum's," he said bleakly. "Dad?"

They walked over together. Sam knew that his father understood – and understood that they had to do this together. Henry was silent, his breath catching, as they moved through the woodland.

When he saw the body across the clearing, horror, sorrow, grief and a kind of acceptance rolled together in a sound Sam never wanted to hear again - a guttural shriek of pain. Henry ran across and leant over Josephine, pulling her to him, her body still warm to the touch. Shock clouded his face as she fell lifelessly back from his embrace.

Upright now, his eyes wet, he stared at the penknife and the wrist, glutted with blood. Slowly, he disengaged himself. Sam was walking around the sunken garden.

"Do you think just here?" he said.

Henry nodded. He knelt down again and kissed Josephine on her forehead and then on her lips. He took her shoulders and Sam her legs as they lifted her over.

"Sweet dreams, darling," said Henry blankly.

"Love you, Mum."

Tears were falling freely, unfettered, from Sam's eyes now. They picked up pine fronds and ferns and bracken and laid them over her. A robin, seeing the commotion, flew to a low branch and sang its sad lament. For some moments the two men stood quietly, arm in arm beside her.

"I'm afraid Josephine is no longer with us," said Henry, his voice breaking, as they got back to the others. "We have buried her in the wood beside the sunken garden. She will be happy now."

He meant that. The pain of life with depression and anxiety was something he had had to observe in her over many years, and he knew that, whatever the medication, whatever the treatment had been, there were few times when she had really been happy.

\*\*\*\*\*\*

Henry pulled in a few miles down the road. He leant his right arm out of the window, and waved the motorhome down behind him. They had been going for barely fifteen minutes. Noone had spoken.

"I think I saw a guitar in the cupboard there," he said to Stef as she got out.

"Yep."

A question, and then a look of understanding, passed between them all. Henry seated himself on a tree stump at the edge of the verge. He picked at the strings, turning the pegs at the end, tuning it until he was happy. He looked up.

"It's for Josephine," he said, his voice choking and his eyes melting. "I didn't say goodbye properly."

He plucked a few notes.

"Sometimes we see death as a world away, separated from us, from life, by a great wall," he said. "And sometimes it is very close, just the other side of a thin curtain wafting in the breeze, so close that it seems you might lean through and touch it.

"I remember the coloured cords that led to the kitchen in a tiny village restaurant Jo and I went to in Spain before Sam was born. We had walked all morning and eventually came down from the hills to follow a stream. The village was folded into the cleft of the valley and a large church formed a bridge across the water, with purple hibiscus blooming from its walls. Its bell tower stood high over the village and perhaps in years gone by its congregation came from miles around.

"We ate a Spanish omelette and drank white rioja and the coloured cords rustled when the waitress went through them. 'She's going to the other side,' Jo said every time and laughed. It was a moment, a period of time in between, when she had seemed almost happy.

"But for her the coloured cords were never far away. She knew that, when the time came, they were not a wall -

she could pass through them; they held no fear for her. And today she did pass through them…to the other side."

He strummed a few chords on the guitar. Everyone recognized them, even Rabiyah, who sat with Noor on the steps of the motorhome. If they could not immediately say the words, they recognised the chords. Even those who had not even been born when they were first released knew them.

Henry began to sing. He did not really sing. He lilted the song as if a poem, the music giving the song its voice, his voice the haunting, broken sound of the bereaved.

"So, so you think you can tell…

Heaven from hell…"

He looked up. The others were staring at him, rapt. Rabiyah was rocking the baby and Lou was tapping her feet to the rhythm.

"…How, how I wish you were here…"

His voice cracked. Sam stood up and moved away, his shoulders heaving. He leant his forehead against the trunk of a tree. Henry reached the end of the song with a final empassioned chord.

"It was our song," he said. And then, as an afterthought, "We'll get to Balmanie, darling."

No one spoke.

"She loved it there. She felt safe there. She wants us to get there – just…not her this time."

He put the guitar down. He looked about him. He looked at Sam. He looked at Shani, Rabiyah and Noor, at Stef and Lou. He looked at the woods. A flock of rooks burst from a nearby oak, cawing and screeching. Sam went over to him and hugged him like only a son can hug his father.

"Thank you Dad," he whispered.

# CHAPTER XXVIII

THE DOGS looked pleadingly at Anne-Marie for some breakfast, and she scraped the last tin into their bowls. Something rustled in the woods across the lawn, and they raced off in search of a rabbit or anything more that they could eat. So far, Fraser's dog Rabbie had kept up with Aragorn, despite his three legs. He was lagging behind now, Anne-Marie noticed. The kettle boiled.

"You're joking," she exclaimed as she scanned an old newspaper that lay beside the aga.

*'With no sign of a break in the drought, further water rationing has been introduced in Capetown, South Africa. As of seven a.m. this morning, with the reservoirs running dry, residents are permitted only fifty litres per day, not enough for a bath.'*

"A bath? Do you know how long fifty litres would keep fifteen people alive?" she shouted at the Scotsman, now five days old.

She picked up the telephone. The line was still dead. She picked up her mobile and tried Henry's number. No signal. No bars. Nothing. She looked at the WiFi. No light. Even a flashing red light would have been welcome. She watched the devotees come out of their morning puja.

They looked tired. A bespectacled woman with lank, wavy hair and a flowery skirt appeared.

"Mira has asked me to be the kitchen coordinator," she said in a hesitant voice.

"The kitchen coordinator? Ah. So what does one of those do?"

"I'm in charge of the food for our group. Noone else is allowed in the kitchen."

"I see."

Anne-Marie wanted to laugh at the concept, but she could see a logic to it. She showed the woman the bags of rice and oats. In the fridge, now tepid, a small wedge of cheddar sat on a shelf and the remains of a two litre carton of milk. The milk was beginning to go off. She showed her a cupboard that held jam and chutney and mustard and mayonnaise, and another that held raisins and a few tins of fruit. She showed her a small stainless steel churn where water from the well could be stored. She took her to the vegetable garden. Two rows of lettuces were ready for eating - the beans and carrots and courgettes were a month or more away.

"That's all I have, I'm afraid. I don't know how long it can last."

"I have to give Mira something special," said the woman.

'Why?' wondered Anne-Marie.

But the woman poured some oats into a bowl, sprinkled some raisins on top and opened a tin of apricots. She poured some of the remaining milk over this and took it out of the room, holding the bowl with both hands like an offering. Leah and some of the other devotees looked enviously at the concoction as the woman passed them on her way upstairs.

When she returned, she set a row of bowls along the sideboard and poured a measure of oats into each, then studied how much was left in the bag. She frowned, took some of the oats out of each bowl again and put them back in the bag. Eventually, she seemed satisfied with the ration and beckoned the devotees forward. She handed a bowl to each along with a mug of water.

Leah was at the front of the queue.

"Where do I find the milk?" she asked innocently.

"There's no milk left."

"But I...and the fruit?"

The woman did not acknowledge her. Leah studied her bowl, then looked up at Anne-Marie with a shrug. Most of the devotees seemed to accept their portions with gratitude. Some sat in silence, eating slowly and chewing endlessly. Others ate in lightning quick time, like a bird swoops on a seed and devours it. Like a dog wolfs the food from its bowl. If there is food in its bowl.

'There is no rush,' thought Anne-Marie.

Two people came back towards the house, the night sentries. They looked exhausted.

"Anything going on?" asked Daniel.

"There was a boat," one said. "I could hear it coming. The engine cut and then voices. I called for Ash here." He inclined his head towards the other man. "It came in quite close to the jetty. They were trying to land. I flashed the torch – it looked like a family. We made a lot of noise. Threw stones and sticks in their direction and shouted. They didn't take much persuading to turn back."

"Wake us if that happens again – that could have been dangerous with just...." His voice petered out.

"A family, you say. Christ!" said Anne-Marie. "How many, can you describe them?"

"I couldn't see clearly. There were some little kids, five or six year-olds. They sounded French, foreign, anyway."

Her shoulders subsided.

"There'll be some breakfast in the kitchen," said Daniel.

The remaining devotees divided into three groups. Daniel took the first in the direction of the sea, another went to the land-ward side. The third, with Mehau, went to dig the latrines.

"Please, you show us the spades," said Mehau.

Anne-Marie led them to a small stone and slated outbuilding next to the generator shed. Its earthen floor held the sweet smell of petrol and rotting grass. A motor mower stood in one corner and to the side a petrol can and a selection of spades, forks, shovels and snow shovels, an edging tool, a crow bar and two rakes. Mehau dragged out the spades and forks and handed them to his crew.

"Where we dig?" he asked.

Anne-Marie had in mind a place close to the vegetable garden. Close enough to the house that it did not involve a long trek, far enough away that it held some privacy. From here, the prevailing wind would take any stray smells out to sea, she hoped. She watched the devotees dig. There was no energy in their digging. She made a decision.

"I am going out in the boat," she said, beckoning to Mehau. "Did you ever fish when you were a child?"

Mehau nodded.

"With a, how you call it, a rod. Yes, in Poland I fished with my father. But I cannot eat fish now. Baba Ji does not allow fish."

"If you do not want to eat fish," said Anne-Marie, "that is OK. But will you help me?"

They made their way down to the secret harbour, the route now familiar to Mehau. At the point, Anne-Marie stopped and raised her binoculars. For a long time she held them, looking North across the sound.

"What you look at?"

"You see the white dot on the shoreline, there on the mainland – my friend lived there. The man who owned your boat...who died on your boat. And my family, my brother and his family, are trying to come up from England. I think they will reach there – it is the place they know. I have left my boat there – it is my brother's boat too."

She handed the binoculars to Mehau.

"Is very alone," he said. "Right on the beach."

Sound broke in the sky to the south, then magnified and magnified until the air screamed. This time it was not a helicopter, but jets, black fighter jets, flying low over the water like a skein of Canada geese. They disappeared into the distance as quickly as they had come. The sky quietened again until far away they heard a loud boom. Then nothing.

"You think is safe to go out in boat?"said Mehau.

"If they want to get us, they'll get us whether we're on land or sea. It's up to you Mehau."

With the tide high, they carried the dinghy down to the water and paddled out to the Lizzie. They clambered aboard and soon were  chugging slowly out of the bay. Anne-Marie punched a button on the control panel, and a screen lit. Her brow furrowed as she tried to understand it. Mehau leant across.

"This, the water, how long it is." He made a sign with his hands.

"Ah, how deep."

"And this – how you say – a picture of the bottom."

Fraser's electronic gizmos had always been a source of amusement to her. She turned her attention to the real sea, noting the strength and direction of the wind. Sunlight glanced off the broken water.

"There," she said. "Over there. You see?"

"Is like a saucepan...boiling."

"Yes, a shoal of mackerel."

In the sky above the shoal was a swirling maelstrom of yellow, black and white.

"Gannets," said Anne-Marie.

They moved in closer. The air was wild with the birds' wingbeats as they dive-bombed the shoal, hurtling into the depths of the sea with barely a splash, transforming suddenly into seals, then emerging, gaining air and diving again. Mehau ducked under the shelter of the wheelhouse, so low did they fly over the boat.

Anne-Marie idled the engine. She attached a string of feather lures to her line and cast. Almost immediately, the rod bent and when she raised it, five mackerel hung from the hooks. She laid it on the floor of the boat. Mehau held one thrashing fish with his foot, while he detached the hook from another. He was smiling.

"I can see you've done this before," said Anne-Marie.

They put the fish in a red plastic bucket and then she cast again. It did not take long for the bucket to fill. They had drifted closer to the bay where Fraser's bothie stood, bereft of its owner. Nothing moved there. She pointed out the white hull of her own boat. Mehau looked back South towards Balmanie. From here, you could see only the chimneys of the house, the wooded point in front and the old castle to the left clear landmarks. He turned again and studied Fraser's bay.

"What are white ... white paint on the cliffs?"

"Waterfalls. The water pours down from the hills. They are there all year. You can hear them when the water is very still."

"I would like that," said Mehau. "No cars. Does it have electricity and broadband?"

Anne-Marie shrugged.

"It did, on and off. Now it is no different to here or anywhere else. Nothing."

"Is nice," he said. "No dead people here. No enemies."

Anne-Marie nodded.

'I'm wasting fuel,' she thought and headed back.

# CHAPTER XXIX

THE ROAD rolled and stretched through the valley, the single track railway to the right, no people and no trains moving. Hills appeared ahead, folding into themselves, then disappeared again. A sign said 'Drive safely in Scotland.' 'Real ale,' proclaimed the Bridge of Orchy Hotel. Henry felt numb. The dried blood of his wife was still on him and now and then he caught its tang.

He drove on. Scattered rocks and lochans punctuated the barren moors and he drove on. He drove on towards Glencoe. The road climbed steeply, the Three Sisters looming ahead, guarding the land. The mountains beckoned the visitors forward, smiling a welcome - then, with a cold laugh, swallowed them in an irrevocable embrace. The ghosts of murdered Maclan clansmen and their womenfolk hung in the air. The steep and lonely slopes rose sheer on either side, engulfing them. It seemed they would crush them completely in some form of final expiation for the treachery of 1692 and for the deaths of those on their own journey; and then, at the last moment, at the point of final suffocation, the gorge spat them out into the valley below and Henry breathed again.

The Ballachulish Bridge was clear and they approached the Corran ferry. He looked at the fuel gauge. The melee of abandoned cars and broken bodies that littered the entrance told him all he needed to know. No pigs would fly, no magic carpets.

"No chance," he said to Sam beside him, but Sam seemed dull and only grunted.

Instead, thought Henry, they must circumnavigate an entire loch just to get to Ardgour - the place he could see with the naked eye, merely 300 metres away across the water to his left.

Shani leant across from the back seat and laid her hand on Sam's shoulder.

"You OK?"

"Yeah…actually no, I feel pretty shitty. I'll be all right."

She squeezed his hand and looked out of the window. The tidy houses and hotels and guest houses that lined the East side of Loch Linnhe seemed frozen in time, caught in a captured moment, like a black and white photograph of something that once was. They were silent now, their neat gardens untended. Heaven knows what had become of their owners. Was their flesh fuelling the pall of smoke that lay over Fort William ahead?

'That stench again,' thought Henry, trying to close off the airflow in the Toyota.

He didn't let up speed when he reached the town. He leant his arm out of the window, signalling to Stef to close up behind him. In tandem, they zig-zagged and steam-rollered their way past deserted cars, over pavements and roundabouts, scattering the few people who tried to approach. An old woman, a toddler in the crook of her arm, held her palms together, beseeching them to stop. Henry swerved violently to avoid her and drove on. Past the M and S food hall in the north of the town, its plate glass windows smashed, and on finally to the A830 on the north side of Loch Eil.

This was the Road to the Isles - that was the name he remembered. It sounded romantic but he didn't care now. The road to safety, to Fraser's and then Balmanie, was all he cared about. At the head of the loch, he turned off onto the single track road that would bring them back, eventually, to Ardgour. A sign indicated a Z bend. Henry slowed. He breasted the corner.

"Shit!" He slammed on the brakes.

Boxes and cans crashed and clattered in the back and the water in the canisters sloshed noisily as everyone and everything was hurled forwards. Shani threw her arms against the seatback in front to protect herself.

A tree trunk lay across the road, its leaves and branches fresh, like a bird just shot, its feathers still carrying their tint, unsullied yet by the crows and flies and weathers. To the left, a fifteen metre bank dropped almost vertically to a sluggish stream. Gulls wheeled and circled over the marshy land that led to the loch and a blue boat tugged gently at its mooring rope in the distance. To the right, a thicket of silver birch, gorse and bracken opened onto hillocks of scrub grass. Beyond, the ground sloped down to the angled, deep green corners of a pine plantation. The road was completely impassable.

With Shani, Henry got out to investigate. It was then that he saw the stump on the verge. Neither age nor wind had felled the tree.

"Sam," he called, but Sam was still in the passenger seat, slow to react.

It was too late. Four men, clothes torn and faces masked in sacking, raced from behind the trunk. Three carried long sticks. From their movement, the shape of their bodies, Henry could tell they were young. The last of them wielded a machete. He yanked open the passenger door and dragged Sam out, shoving him forwards. With a jolt, Henry saw that he did not have the twelve bore.

"Over there, all of ye," whinnied a rough voice. "Where is yer food. Yer water?"

The motorhome lurched to a halt a few yards behind on the other side of the road. Lou leapt down, knife in hand. One of the men saw it.

"This yin's got a knife," he shouted, slamming his stick down hard on her wrist before she could set herself. The knife tumbled to the ground. He slammed her again across the neck for good measure.

"Bastard!"

"You – out," he was almost screaming, pointing his stick towards Stef in the driver's seat. She stepped down and moved towards the others, helpless.

"Right, all of ye," the man said, suddenly calmer. "Let's make this real friendly, shall we? I dinna want to see any more knives or anything else. So - clothes off. Slow. Throw them on the ground away from ye."

The man with the machete had moved to the back of the Toyota. He was ransacking the boot. Clothes, ropes, anything that was not food or water flew onto the road or down the bank. Henry looked at the others.

"We're going to have to do it."

'Shit, shit, shit,' he thought. Had he come all this way for this? He pulled off his shirt and then his trousers and underpants. He didn't care about himself. Too much had happened. But Shani, Stef, Lou...these young men?

Sam was sitting on the ground, struggling to get his shorts over his injured leg. Shani, her long black hair flowing over her bare skin, bent to help.

"Dinna move." The man raised his stick again.

"C'mon on now, faster!" he shouted at Sam, landing a blow across his back.

Henry looked across at his son. Though the maggots had gone, his thigh was swollen around the edges of the bandage and a purple rash was visible on his inner groin. It seemed to be tracking towards his stomach. Another purple rash the size of a fist had formed above his left ankle. The men moved forward in a line, looking left and right at the girls.

"Run," Henry shouted, but he was a split second too late. Two of them lunged forwards and grabbed Stef, dragging her behind the log.

"Sam!" But Sam was helpless, his naked body fading.

There was a sudden crack. The skull of the man left in front exploded, blood and fragments of bone and brain matter bursting over the leaves, turning them to the colours of autumn. His body crumpled headlessly backwards. For a split second, the silent air charged, Henry tried to process what had happened.

"Shit! Get doon!"

"Get the fuck off me! No!" Between the branches, he could see glimpses of Stef tearing and scratching at the men. Then a muscled arm locked her into a strait jacket grip. Lou crouched low, sweeping her knife from the ground.

"We're coming Stef!"

The man with the machete had slipped down the bank out of sight. In the motorhome, the baby began to wail.

"He's in there," came a shout from behind the log. "The gun's in the caravan."

Henry tried to focus. He wondered what Rabiyah's next move would be – he could not see her. He scanned the lie of the land beyond the tree. At the apex of the bend ahead was a bothie, its plaster a dirty stain of grey. Weeds grew all around it and the shell of a Land Rover rusted in the driveway. It looked a suitable rathole for these men.

A head appeared above the bracken on the bank. The man looked nervously about him, then sprinted across the road to the back of the motorhome. He edged around it, creeping, his back flat against the side. The machete was poised as he ducked low under the window. The baby was still crying inside.

"Down the left...shit, Shani!" Henry shouted, his words fading as he realised Rabiyah would not understand.

Shani called out. Just one word.

"Yassar!"

The man glared at her and glanced behind him. He slipped his palm, backhand, through the polished C-handle and gently pulled outwards.

Henry glanced across at Lou.

"The baby," he whispered.

She nodded, ready, but the door did not open. The man bent and picked up a stone. He threw it behind him right over the vehicle, gesturing towards the log, trying to convey his plan. Noone moved. Only the sound of Stef thrashing against her captors disturbed the air. His cheek hard against the metal, the man peered through the edge of the window. He bent again.

Another whiplash crack.

The shot came from the roof. He had not been expecting that, thought Henry. He had not expected that himself. The machete clattered to the ground as the man's grip on life disintegrated.

Rabiyah thrust her hand into her robe, reloading, but, in those few moments, Henry caught a glimpse of Stef's torn body being dragged through yellow gorse. The two remaining men were retreating – but not to the bothie. Inland instead towards the pine forest.

She fired. There was a dull thud as the bullet hit a tree.

"Lou! Sam! Help me!" Stef's baneful shriek was close.

"Wait Rabiyah," shouted Lou, seeing her re-loading again. "Wait. I'll go in."

Rabiyah did not understand. She stood now on the roof of the motorhome, her green robes flowing about her like some sort of female Lawrence of Arabia. Raging. Raging for her country. Raging for her lost husband. Raging for her lost son. Raging at these men who had grabbed one of her final band of brothers. Another crack. This time the sound of it seemed to fracture and dissipate, its impact thwarted by the ferns and the bracken and the gorse and the woods.

Shani shouted up to her in Arabic. Lou swept up the machete and dived into the undergrowth, naked still.

"Nooo, fuuuuck....Lou! Get off me you bastard."

Henry was struggling to get into his trousers and boots and load the twelve bore. He could hear Lou ahead of him fighting through the scrub. He followed, trying to pinpoint where Stef's cries were coming from, but they seemed to circle and echo all around the empty hills, receding. He saw something, a flash of colour, momentary movement, on the edge of the pine forest. He scrambled forwards, raising the gun - but the target was gone like a fleeting bird.

"No...noooaaaah," Stef's scream now was elemental, deep and distant, the scream of an impala at the end of the hunt, the lion poised at its throat. And then an awful, pitiful whimper across the land.

Sweating from the run, his hands on his knees, gasping for breath, Henry stopped. Lou appeared above a mound of gorse. Her arms and legs and chest were torn and scratched, trickles of blood weeping from the cuts of a thousand brambles. She was limping. She came up to Henry and laid her head on his shoulder. She sobbed, her whole body heaving. He could feel her breasts beating against his chest and hugged her like a daughter, his own silent tears coming in waves.

******

*Why am I sweating? I feel awful, but I can't tell Dad. Not after all this. Losing Mum. I can't remember...Shani was there wasn't she? Everything is so slow. Is it slow? I don't want to lose it here. I have to help Dad get to Balmanie. We have to move that log. Did I say that or did I think it? It's obvious anyway. Where's Stef gone? Has she gone? Did they catch her? What's that noise? A baby. Is the baby in the motorhome? Did Shani and I make a baby? Is it our baby? Can anybody hear me? Christ, I'm bloody freezing.*

******

172

"Did you get to them?" Shani asked, but the tone of her voice told the story she already knew.

Lou shook her head and, ignoring her bruises and scratches, threw on her clothes. She grimaced as she pulled her boots over a ragged cut in her heel.

"Too far ahead. We had no fuckin' chance in those trees…she's gone."

Her face set, she inspected the log.

"Let's see if we can swing it around."

They hauled and heaved, but it was far too big. Too big, too thick and too heavy.

"There might be something in the bothie."

Lou ran towards the place manically. They ransacked the outhouse. A rusty bow saw lay in a corner.

"If we have to use it, we have to use it, but it will take forever to get through that trunk," said Henry.

"That or we're going to have to go back."

"Where to? There is no back."

They went into the house. Faded curtains that once might have been cream were half-closed to the world and on the sill was a candelabra, the candles long ago extinguished. They moved through the dirty rooms, grey sheets and syringes and empty bottles littering their path. They rummaged through the bathroom, but there was no medication, no bandage, nothing.

The sound of another vehicle coming up the road interrupted their search.

"Quick," said Henry. He grabbed the twelve bore. He knew that Rabiyah, hidden somewhere out in the scrub, was covering them.

His arms were shaking as he pointed the gun towards the old Daihatsu pick-up, burgundy and dented, that appeared. A collie barked excitedly in the back amongst a pile of old sacks. A gnarled man with a craggy beard sat in the cab. He wound down the window as if to pass the time of day.

"What's gen on now? It's all right. I will not harm ye."
He raised his arms inside the cab.

His eyes alighted on the bodies on the road in front of
him. The collie too seemed to sense the blood and fear,
and raced from side to side.

"If ye want to harm me, then so be it – I don't suppose
I have many years left; but I've nothing I can give ye
except some bread and a few wee tins. But they're way up
on the hill."

"Ambush," said Henry simply. "Four men."

The man leaned out of the window, bending his neck,
and squinted at the closest body. He nodded.

"Aye. A family o' ne'er do wells. Always were. They'd
ha' had me next."

Henry lowered the gun.

"We don't mean you any harm. We just want to get
past here." He waved his arm in the direction of the log.

"Aye," the man said, "that's a problem. But it's no a big
problem for a woodsman."

He seemed to live in a parallel world, the horrors of the
past few days passing him by.

"I dinna ken what's become of old Angus, but I know
where he keeps his chain saw. If he's got some fuel, we'll
do fine. It's only a couple of miles away."

He turned the pickup and disappeared the way he'd
come. Henry stood helplessly by the blockage.

"How do we know the old guy's not going to come
back with a gun or a bunch of other guys or something?
This could be the biggest fuckin' trap," said Lou.

"You're right, but I trust him. Just gut feeling. What
else can we do?"

"I hope you're right."

\*\*\*\*\*\*

Henry paced up and down, the seconds passing like the
padded, measured footfall of an elephant. Lou busied

herself collecting the clothes and ropes discarded from the Toyota by the machete man.

As she clambered up the bank, Henry heard an engine in the distance. He raised the gun, taking cover behind the Toyota. The Daihatsu re-appeared. He blew out a long slow breath, puffing out his cheeks – the old man was on his own.

He put on an orange helmet and goggles. Then he put on some gloves, pulling every finger through. The chain saw was orange too and had a long blade. 'Stihl' was printed on the body. He opened the fuel cap and studied the level. He went to the back of the pickup and took out a green plastic can. Methodically, he poured the fuel in through a funnel.

Lou was drumming her fingers against the bonnet of the motorhome.

"For fuck's sake get a move on," she whispered.

The man looked up at her quizzically, then opened another cap.

"Blade oil, lassie," he said, "That needs filling too."

Again he went to the back of the pickup. Again he poured, this time from a smaller grey bottle. At last he was ready. He pulled the cord. The motor coughed, then nothing. He fiddled with a lever on the controls. This time it fired.

"When the branches come off, get them away," he shouted above the motor.

He moved along the tree, severing every last limb and shoot. Henry and Lou dragged the wood and brush to the side, hurling it down the bank as if casting off demons. Shani had installed Sam in the Toyota, and she too came out to help. Between them, they could now roll the tree half-way over.

They repeated the exercise. The man cut a four-foot length from one of the larger branches, then turned to the main trunk, choosing a spot where a gap sat beneath the uneven tree and the road. The saw bit hungrily into the wood and soon he was two-thirds through.

He placed the log into the gap to one side of his cut and sawed further. The two sections began to pinch and close together, but the man withdrew the blade. He started from the top again, this time at an angle to the first cut. Now he was able to saw right through, the unsupported side falling to the ground.

"Right, let's see if we can move these wee logs between us."

They moved into two teams, one at either end.

"Roll it," said the gnarled man, and with a lot of pushing and shoving, the left-hand section of the trunk rolled down the bank.

They moved the other half to the opposite verge. Only a mess of leaves and twigs and sticks was left. A sorry pile of clothes lay on the tarmac too, covered now in sawdust. Henry did not want to think about what had happened to their owner. Stef's mobile peered from her jeans' pocket. He felt like a criminal, but pulled it out and handed it to Lou.

The bloody remnants of the two men they left. They looked little different to the pheasants and badgers he was used to seeing mashed into the tarmac every day, only bigger. The crows and foxes of this place were welcome to them. He felt as shredded as these entrails that, little more than thirty minutes previously, had been human beings, himself.

"Thank you," he said to the gnarled man.

He wanted to give him a hug, or some chocolate or whisky, but he didn't.

"Nay bother."

Lou turned to him.

"Those men…the other two. They took my friend. Out that way."

She waved her arm towards the pine forest and the hills behind.

"I don't know if she's...we tried to chase them but they disappeared."

"Och, I'm sorry. They'd know every wee spit and spot of this land. Ye'll never find them."

Lou looked to the ground.

"Where are you headed, anyway?"

"Mull," said Henry.

"Aye, ye'll need a boat. I canna help you with that. God speed."

And with that, the man murmured something to the collie, stroking it, and climbed into the pick-up. Henry shook his head as their guardian angel disappeared around the bend where the dirt-grey bothie stood. He was not a religious man, but he wanted to say a prayer.

.

# CHAPTER XXX

MEHAU carried the red bucket back to the house. Some of the devotees had built a fire on the lawn and the smell of wood smoke greeted them.

In the kitchen, Anne-Marie pulled out one of the mackerel. She placed it onto a chopping board. With a knife she cut off its head, and then its tail. Expertly, she turned it on its back and sliced a line from its anus to what was left of its neck. She scooped the bloody innards from the fish and placed them on a sheet of newspaper along with the head and tail. A photograph showed people queueing for water from a tanker. Streaks of red dribbled across the image.

"Yuck, that's gross."

It was Leah.

"Did you eat fish before you joined the group?" asked Anne-Marie.

"Oh yeah. But my Mum bought them. They came from the supermarket, all ready, with a pat of garlic butter or something."

"That would be nice."

The kitchen coordinator woman walked in.

"What are you doing in here?" she asked Leah. "You are not allowed in here."

Anne-Marie looked at the woman and then looked across at Leah.

"She's helping me gut these fish," said Anne-Marie.

"Fish? We don't eat fish – Baba Ji says, no fish."

"Well, whether you eat them or not is up to you. But Leah is helping me gut them."

"I…I must speak to Mira," said the woman, and slunk away, her authority holed.

"You want to learn how to do it?" asked Anne-Marie.

Leah screwed up her face.

"OK."

She took a knife and followed the older woman's movements.

"Harder," said Anne-Marie, as she struggled to cut through the neck.

"Now, slit from here…to here."

The innards of the fish were exposed.

"Just take them from the top, and pull down against the backbone. It will all come away. They're just like us – heart and liver and intestines."

Her hands now bloody, Leah drew the membrane down, then flicked the contents onto the newspaper.

"Want to do another one?"

A dozen fish and more were gutted, and Anne-Marie took them outside. She spread three out across a large frying pan and held them over the fire that burned between two brick pillars. The fish began to cook in their own oils and the smell of their cooking filled the hungry air. Mira strode across the lawn. The kitchen coordinator intercepted her and muttered some words.

"What is this? Why are you cooking these fish in front of the devotees?"

"Mira, I don't know about you, but your group is hungry. The rice is cooking too, but if you want, if any of your people want, fresh mackerel with it, it is here."

Mira shook her head. Anne-Marie looked across at the Cedar of Lebanon and out over the sea. 'For heaven's sake, woman,' she thought. 'There's virtually unlimited food out there.' She turned the mackerel in the pan.

"We need all the energy we can get if we're going to survive this situation," she said out loud. "Do you not think your Baba Ji would agree?"

Mira stared at her, then walked across the grass, her back to the devotees. She seemed to be sharing her thoughts only with a sprawling border, mauve dahlias and orange chrysanthemums rising triumphantly above a tangle of weeds. She paced up and down for minutes. Eventually she returned.

"Any devotee who wishes to eat the fish may eat the fish," she said.

She ran her hand through her proud hair.

"I will explain to Baba Ji."

With this pronouncement, Leah leapt up, pulling Daniel to his feet. Mehau stood up too.

"Steady, we will allocate the fish in equal shares to those who want it," said the kitchen coordinator, endeavouring to retrieve some of her authority.

Two other devotees stood up. Their faces were set.

"Baba Ji says no meat, fish or eggs," said one of them. Both were men, and their sagging combat trousers, bulging stomachs and faded t-shirts did not belie their age.

"Mira is not a true devotee of Baba Ji if she is saying we can eat fish. Eating fish is killing life, Baba Ji says."

In the firelight of the dusk, a woman looked around uncertainly, nodded and went over to join them. The three hesitated.

"Anyone else?"

Noone. They conferred briefly in whispers.

"By Baba Ji's grace," said the man, "We have seen the false message of Mira. We will take His grace away from this place. May Baba Ji protect you."

And with that they walked purposefully across the lawn towards the road that ran inland.

Mira's eyes, Anne-Marie could see, were filled with tears. But the kitchen woman, refusing to acknowledge what had just happened, picked up a tray and a knife and fork. From the mackerel that were already cooked, she selected the largest and most succulent. She spooned out a generous helping of rice and set it in front of Mira, bowing her head.

The remaining devotees could scarcely hold a line, shuffling impatiently towards Anne-Marie. As their turn came, they barely glanced at the meagre ration of rice they were given, holding their plates out ravenously for the fish.

There was not enough cutlery for everyone. Some tore into the mackerel with their bare hands, flinging the skin aside and stuffing the flesh into their mouths. Some ate the skin itself. And some, scouring for more, found the severed heads and necks in the newspaper and put them in the pan and sucked and levered every last millimetre of flesh from the bones and crevices.

# CHAPTER XXXI

SHANI went across to the motorhome and picked up the baby, cuddling her. She called out to Rabiyah in Arabic.

"Shukran," came a voice from the scrub.

"She's going to stay there covering us till we're ready to go."

Sam leaned towards Henry.

"Dad," his voice was faint. "There's no point in two vehicles now. We have to dump one of them."

This time Henry nodded. His mind was a maelstrom. He looked at the fuel gauge of the Toyota and shook his head.

"Aaargh, we're nearly on the red and we used the last can back at the hotel. What do you think – there's more space in the motorhome, there's water in it and beds. But it's going to use more fuel and it's got no four-wheel drive. We've got about thirty miles to go to get to Fraser's, and the last bit is tough going."

"Landcruiser. It's got to be…"

"If we can get fuel into it."

He looked at Lou.

"You OK with that, Lou? You come with us?"

It was a rhetorical question. She had no choice.

"Yeah…thank you. I… I wish I could tell Stef's Dad she tried to look after it. Ah shit…I'll pull everything I can out of it."

"Quick as you can. We need to get out of here."

"I'll change the baby in there while we have it," said Shani.

Through the open door, Henry could see Lou moving back and forth. She set down blankets, a blue plastic supermarket tray filled with what was left of their food, a turquoise fleece and other clothes. She held the guitar up, a question in her eyes. Henry nodded and took it quickly, though there was no space for it. He squeezed it down the side of the other paraphernalia in the back. It was a reminder for him, through Wish You Were Here and the few other songs he could play, of Josephine. Subconsciously perhaps, something told him too that, whatever happened from here on in, they would need music. So long as there was life, they would need music.

"Do you have any empty water bottles?" Lou shouted, her words rushing.

Henry handed her two that they had drained and she filled them from the motorhome's tap.

"It's the fuel we need, though, Lou. Somehow we have to get it out of the tank."

"We need hosepipe," said Lou. "Have we got all the water we can take? Any more empty containers?"

Henry pulled another from the back of the Toyota. It was still half full. He knew there was fresh water at Fraser's and at Balmanie. That water could surely not have been tainted.

"Fill this one. But it's fuel we need Lou," he said again, irritated now.

"I know," she said. "That's why I'm asking. That's it for the water."

She pulled out her knife, then bent under the sink and sliced off the pipe that fed the cold tap.

"Let's have the fuel cans."

Henry pushed one end of the pipe into the fuel point. Holding the can close, he sucked on the other end. Nothing happened. He sucked again. A trickle of gaseous liquid dirtied his tongue.

"Ughh."

He spat. Sam tried to lean across, but Lou held his arm.

"Wait," she said.

She moved inside and when she reappeared she held the severed shower hose. She pulled the pipe out of the fuel tank and studied its length, then replaced it with the shower hose, feeding the outer end back into the fuel can.

Picking up a couple of old socks from the discarded detritus inside the motorhome, she pushed one end of the pipe back into the fuel point alongside the feeder hose. Then she stuffed in the socks, closing the aperture. Squatting, she blew into the shorter pipe. Nothing happened. She blew again. Something seemed to change, the hint of a sound - a kind of puff. She blew for a third time

"What the hell are you…?" shouted Henry. But he was silenced. A dribble, and then a steady flow, of fuel began to run into the fuel can. They switched cans quickly when the first was full, some diesel dribbling onto the road.

"How did you do that?" said Henry, pouring fuel into the Toyota. He didn't wait for an answer.

"OK, let's go. Now!"

Lou climbed into the vehicle for the first time since they'd rescued Stef from her mum's village. She looked quickly back at the motorhome. If she had been the sort of person who crossed herself, thought Henry, she would have crossed herself now.

\*\*\*\*\*\*

*Smells like sweat. Not Mum's smell.*

184

*Can't blame her. Chasing after Stef. Did they rescue her? Where's Mum? Oh yeah.*

*The gun. I had a gun. Dad's got it. Where are we going? Mum said we're going somewhere. To Aunt Anne-Marie. Balmanie. Boat, we need a boat. I'm cold, really cold. Why am I so cold?*

******

Sam moaned. His neck moved slightly and his eyes turned, so far as they were able, towards Shani. She seemed to understand and wrapped a blanket around his shoulders.

Henry glanced in the mirror. The girls were squashed in the back with the baby. One of the fuel cans was on Lou's knee. Rabiyah was feeding Noor and finally the baby was quiet, the contented sounds of her sucking filling the silence. She looked hard at Sam over the seat top. She studied the purple rashes that had appeared now on his neck and above his stomach. She said something to Shani.

"Poison...blood. Oh Christ, blood poisoning."

On automatic, Shani flicked her mobile on. She stared at the blank screen and the circling circle over the Google icon. Lou pulled a book from her bag.

"What's that?" asked Shani.

"Wilderness Medicine. It's kind of a handbook."

She read for a few moments.

"Look Shani, from everything it says here, seems like Sam has sepsis. Septicaemia. Disoriented. Cold … shivering, means low blood pressure. The infection isn't local any more; somewhere along the line it's got into his blood. It's potentially... it says get him to a hospital immediately. Call in a medevac helicopter if possible."

"No chance," breathed Shani.

"So...we have to get him to Balmanie. Hope his aunt has a load of antibiotics. Unless there's some hospital or surgery that's operating on Mull... but I don't think that's going to happen. We need to be quick. Really quick."

185

"Henry? Did you hear?"

He nodded. He was exhausted – physically and emotionally. He was too tired to feel the pain of Josephine's loss, or to think about Sam and what might happen, but he had no thought of stopping. Darkness was falling but he would drive through the night until they reached Fraser's place or perished on the way. Then, he would have to figure out how to get to Balmanie across the water. Now, he just had to drive. Faster.

They passed the buildings of Fort William to their left across the waters of Loch Linnhe. They reached Ardgour and the other side of the Corran Ferry that they had seen, just three hundred metres away, many hours earlier. The road became single track. For miles, it wound along the edge of lochs, up mountains and down through valleys. Occasionally, the flickering light of a candle seemed to beckon them from the whitewashed walls of a bothie. Otherwise nothing, no sign of life.

Sam woke for a few moments. He held up his hand.

"Are you sure we're on the right road, Dad?"

His voice was breathy. His breaths seemed to come from some deep mine, begged from the universe. He held his thigh, rubbing the injured area for some relief, then scratched at his stomach. Shani leant forward and held his head in the crook of her arm.

"We'll soon be there," she said, stroking his hair.

Henry raced on. At times, the moon appeared from behind the clouds and lit up the barren landscape. At others, he had to blink to adjust his eyes to the looming shadows of hill and water.

******

"Lou, Shani –talk to me. Tell me something. Keep me awake."

"What shall I tell you? What would you like to hear?" asked Shani

"Anything. Tell me how you met Sam."

"Ah – I can do that. We were both so stupid.

"I was in the Cross Keys with my boyfriend at that time. Well, he was, and then he wasn't. He left. Dave Crannock, the philosophy lecturer, was there with a bunch of his students. They were all in a big circle, drinking and talking. He said come and join us and bought me a beer.

"They were discussing all this stuff about anarchy and chaos in relation to Plato's theory of forms. Are you familiar with Plato's theory of forms, Henry? In the cave?"

Henry nodded. "Somewhere I read about it. Got the general picture."

"How could there be a form of chaos? That was what they were discussing."

She laughed ironically.

"If I could bring them all here... we're probably living right now in the form of chaos. Anyway, I wondered if this was a tutorial or just a chill-out. If this was the way he ran his tutorials, I was up for it.

"I kept catching the eye of this guy who was at one o'clock to my seven o'clock. Or he kept catching mine. You don't know, do you. 'What's your name?' he said. 'Shani,' I said. 'Nice name,' he said. When everyone slipped away that night, he asked me for my number.

"He wrote it down on the palm of his hand, and touched my shoulder as he left."

"Silly boy," she said, turning to face Sam.

His lips moved slightly, and she squeezed his hand.

"Henry – you awake? You OK?"

Henry grunted. "Did he call you?"

"No, Henry, that's the point. I think I glimpsed him once or twice, in a bus queue or a passing face in a crowd, a second, then gone. I did see him once, in a restaurant, but he was with a whole group of people, other girls too. It sounded like they'd all had a lot to drink. I decided it wasn't the right time.

"I went into the Cross Keys a few times, but they were never there again. I think I thought – if he wants to find me, he will. I don't know why I didn't go hunting for him. It can't have been that difficult, even with twenty thousand students."

The road veered to the left and for a moment Henry lost sight of the tarmac.

"And…"

"It was three years later. We'd both graduated. I was at this nightclub in London called Seven Steps. I saw his face across the dancefloor, flashing in the strobe lights.

"I watched him and when he went to the bar, I followed. I sat down beside him as he ordered. I did not say a word. Eventually, his eyes turned to me. He looked, and then he looked again and his face lit up.

" 'I'm so sorry', were his first words. 'I went for a pee and washed my hands. Properly brought up, you know. The people I was with couldn't understand why I was so upset that I'd washed my hands. I tried to look for you but I didn't know your surname. I just had Shani. I didn't even know how to spell that.'

" 'It's OK,' I said.

"We danced. His dancing was kind of weird but I didn't care. We were dancing in each other's rhythm. He came back to my flat that night. And, well…here we are."

"Henry – you OK?"

"We were never very good at dancing," said Henry. "Any of us."

******

At the head of Loch Aline a small road forked to the left before they reached the village. An old stone bridge, etched in moss, wended over a boulder-strewn stream. The headlights seemed to pick out each stone, their different sizes and colours, as they crossed. Henry remembered looking over this bridge in his youth – it was the first time he had seen an otter hunting, oblivious to him in the noise of the waters.

A few hundred yards further and a track followed the south bank of the loch. This was the final stretch of the haggis route of his childhood. There were more pot holes than he remembered and, with every lurch of the Toyota, Sam groaned. A bothie sat on the edge of the loch, a slipway beside it. The body of a man was slumped against a boat, torpid. On the bank a heron and a seal seemed to look on unconcerned. Henry could not understand why they did not fly away or swim until he realised they were moulded in wire.

He drove on. He felt a pang now. Would Fraser recognize him? Would he welcome them? The track turned at the end of the loch inland, above the cliff. A gate here, marked by a deer fence, blocked their way. Shani got out. There was no lock and she pushed it open through the thick grass.

Now the way was cobbled and rutted. In places it dipped into fords, deep muddy puddles slewing the Toyota sideways. In other places, a steep incline. The headlights picked out the yellow flowers of the gorse, and sheep scrabbling to their feet and scurrying to the side. Henry was glad they had chosen the Toyota.

At the western end of the track lay an N-shaped steading, built of stone. There were cattle and sheep here in his younger days, but it lay empty now. An old tractor rusted in one corner, some sacks of feed, damp and useless, and a cattle trough slumped on the bare earth.

From somewhere in his mind he remembered Fraser saying that this was not his land. It was the land of the man on the hill. But he looked to the right. He knew where to look. The old five-barred gate was still there. He felt a kind of resurgence. He was nearly home.

Stones had given way to grass. Tall trees loomed over them to either side. The track wound steeply down the cliff left then right, then left again, the headlights picking out the trunks in sharp relief and tyre tracks in the wet ground. Suddenly the land flattened and the bay opened out ahead. The house stood white and luminous and solitary, the water spreading beyond it – out towards Mull.

The Toyota crunched across the sand-strewn driveway. A pick-up was parked in a corrugated lean-to behind the house. Henry left the headlights on and went to the door. All he could hear was the rhythmic lapping of the waves against the shallow beach. He knocked. There was no answer. He knocked louder again.

"Fraser...it's me, Henry."

Still there was nothing.

He pulled the torch from the Toyota. He remembered that Fraser never locked the door. In that, at least, he was right. It opened with a squeak. A dandelion was growing in a crevice of the doorstep. There was a hint of damp in the air. He shone the torch around the living room and the kitchen. Nobody. Nothing.

He went up the narrow uncarpeted stairs, his footsteps breaking the silence. In Fraser's room, the duvet was thrown back, the sheet crumpled. In the other bedroom, the old wooden bed that had been in the family for years, lay neatly made up, a yellow eiderdown spread across it.

He went outside again. He cast the torch across the beach and across the water. He could see a boat, but he was too exhausted. In any case, they could not attempt a crossing in the dark. He went back to the Toyota.

"Noone here. No sign of him. But a boat's here, thank God. Let's sleep for a few hours and cross in the morning."

Together they lifted Sam over to the house, stumbling in the half-dark, and laid him on the sofa. Lou took the torch and scoured the shelves and cupboards in the bathroom.

"Hah!" she said, holding up a small white box. Flucloxacillin. She pulled out the silver foil packaging. It was torn and out of date. There were only six tabs left. The dosage was one every four hours.

Shani spoke to Rabiyah. She looked towards Sam, then back at the antibiotics.

"Thalaatha."

"Thalaatha?" cried Shani.

The Syrian woman nodded.

"She says three now and the other three in four hours. It's the wrong anti-biotic but it's better than nothing."

Shani filled a mug from a tepid water can and fed the capsules to Sam. He could barely swallow. Now they could only wait. Sleep and wait.

Rabiyah and Noor took the spare room.

"I can sleep on the floor," said Henry, entering Fraser's bedroom.

"Who fuckin' cares," said Lou. "I'll go this side."

And she pulled off her boots and lay on Fraser's double bed.

# CHAPTER XXXII

THE MORNING was fine, with just a slight breeze from the south. Anne-Marie studied the tide, then went downstairs. Devotees were peeling out of the sleeping rooms in underpants and bras. Some were filing towards the newly dug latrines, barefoot over the daisies thick with dew.

Aragorn came up to her in the kitchen. He was whining and pulled at her trousers, then ran outside towards the woods. She followed.

"Where's Rabbie?" she asked him.

Aragorn led her on, looking behind him from time to time to make sure she was following. In the shade beneath a spreading branch of the Cedar of Lebanon, Rabbie lay. His brown fur was scuffed and standing on end in places, streaks of grey around his nose. His body was still. Anne-Marie bent down to stroke his head.

"I'm sorry Rabbie. We did our best. You can join Fraser now."

She hoped that, whatever dogs understood by instinct, Aragorn would know that this was the end. That he would not mourn Rabbie's loss. She fetched a spade from the shed. There was a cough behind her.

"I help you?" asked Mehau.

She handed him the spade. He dug deep into the ground and a mound of soft brown earth formed to the side. A trickle of soil began to slip back into the hole. Gently Anne-Marie laid the dog inside. Mihau shovelled the earth back. It looked incomplete. She picked up stones and pebbles and, patting down the soil, formed an 'R' with them.

"I am sorry. Nice dog. Brave dog."

"Yes," said Anne-Marie. She paused.

"Mehau, do you want to come fishing again?"

"Yes, but is puja now. After puja."

"We need to go now. Now is when we can get the fish."

"I speak to Mira."

Mira was standing on a rock at the edge of the lawn, silhouetted against the sea like some sort of mermaid princess. Her hair was wet and the bottom of her trousers clung to her ankles.

"It is puja time Mehau."

Mehau held his hands together and bowed his head.

"Yes, Mira. Anne-Marie says now is the time to fish if we are to catch fish today. She has asked me to help."

"Puja is time with Baba Ji. By His grace, you will find fish after puja."

"Look Mira, Baba Ji might help Mehau to find fish after puja, but I am going now and I need help. The tide is out right now. It will turn very soon and a rising tide is the time to find a shoal. Can puja not happen later for Mehau?"

"Puja is at 6 o'clock, this is what Baba Ji says."

"But does Baba Ji control the tides, Mira? If we do not go very soon, we will not be able to go for twelve hours or more. You saw the hunger in your group last night. If you want to keep them strong, they need to keep eating. None of the other food will last long. You're the only one getting proper meals."

"What?" said Mira. A flash of anger passed her face. "What do you mean?"

"The kitchen woman is giving you larger portions, tasty portions with extra bits that none of the others are eating."

Mira called the kitchen coordinator over.

"Is this true? Are you giving me larger portions than everyone else? And special extras?"

She nodded.

"Why?" Her eyes drilled into the woman, unblinking. "Baba Ji says we are all equal. There is Master and there is devotee. There is not senior devotee and lesser devotee. He does not differentiate between the man who sweeps the floor beneath His feet and the man who gives his money to build a palace for Him."

The kitchen woman's eyes filled with tears.

"I was trying to do it for Baba Ji. I…"

"From now on, I eat what you eat. And if there is nothing to eat, then I eat nothing."

She turned and walked purposefully across the lawn towards the rest of the devotees, then stopped and looked back.

"Mehau, you may go fishing with Anne-Marie. On your return, you will do private puja for one hour."

"Thank you, Mira."

He looked up. A persistent humming had broken into the skirl of the gulls and the breeze in the trees. A black drone, perhaps half a metre in diameter, was circling the house and garden like an angry stag beetle.

"Look out, Mira, it may be armed," shouted one of the devotees, diving into the spread of a rhododendron.

Mira stared at the intruder for a long time, upright and impassive.

"Baba Ji will protect us," she said.

\*\*\*\*\*\*

Anne-Marie and Mehau made their way along the narrow path to the secret bay, ducking under low pine branches and skirting roots that looped above the dirt. When they were clear of the woods, she raised her binoculars to the north-west. A mist hung over the water and Fraser's house was not visible.

They headed out of the bay south this time past the old castle and Grass Point towards the Firth of Loon. Anne-Marie scanned the sea in front of them. A sea eagle flew overhead, high, its outstretched wings like a great signpost in the sky. It was some time before they found what they were looking for. Mehau's face lit up in the sort of smile that she had not seen in many of his group.

"You like fishing, don't you?" she said, as he pulled the mackerel in.

"I do Anne-Marie. Is very simple. I do not have to think. I do not have to think 'What Baba Ji want? What Mira want?' I just fish. We catch fish. We eat fish. Is normal. Is man, right?"

The sound came from the west. A churning. A RIB* raced into the narrow channel that led to Loch Spelve. It was black, apart from a white motif that she did not recognise on the bow – a reverse crescent.

"What is?"

Anne-Marie idled the engine and for some minutes the boat rocked in the water, drifting with the wind. She trained the binoculars on the channel. Gulls flew and circled overhead. Mehau landed another line of mackerel and began to unhook them. Nothing else moved.

And then, from behind the curved spit of rock that marked the entrance, the RIB reappeared. She could see it clearly now. On either side, a line of eight people, black gear and fully hooded, sat upright, staring ahead. Some might have been women. A shiver ran through her.

* RIB *(Rigid Inflatable Boat)*

"Just keep fishing," she said. "Pretend you have not noticed them."

The boat circled them. One hundred metres. Fifty metres. Thirty and closing on the third pass. Her eyes were drawn to the cold, hard faces.

'So this is how it ends,' thought Anne-Marie.. She could feel fish struggling on the end of her line but her arms would not raise the rod, her brain frozen.

The pitch of the RIB's engine rose suddenly to a crescendo. Anne-Marie braced herself. A curtain of water sluiced across the divide, showering her face and the screen of the wheelhouse. The salt spray tasted oily, unclean. She swiped it from her lips as the RIB veered sharply away and sped north up the Sound, the ripples of its vortex flinging the boat from side to side. All colour had drained from Mehau's face. His rod lay on the deck, his hands gripping the side rail.

"These are not good people," he said, his voice quavering.

Anne-Marie nodded, unable to speak. Her arms shook as she pulled the fish in. One of the mackerel slipped from her grasp. She watched blankly as it thrashed about on the deck, desperate for oxygen. Its tail slapped the wet planks and a trail of silver scales formed a random pattern on the wood. With one final, desperate curl the fish succumbed and lay still.

Her eyes met Mehau's. She turned the wheel back towards Balmanie. It was not until they had rounded the point where the old castle stood that Fraser's house came into view. Sunlight glinted off something to the left of the building. Frantically Anne-Marie focussed.

"Someone's there!"

She handed the binoculars to Mehau.

# CHAPTER XXXIII

HENRY woke to the piping of an oyster catcher skimming across the bay. Lou was snoring rhythmically beside him. He got up quietly. He was impatient now to get across, but he was aware too that everyone was exhausted.

He crept down the stairs in his stockinged feet. On the kitchen table, visible now in the daylight, lay a crumpled sheet of brown paper, a note discarded. He recognised Anne-Marie's scrawl. He remembered his mother's anguished cries as she tried to decipher her daughter's missives from school. It was to him that she passed them for translation.

*'Have taken the Royal Yacht and looking after Rabbie. Call me when you get back. Will explain. A-M.'*

He felt the kind of wound in his chest that only a twin feels. Anne-Marie had been here recently; Fraser cannot have been here at the time, yet it seemed he had read the note. There was a finality in this.

He inched the door open. Outside he pulled on his boots. He looked across the Sound. On a clear day, the chimneys of Balmanie could be seen peering above the

197

pines on the other side, but a mist hung over the water, and for the moment they were hidden.

At the sea's edge he splashed his face in the salt water again and again. It was not just the dirt he was trying to wash away. A stream strolled out at the bottom of the cliffs below the waterfall, tumbling over the stones. Surely this water must be clean, he thought - they'd always drunk it. Cupping his hands, he bent his head to suck in a great mouthful...then stopped. With a wrench, he threw his hands aside, casting the water back. He was too close to the prize to gamble.

On the north side of the bay lay the ruins of a boat, devoid of paint and weathered to the colour of the beach. It had not been there twenty years ago when he was last here. Its back was broken and its timbers fell away to the side like the ribs of a long dead sheep that has been eaten by crows and foxes.

He walked to the end of the jetty. With a surge of recognition, he realised that the boat moored against the orange buoy twenty-five metres away was his boat, his and Anne-Marie's. Was she now on the mainland? Had she left it for him?

The sea was over a metre deep at the end of the jetty and the tide was coming in. He looked about. Fraser must have a tender, a dinghy of some kind, he thought. Unless he'd taken it with him for some reason – wherever he was. If Henry had to, he could swim out and somehow clamber aboard, but a dinghy would be a lot simpler.

There was nothing in the outbuildings at the back of the house. He walked across the beach to the stone boathouse that stood behind the wreck. He'd thought it too was now a ruin but, as he approached, he saw that it was just a section of roof that had caved in. At the entrance, the flotsam and jetsam of a thousand tides had gathered in a mattress of litter, but, inside, a tiny wooden dinghy was tethered to one of the undamaged roof timbers. A metal trolley, the mudguards of its two wheels painted in an incongruous sky blue, was stowed vertically against the side wall. In the far corner, lay discarded cans of coca-cola and spam beside a pile of ashes, as if someone had taken refuge here. Henry could find only one oar.

He released the dinghy and manoeuvred it down to the sea. Long-buried skills of life on the water came back to him. Instinctively, he knew what he had to do. He paddled out to his boat and, securing the dinghy, climbed across.

A plastic bag, a note inside, clung to the gunwhale, somehow unmoved by the weathers. Anne-Marie's scrawl again. He pulled out the sheet. She had sealed the bag well and only the outside edge was damp and etched with the water. He read:

*Henry,*

*I don't know what is going on. I do not know what has happened to Fraser. He must have left here in the pickup on Tuesday, but he had not got back when I came over to pick up my things. I have taken his fishing boat. I pray that you and Josephine and Sam are OK. If, by the grace of anyone who has control over these things, you are reading this, then you've made it this far. Take the boat. It is the same old boat, our boat, though the outboard is new.*

*I will be at Balmanie. I will be looking out for you through Dad's binoculars. Please make it through. If you have a problem on this side, light a fire or do something to show me you're here.*

*XXX*

*A-M*

He felt a pang of love for his sister as he lowered the black and white outboard into the water. It started easily and within minutes he had the boat moored at the jetty.

******

Back in the house, Rabiyah was showing Noor the butterflies that hung in cases on the walls. The baby was giggling, trying to touch them.

Her mother took her to the sea, dipping her backside gently in the waves to wash her, then laid her on her back on the pebbles outside and studied Sam. She felt his pulse and his forehead, and touched his stomach. She looked Shani in the eye and spoke in Arabic.

"What did she say?"

"Liquid," she said. "He must drink liquid. His blood pressure is very, very low."

"I've been giving him water all night. Can we heat any water? I saw some mint tea."

Henry studied the kitchen. An electric kettle stood on the counter. He flicked on the switch expecting nothing. He got nothing. He followed the line of the hob. It seemed to reach into the ground.

'Calor gas,' he thought.

He turned on a bar, and lit a match to it. A blue flame darted about the pan as if refusal to light was a sin.

"Wow!" He had not expected that.

He poured water from one of the containers in the back of the Toyota into a saucepan. Shani supported Sam's back. One by one, she placed the last three antibiotics in his mouth. He was barely able to lift his chin to drink, but with a struggle he swallowed.

"We're going to be there soon," she said. "It's just across the water."

"Shani's right, Sam. Anne-Marie has left my boat here…with a message. She's expecting us. All I have to do is remember how to work the damned engine."

Sam grimaced.

"You can do it Dad," he whispered. " 'Just turn the key and pull the starter'. That's what you always said."

Henry looked at Shani. He pursed his lips and nodded… there was life and fight in Sam yet. Lou came down the stairs. She read the two notes lying on the table then headed straight for the sea. She took off her top and sluiced water across her face, around her neck, over her breasts and under her armpits.

Seaweed reeked in the morning air and flies buzzed about the surface of the shoreline. The trees behind the bay were thick with the calls of the land birds while the sea birds swooped and dived and screeched over the water. Henry wondered, as he had idly wondered many times in his childhood, what they thought of each other – the swooping trapeze artists of the waves and their raucous country cousins - the bowler-hatted civil servants, the waddling landlubbers. Lou jogged back.

"Let's get going," said Henry,

They lay Sam onto the back seat of the Toyota. Henry flicked it into four-wheel-drive mode. It grabbed the stones and pebbles of the beach and the wet sand as if this were its home. It reminded Henry of why he'd bought it in the first place. But now his sick son was in the back and he edged the vehicle gently across the shoreline to the end of the jetty. They began to unload.

"How much can we take?"

"Leave the fuel. It can stay here. Just one water can for on the way over – there's a well at Balmanie. Bring all the food and warm clothes for everyone. We can come back for the guitar."

Lou moved quickly up and down the jetty.

The boat was lower in the water than Henry would have liked. He looked out to sea. There was no GPS or weather forecast he could rely on now. Instinct, childhood lessons of tide and wind, were all he had. The sky looked clear with only small cumulus clouds to the south; there were no rag tops on the waves beyond the bay.

"Get Sam on and then everyone else, and let's see how it looks," he said as he fiddled with the controls.

Lou supported Sam's legs and Shani held his head and shoulders. She stepped backwards onto the rocking boat gingerly, first her left foot. Lou waited as she found her balance, ready to catch Sam. Shani steadied herself and pulled her right foot across, Lou moving forward with her. They laid Sam towards the prow, cushioning his back. The reek of his son's leg passed across Henry as he checked the engine, and he winced inside.

"We're nearly ready," said Shani, stroking his hair. "We'll be at your aunt's house really soon. I can't wait to see the famous Balmanie for real."

Lou looked at the island across the water, to the point that was visible now that the mist had lifted. Then she looked back inland towards the bothie and the bank of trees behind that hugged the bay.

"Give me the keys," she said.

She turned the Toyota towards the bank, then swung it hard right onto a patch of broken concrete beside the house.

\*\*\*\*\*\*

*I can hear them talking. They're trying to humour me, pretend they're not worried, like I was when I called from London. That's so long ago. Dad's trying to start the boat. Go on Dad, you can do it. The old castle — head for the old ruined castle on the point. That's what you used to tell me when I was a kid.*

*What's that in the sky? Those wings, like carpets. Have the angels come? Eagles, they're eagles. Have they come to fetch me off the burning mountain? Will they bring Shani too and Dad? No, don't go away. They're flying away. Come back! Oh I am so thirsty.*

\*\*\*\*\*\*

Rabiyah stepped in with the baby. She looked back to the house, wary. Her eyes searched the boat. Her face seemed to relax as she spotted the .22 lying on the floor boards, the box of orange bullets beside it.

Henry held the boat in neutral.

"Push us off, Lou."

She released the ropes and in a single fluid movement lunged forward into the stern. Henry swung the boat round and they headed across the bay. The sea rose and fell quietly, like the purring breath of a sleeping cat. He had seen it otherwise, when it would rage like a caged lion against the confines of its shores, rage at anything that dared set foot on it, rage in concert with the wind and the skies in tormented fury. He was glad that, on this morning, the lion was still.

But the wind, as they moved into the open sea, out of the shelter of the bay, was unexpected. Henry felt the boat move and struggle but he set his course firmly. Whatever it took, if they were all going to have to swim, if they were going to have to support Sam in the rescue position across the Sound, they were going to Balmanie. He could see its trees and feel its pull, and he was not going to let the wind stop him.

It was colder out here. He wrapped his fleece around him. The others were crossing their arms against the chill and Rabiyah had Noor wrapped tightly into her breast. He looked across at Shani. He raised his eyes.

"Is he warm enough?"

"He's shivering."

Henry began to pull off his fleece again but Lou was looking around the boat. She delved into the prow - a heavy oilskin hid behind the small door. She dragged it out and laid it over Sam.

The black shadow of a helicopter played deep and low across the high hills of Mull ahead. Henry wished it were only a shadow, a shadow of nothing, but then he saw the reality following the contours of the island coastline. So close to Balmanie. 'They are here too,' he thought, and a part of him died.

A boat, a speck in the distance, lay way south, to their left. Otherwise, the sea lay empty. The CalMac ferries that normally plied their trade from Oban were nowhere to be seen. Noone was fishing. No white sails scudded over the water or hung becalmed in a fading wind. Henry looked at his son. His eyes were closed, his head slumped to the side.

"How long, do you think?" asked Shani desperately.

"Fifteen, maybe twenty, minutes."

He turned up the throttle and now the boat rose and fell in the swell, spray flinging about them. Noor seemed to like it. She was giggling again as Rabiyah held her tight. Henry continually corrected their course, fighting against the wind heading up from the south. He watched the green-black water skirl and eddy against the hull.

He remembered the first time he had done this. He was barely out of short trousers. 'Just aim for that headland,' his father, Sam's grandfather, had said. 'Keep the old castle on your left. Use the prow as your sight.' He had handed over the tiller, the outboard, everything, moved to the prow and closed his eyes. That was the way he taught him. Familiarise, give him confidence, then give him control.

Henry could remember the fear he'd felt at the time. But the excitement too. It was one of those memories that imprints itself on the person, that is not deleted by passing life or trauma. A piece of music, for instance, played on the radio at a moment in time, that connects itself to one particular image or emotion, such that, forever after, when that music plays, that image or emotion comes to mind. Tristan und Isolde plays - a male kestrel flies from a perch on a tree above a canal bridge and hovers, then dives. Or drive over the canal bridge and the music sounds, the kestrel flies.

Why are these particular things imprinted on our brains, thought Henry, while others are long forgotten? And why now does my son have to endure this pain? He looked at Shani. She was talking to Sam, encouraging him, putting water to his lips, her eyes flicking up from time to time to the approaching shore, willing them forward.

Lou and Rabiyah stared at the headland and the chimneys that peered now from the trees that shielded Balmanie, the hills of Mull towering behind them. The roof of the house that had been their destination since the start of this journey grew ever larger, the individual tiles clearer; but, for the moment, they were disarmed, captive in the boat. There was nothing they could do to change their fate.

\*\*\*\*\*\*

Henry dead-headed straight for the old pier. It was the quickest way to get Sam out and up to the house. They could sort the boat out later.

As they rounded the headland, they could see more of the house. A wave of nostalgia hit him. For the holidays he had come here. The summers from school. The summers with girlfriends, some of them looked down upon. Grandpa and Granny there. Mum and Dad there. He almost expected them now.

He slowed the engine and began to glide in.

"Now!" he heard a cry.

From the bushes that masked the start of the pier, from the trees on either side, from the shore to the left, people came running. They were shouting and throwing sticks and rocks – anything they could pick up from the beach. Much of the fusillade landed well short, splashing in a curtain in front of the boat, though no less of a threat.

"Private land," shouted a voice. "Go, leave, you are not welcome here."

"Who are you? This is my land. Where is Anne-Marie?" shouted Henry, but the fusillade did not let up. He saw Rabiyah, sheltering the baby between her legs, slide the rifle from under the seats and pull some bullets from the orange box. Shani shielded Sam's head with her arms.

Henry began to turn the boat to gain time. A stone, barely more than a pebble, landed on Sam's legs. There was no time for this. He picked up the twelve bore and loaded. He fired into the air, but it generated only another volley of missiles.

He raised the gun again.

\*\*\*\*\*\*

"Is a car, gold colour," said Mehau.

"Jesus!" As they rounded the point by the old ruined castle, Anne-Marie pointed to the bay below Balmanie. She rammed the throttle forward, then forward again into the red. The boat bucked and kicked, bouncing off the water.

"Hold the line," she said, handing the wheel to Mehau.

Through the binoculars she could see a boat, her boat, her and Henry's boat, close to the pier. To either side, from the bushes on the shoreline and on the pier itself, she could see the devotees swirling like crazed ants. Henry was in the boat. There were others. Someone was lying at the front. She saw Henry raise the gun.

"Nooo," she breathed.

"Is problem?" asked Mehau

"No, Henry! No!" she shouted, this time.

But the rush of the breeze and the splashing of stones and sticks in the water on the shoreline drowned her call and swept it helplessly down the Sound.

She shouted again and again.

\*\*\*\*\*\*

It was too late.

One of the people on the shore had found a source of flat stones. They were playing a deadly game of ducks and drakes. Stones thudded into the boat's timbers, peppering the side like a discordant drum solo. But one stone, bronze coloured, seemed to take flight. It skimmed faster and faster towards the boat, gathering momentum. It hit a wavelet, and, before anyone could react, leapt into the boat, glancing off Noor's forehead.

The baby screamed.

Rabiyah, enraged, raised the .22 to her shoulder. Very deliberately, she targeted the thrower. He seemed to sense the danger. He moved from one leg to the other. He looked to his left. He looked to his right. He looked behind him. Broadside on, the boat rocked in the swell. Rabiyah held the gun still and, in the moment between the rise and the fall, in the moment that the thrower turned to run, she fired.

\*\*\*\*\*\*

A devotee fell violently backwards. An arc of blood rose in slow motion from his chest, like the momentary sweep of a dancer's veil, then settled onto the stones and seaweed.

Anne-Marie could see the kitchen woman running to help. Some of the devotees raced to the edge of the beach to seek cover; but the ones on the pier kept hurling stones at the boat, bigger stones now, it seemed, and somehow with more intent.

Henry was shouting at them though she could not hear his words, gesticulating wildly and waving his gun.

\*\*\*\*\*\*

"We have an injury on board, medical emergency. This is my home. Let me in," he screamed, but the people looked back blankly.

Another stone, this one the size of a tennis ball, smashed into the timbers. Rabiyah raised the gun again. A young man seemed to be directing the attackers, a blonde girl beside him. Rabiyah took aim, but amidst the chaotic noise of man and sea, Henry heard a call. A call of his name. He would know that voice in the loudest of crowds.

"Wait!" he said urgently, holding up his hand to Rabiyah.

"Stop! Mira, Daniel – Stop!" roared the voice. "This is my brother. Let him land."

On the beach and on the pier, the attack suddenly subsided, the stones ceased and the people withdrew. Henry looked behind him to see his twin sister standing in the prow of a larger vessel. Somehow, he could see, she held the ear of these people and they obeyed her.

He glided the boat into the shore and cut the engine. Lou, her knife drawn, leapt out into the shallow water with him, and pulled the boat forward. A tall, stately woman in a torn coral shawl approached. Her face was smeared in tears and blood.

"Don't you dare come fuckin' close," said Lou.

But the woman held her hands together and bowed her head.

"I am sorry," she said. "These are my people by Baba Ji's grace. They mean you no harm. We did not realize – Anne-Marie was not here."

Lou looked at her.

"What the fuck?!" she said, but stood back, guarding the group.

"Can you help?" said Henry, looking at the woman. "My son is really sick. We need to get him into the house. Take his legs. As quick as you can."

She waded into the water without question. Shani took Sam's shoulders and neck and together they moved across the shoreline. The young man who had been directing the attack from the pier was deferential now. He offered to take over from the tall woman, but she waved him away.

"Just get Ash buried," she said.

******

Anne-Marie appeared on the beach beside Henry. They embraced. Tears were welling in her eyes, but he pulled himself free.

"Sam is sick - really sick. Sepsis. Is there any medical…"

Anne-Marie was already shaking her head.

"The island's broken – people are roaming about hunting for food and water. We've had to ward off attacks from inland and from the sea. We have to protect the well

208

and the house and the boats, otherwise we're all done for. That's why…"

"Have you got any antibiotics? Anything? We need to be quick."

"I think I've got something - I don't know how old it is. We'll find it, Henry."

He looked across the beach as they walked towards the house. The body of the shot man lay on the stones, blood still oozing into the sand below. A tall young man with wild dark hair had been standing in the background. Now he pulled the corpse up above the tideline, unsure.

"Who the hell are these people? What's going on here anyway?" asked Henry.

"I had to let them in – to share the house – or I'd have lost it. They're some kind of sect. They follow someone called Baba Ji, but Mira, the tall woman, is their leader here. They were vegetarian but there's no food. That's why I went out fishing. We need to keep them on side."

"But Rabiyah shot one of them."

"I know but, Henry, they're strange. I don't think they are going to hold it against you. Who is this Rabiyah anyway? Who are these other women that have come with you? Where is Josephine?"

Henry told his story.

"I'm so sorry," said Anne-Marie quietly as they reached the front door. "It would not have been any easier for her here."

They entered the old dining room.

"We need this room," she said to some devotees. They trooped out obediently and she adjusted the cushions as Shani and Mira laid Sam down. With Henry she went straight to the bathroom upstairs.

"It's got to be here somewhere."

She rifled through packs of plasters and aspirin, tubes of toothpaste and germolene in a plastic tub. At the bottom - Amoxicillin.

"Here!" she said, holding it up. She squinted at the expiry date.

It was close enough. Only three months past. It said four per day for fourteen days. There were ten tabs left.

# CHAPTER XXXIV

SAM LAY on the cushions naked, a rainbow-patterned duvet covering him despite the heat outside. The purple patches on his body were angrier now, almost black, like a starling's feathers. They were growing in size and coalescing. The tip of his nose and his toes, the furthest distal points, had succumbed. His heart was no longer getting blood to them, his organs were failing.

Shani looked at the label on the box of Amoxicillin and sighed. She popped out one, then two tabs. Then a third. She looked up at Henry. 'A strong dose or make them last?' her eyes seemed to ask.

"I don't know," he said, his face etched with the pain of not knowing. "I just don't know."

Shani took the three pills to the kitchen. She laid them on a bread board and with a rolling pin crushed them into a powder. She filled a glass with a few centimetres of water, then carefully tipped in the powder, stirring it vigorously.

Henry piled more cushions behind Sam and together they hauled him upright. Holding his cheeks, Shani poured the medication gently, sip by sip, into his mouth, willing him to swallow. She peeled the bandage from the laceration on his thigh, the origin of the problem. She tried to clean it up, dabbing it with cotton wool and TCP. He did not even flinch. The wound was a mere footnote now to the battle raging across the rest of his body. Henry knelt on the carpet. He put his palm on his son's chest.

"I'm going outside to talk to Anne-Marie to try to understand what's going on here. Shani's here with you. I'll be back very soon."

\*\*\*\*\*\*

He sat on an oak bench on the lawn, waiting for his sister. The bench commemorated, so far as he could remember, his parents' twenty-fifth wedding anniversary.

'Wood's better than silver,' someone had said.

A throbbing arose in the air, quiet at first but relentless. The sound grew and reverberated. It was deafening now, a merciless staccato beat.

From behind the trees, a black Chinook filled Henry's vision, thundering low over the house. His hair, unkempt though it was, ruffled and tousled with the sweep and slap of the two huge rotors. The helicopter seemed to stoop like some giant cockroach in the sky. He could feel the heat of its engines as it bent away to the north. Anne-Marie appeared from the kitchen door.

"I don't know how long we've got," she said. "Drones have been overflying, jets. There was a RIB when we were fishing…they know we're here."

"Can we get across the island? Is the pick-up working?"

"Yes, but, as I said, inland people are fighting for food and water. There's nowhere to go – we're safest here."

"Safest and trapped?"

"Yep."

Henry sighed. He did not know if he had the strength left in him to run again anyway.

"What have we got?"

"We do have boats. Our boat and both of Fraser's boats. We have the guns that you brought."

"And not much ammunition. I don't think we are going to fight off drones and helicopter gunships with a twelve bore and a .22 for very long. Where's Fraser?"

"Gone. He got into some fight in Oban. He died on the way over with Mira and the Baba Ji's. Sounds like he was trying to bring them here. They had no idea what they were doing. He gave them directions. They were lucky to get across."

Henry nodded. Almost unconsciously, they moved together, brother and sister, up the meadow and on through the woods to the secret harbour. Fifty years previously, this would have been two teenagers creeping surreptitiously through the rhododendrons on a summer holiday escapade. They brushed aside the fronds and made their way along the dark path thick with the scent of the loam. Years of fallen leaves and pine needles and ferns decayed to a soft carpet. It felt no different to Henry - except the end-game.

An otter swam playfully in the water below them. It dived, re-appearing a few moments later to the left, and turned on its back as if sunbathing, its white throat exposed to the sky. Further out, a seal flopped lazily into the Sound from a seaweed-strewn rock. Overhead, a small flock of greylags, honking loudly, flew inland. The Lady Ffiona floated serenely, her movement barely perceptible in the water.

"The propeller's fouled up with fishing net. There was no time to fix it. We had to row her round," said Anne-Marie.

"I'll look at it in the morning. I need to get back to Sam. I…I don't know if he's going to make it."

As they made their way up again through the woods, they could hear a female voice ahead of them. Anne-Marie saw them first – Daniel and Leah in a clearing. She raised her hand, bidding her brother to stop, and moved backwards out of sight.

Daniel sat on the trunk of a fallen pine. Leah stood in front of him.

"I'm scared Daniel. Not Anne-Marie's family but, but…everything. The helicopters, the drone, the…"

"That's the guy who was on the pier," whispered Henry. "They could have killed us."

"I know," said Anne-Marie. "But they're OK. Leah is with me."

Daniel stood up and held out his arms to his girlfriend. She lifted her face, offering her soft lips, but he turned his face to the side.

"Noone will know," she said.

"That's not the point. Baba Ji says no sex on retreats."

Leah broke away from him.

"Yeah but this isn't exactly a retreat is it? And Baba Ji can't see, can he? Mira said Baba Ji would protect us, but he didn't protect Ash, did he? It's not like it's kind of normal out here is it?"

"Leah…" He held his arms out again.

"I don't want a bloody hug," she said vehemently. "I want to fuck, like we used to. This stuff is OK…I promised I would do it for you. World peace – cool. Peace inside – cool. But this is for real. A drone could kill us in the next five minutes for all I know, and all I ask you for is one more time. If Mira sees us, who the fuck cares? Where does she stand in the millions of people on this earth making love right now? What's she going to do? Tell you you are a naughty boy and do extra puja? It's not like she has a whole load of options. Perhaps someone should make out with her – tell her she's beautiful, tell her it's OK, she doesn't have to be so uptight. Maybe I will."

Daniel breathed a deep sigh and pulled Leah towards him, his hands dragging on the waist of her turquoise jeans.

"Shit," whispered Henry. "Let's go the other way."

It was afternoon when Shani heard footsteps outside. The tall Georgian sash windows were open at the top, anything to clear the fetid, stinking air and warm Sam.

"I'll show you where the water is," said a muffled voice.

"This is where we used to sleep. Let's see if any of the others will come with us now," said another.

A man's face appeared at one of the windows. He seemed to be shielding his eyes. He started pulling at the lower frame, trying to lift it.

"Jammed solid," he said.

He held something soft, a fleece perhaps, against the left-hand pane, smothering it. He raised his fist. The glass burst into the room with a crash, splinters littering the carpet, barely missing Sam. Only a triangle of glass at the bottom of the pane remained in place. Shani screamed.

The man stuck his head through the hole. For a second he looked around as if he was somehow familiar with the place. She leapt across the room.

"Get out," she shouted.

She slammed the top frame down.

In slow motion, as if she were watching some old black and white movie and realising its ending, she tried to halt her arm, to stay its momentum.

"No, no, no! - I'm sorry!" she screamed.

But the force of her closing took its full course. She heard the throttled gasp, saw the first red droplets. The man's head slumped forward across the triangle of glass, hanging loose. Blood spurted from the cavity that had once been his throat, catching her face and drenching the carpet. On and on the blood poured. His eyes stared blankly at the wall, wide in silent surprise. Only a few sinews seemed to keep his head attached to his body.

In a daze, wet with blood, Shani heard the blast of the twelve bore, then Henry's voice above her.

"We do not want to harm you. Leave now. That shot was in the air. The next will not be. Leave now and you will be safe."

For some moments, there was no sound. There was no movement either. Then two shots in quick succession - the blast of the twelve bore and the crack of the .22. Now people raced across the lawn beyond the shattered window, zig-zagging and screaming. Behind them, two bodies lay prostrate on the unmown grass.

Anne-Marie came into the room. Shani knelt on the carpet sobbing. She was holding desperately to Sam's hand.

"It's OK," said the older woman quietly. "They're leaving now."

She moved towards the window. She lifted the severed neck over the sill and pushed the body outside.

"We'll sort that out later."

"I killed him," said Shani. "I'm so sorry. He stuck his head in and when I closed the window…"

Her voice trailed off.

"It's not your fault," said Anne-Marie. "Not even his fault, really."

Henry came downstairs. He saw the blood on the carpet and the body outside, flies already settling on the corpse.

"I didn't mean to kill him."

"No," said Henry softly, putting his arm around her shoulders. "But what if you hadn't? What if I hadn't shot one of them, what if Rabiyah hadn't?"

He knelt beside Sam. His son's eyes were closed. He held his hand.

"Sam, it's Dad." A glimmer of movement on his face.

"We wouldn't have made it here without you. I just want you to know that we'll look after Shani if anything happens to you."

Sam's breathing faltered. Shani smoothed his hair. For long seconds there was nothing. She leant to kiss his forehead, her tears falling onto his ravaged face. He seemed almost to choke, then a breath emerged from the void. But the breathing was shallow and the spaces between the breaths longer. Shani lay beside him, her arm across his chest, her cheek against his cheek.

She could feel the tiny movement of his chest. She could feel him sway. She could picture him swaying. They had swayed, arms linked aloft, in a huge crowd as the candles flickered in the dark Somerset night and they sang together: 'Lights will guide you home...'

She could see the candles; she could feel the tiny movement of his chest until, like the silence at the end of the song on an old LP, there was no further song. She could no longer fix him.

# CHAPTER XXXV

DANIEL came running from the trees.

"I heard shots."

His eyes alighted on the corpse outside the house - Scott, one of the men who, until the previous evening, had been part of their group - and two more bodies on the lawn.

"What happened?"

"He must have gathered together, how you say, band, a band of people," said Mehau. "I suppose he knew where water is. They tried to attack."

He pointed towards the smashed window.

"Scott died there. Anne-Marie's brother and the Syrian woman shot these two. By Baba Ji's grace, the rest of them ran before they get to us."

Mira looked on, distaste marking her face.

"Have these bodies out of sight before evening puja," she said.

Daniel folded his hands together and bowed his head.

"Yes, Mira."

The kitchen coordinator had crossed the lawn. She studied the first corpse - a male. A mess of bone, flesh and indiscriminate matter was all that remained of the right side of his head. Strands of lacerated ear hung limp and his face was pockmarked with shot. Eye jelly dripped from a vacant socket and a stain of blood spread across the top of his chest beneath his perforated shirt. She gasped.

"It's Damian," she said. Another of those who had left.

She turned to the other body. It was a young woman, a girl really, of perhaps twenty. From a distance, it seemed that she lay in deep repose, her arms spread behind her as if recently ravished. A small, dark circle - like a bindi, but slightly off centre – tarnished her forehead. The wound seemed to be closing already. The kitchen woman raised her wrist and felt her pulse. The arm dropped lifelessly. She turned her over. At the base of her skull, above the hairline, the exit wound gaped. A gash of fleshy fragments, of shattered brain and tissue, exuded in a slow stream down her neck.

She raised the girl's t-shirt and pulled down her shorts. She gripped the flesh of her buttocks and waist, seeming to test them. Standing, she went over to Mira and Daniel and spoke.

"No!" Mira shook her head.

Daniel screwed up his face.

"We can't!"

"Mira Bai, we have very little food in the kitchen. By Baba Ji's grace, you have given me this service to provide food for everybody."

She held her hands together in front of her, then gestured towards the devotees and the family.

"You have already said that Baba Ji will allow us to eat fish."

"That is not the same," said Mira. "Is there not enough fish for tonight?"

The kitchen woman persisted.

"It's not like she was killed for food. She's dead anyway," she said.

Daniel turned to Mira.

"She has a point, Mira."

"If we're going to do it, we'll have to do it now," said the kitchen woman, emboldened. "Otherwise she'll go off in this heat - she'll be no use to anyone."

Finally, Mira nodded.

"Do what you have to do," she said, turning away.

Daniel called two devotees over. He asked them to carry the girl's body towards the kitchen. He instructed others to move the two dead men.

"Leave one outside the gate and the other a bit further along the road. No one likes skeletons."

The girl was laid on a sheet. The kitchen coordinator came out with a large knife and a pair of scissors. Leah ran over.

"You can't do that!" she protested, her arms gesticulating wildly. "That's a human being."

But the kitchen woman ignored her. With the scissors, she cut away the clothes from the body and flung the remnants, soiled and ribboned, to the side. She asked for buckets of sea water and, when they came, sluiced them over the now naked corpse, cleaning it of blood and matted faeces.

Leah ran back to Daniel, beating her fists against his chest.

"Stop them!" she shouted. "You've got to stop them."

"It's just food," he said, but he too looked away as the kitchen woman began to hack at a buttock.

It did not cut easily and the kitchen knife was blunt. A small mush of bloody flesh was all she could achieve. She dropped it onto a large dish. It was, Anne-Marie noted, the ancient enamel dish, chipped around the edges, that her mother had always used for casseroles at big family gatherings.

✳✳✳✳✳✳

The kitchen woman raised the knife again.

"Stop," said Lou. "You need to bleed it and gut it if you want to get any proper meat from it."

Mehau nodded.

"Is like wild pig I kill with my uncle in Poland. I will find rope."

"Rope? Why do you need rope?" asked the kitchen woman.

No one answered her. Mehau spoke to Daniel.

"You keep Leah this side of house, OK?"

Lou waved away the knife that was held out to her.

"I don't need it, I have my own."

They carried the body to the edge of the wood behind the outbuildings. Mehau fetched a coil of blue rope from the tool shed. They selected an oak. A low branch stretched horizontally above the bare earth.

He looped the rope around the ankles. Lou lifted the body as he stretched the ends over the branch and tightened the knot. The girl dangled now like an inverted crucifix, the backs of her hands and her long hair brushing across the loose soil and the few sparse patches of grass surviving in the shade. They stood back and checked. The kitchen woman and some of the other devotees were watching them.

"Is better you not watch," said Mehau.

"Fuck off!" said Lou, waving her arms. "Ready?"

Now she pulled out her hunting knife. With one deft sweep she slit the girl's throat, deep and firm, severing the jugular and stopping only when she hit the spine. The head tilted back a little. She drove the knife in again, this time feeling for the small gap between the collar bones where the arteries lay. She plunged it in to the hilt and hinged it up and down, left and right. Blood poured out, spreading across the underside of the girl's chin and veiling her face. A pool formed on the soil, rivulets sliding off the dry earth, collecting in puddles in their foot prints and around the exposed roots, as if feeding them.

It took an hour or more for the flow to become a trickle and for the trickle to become a few slow drops. They carried the blood-drained body to the seashore, well beyond the latrines, and laid it on a rock. Lou took the knife again. From the breastbone, she drew the blade down, cutting only through the skin and stomach muscles, careful not to rupture the intestines or the bladder.

"Urghh!" she said as the corpse split open.

The stench was overwhelming, a putrid cloud spreading through the air around them. She turned the girl on her side, towards the sea, and let the intestines spill out. Mehau turned away retching and coughing.

"We all smell like this inside?" he said. "She so young?"

Lou withdrew the knife. It was smeared in body mucus and tissue and she wiped it quickly on the rough grass that grew beside the rock. Mehau took over. He removed his shirt and knelt over the body. Some of the intestines slipped away from his hands like mercury.

"Careful you don't break them. She'll taste like shit if they split."

With two hands, he scooped out the remainder. He laid them to the side and felt for the bladder. He pulled gently, careful to keep it intact. The liver and kidneys and pancreas came next. He separated the pancreas and laid the liver and kidneys to the other side. Finally, holding the body with one hand, he reached under the rib cage.

"Aaarh!"

Blood spattered across his midriff as he hauled at the heart and lungs. A tube of severed artery came with the organs but he could not quite release them. Lou handed him the knife and he cut the other side.

Now they carried the body down to the sea. They paddled in until they were more than knee deep. They turned the body over and over in the water. Then Mehau held the girl's hair, raising the head, and they swilled her back and forth, allowing the water to sluice through the empty cavity, little pockets of skin and mucus detaching and floating away.

Mehau took the liver and kidneys and heart and rinsed these off too. The rest of the entrails they left on the rock for the crows and buzzards. They carried the carcase back.

"I think here," said Mehau when they reached the stone outbuilding that held the tools and the mowers. "I think will be cool enough."

They roped her up to the rafters, well above ground level, out of the way of Aragorn and any other visiting wildlife. The liver and kidneys he took back to the house. He gave them to the kitchen coordinator.

"These best cook now, I think," he said.

# CHAPTER XXXVI

THE DEATH of Sam, though not unexpected, hung heavy over Henry's extended family. Shani was in a daze, her face closed. Grief, guilt, pain and fear were not allowed to enter.

"Where can we bury him?"

Anne-Marie and Henry walked round the garden with her. She chose a spot that looked out to sea, the house behind and the Cedar of Lebanon to the side. A tiny butterfly, its wings a celestial mauve, fluttered from the harebell that grew there and she knew she had chosen the right spot.

"Perfect," said Lou when they showed her the place.

She had brought two spades and started digging. Henry picked up the other spade but the soil was hard and he dug slowly. Mehau appeared, carrying a pickaxe.

"You give me," he said, pointing to Henry's spade.

Henry would go to the ends of the earth, Shani knew, to ensure his son had a complete burial. He would dig every last cast of soil if he had to. But he was exhausted. And so the grave was dug by a young woman who he had travelled with for just the previous five days and an ungainly young man who he had only come across that morning.

For thirty minutes they dug. Pouring with sweat, they flung shovelfuls to the side. The pile of earth grew higher and higher. Shani handed them water. Lou gulped it down, a trickle running from the side of her mouth to join the beads of sweat below. Mehau pulled off his sodden t-shirt, breathing heavily.

Shani watched in a trance as a worm, pink and vulnerable and suddenly exposed to the day, slithered back into the brown earth before the next spade-cut.

"It's ready," said Lou eventually, emerging, her legs and chest stained with soil.

The grave was a metre deep and half a metre wide and long enough to accommodate Sam.

"Thank you," said Henry.

"Thank you so much," whispered Shani.

She looked for the butterfly but the butterfly had flown. She picked some yellow rattle and harebell from the wild ground where the garden met the shoreline. She picked thrift from the rocks. Some of the flowers she scattered in the bottom of the earthy coffin.

"OK?" she said, looking up.

With Henry she carried Sam's body, the duvet still around him, out of the house and across the lawn. She placed a cushion at one end of the bare soil and gently they laid him down. The pain that had wracked his face only hours previously had fallen away and his head now rested at the end of the rainbow.

Anne-Marie, Lou and Rabiyah, Noor in her arms, joined them at the graveside. Mira stood at a respectful distance behind with Daniel and Leah. Mehau crossed his hands quietly in front of him.

The slow beat of the sea, the screech of the gulls, the sweep of the breeze through the Cedar of Lebanon, did not falter. But, to Shani, it seemed that sound held its breath, took a pause, and for a moment was still. One by one she placed the remaining stems, yellow, blue and mauve, along the length of the grave and beside Sam's head.

"My love," she said, tears falling freely.

"Fuckin' legend," said Lou.

Anne Marie pulled a notebook from her pocket.

"Ah Sam," she said. "Sam, my good-looking brave nephew. We always knew you were special, even when you were in your mother's arms. This is what I wrote when you were two ...."

'He's a lovely bouncy blonde boy. Very intelligent. Sometimes he does wild things, and then he giggles.'

"So now, Sam, unleashed from life, do wild things out there. And here, where you have left us, we will look after Shani, we promise. We'll look after your old Dad too."

Henry was shaking. He didn't have a guitar now. The guitar was the other side. He bent and scooped a handful of soil into his palm.

"Thank you, Sam," he said simply, his voice quavering.

He allowed the soil to dribble through his fingers onto his son's body. He looked up at the outline of the hills in the darkening sky behind, and, when Lou and Mehau began to shovel the earth back into the grave, he had to turn away, bent over in his grief.

# CHAPTER XXXVII

"BLACK, I'm afraid," said Anne-Marie, passing Henry a cup of tea. "Milk went off."

He grimaced at the bitter taste. The sun was burning off the night mist and from their parents' bench they could hear the chanting of morning puja.

"Twice a day," said Anne-Marie without him asking. "Six o'clock."

"If you just close your eyes and listen, it's actually very soothing," he said.

He leant his head back against the mauve wisteria that climbed the wall. Mira began to address the devotees.

'We are on a journey,' she said. 'A journey back to Baba Ji. By Baba Ji's grace, we have come to this point. New dangers appear every day, but we are held in the cup of Baba Ji's love. There is no signpost here. Without a signpost, you might think that we are lost. But we are not lost. Baba Ji has given us instructions – to practise devotion to Him, to do service, to listen to His words and to practise meditation. Sometimes we stray...'

"Hmmm...." said Henry.

They moved away and sat on the rocks on the edge of the lawn, close to the freshly dug earth that marked Sam's grave.

"Well... you made it here somehow."

Aragorn appeared from the woods. He sat, panting, looking out to sea. Anne-Marie stroked his head. He was quiet, as if he understood that someone was buried here, as Rabbie had been too, not far away.

"There were many times when I thought we wouldn't... but we lost Jo. We lost Stef too – Lou's friend. And now Sam. He didn't really stand a chance, once the infection took hold."

Henry stooped to pick a stem of bell heather and tossed it onto the grave.

"I'll tell you the whole story sometime."

He glanced to the sky. A black drone, perhaps the same they'd seen the day before, was circling.

"If I get a chance."

Anne-Marie nodded. Neither of them moved. There was no hiding place from this thing.

"Safest here but trapped – that's what you said yesterday."

She gestured towards the drone that now curled away inland.

"Yes – as far as I can see there's only one place we could escape to."

"Where?"

"Back to Fraser's."

She stared across at the mainland.

"How was it there?"

"Quiet, all quiet. He'd read your note. It was scrumpled up on the kitchen table."

"Was the pickup there?"

"Yup."

"He must have gone off in it. Couldn't get through, came back and took the boat. Anyway, there's no guarantee it would be any safer – if they can get us here they can get us there - but there's plenty of fresh water from the burn, and it would be easier to defend on the ground. I just don't know…"

Henry sighed.

"Ten steps forward and one step back," he said. "We'd better get the Lady Ffiona fixed. Is there fuel in it?"

"Some. They said it cut out before they landed, but that was probably the net."

"Let's take some anyway. Is there a tool kit still in the top shed?"

"Think so."

They walked over and he unlatched the faded red door. "Jeeesus!"

He turned round, white-faced.

"That girl that Rabiyah shot. She's hanging in here."

"Ah….yes…sorry. I should have told you. Mehau and Lou did it yesterday."

"The things…I suppose…"

Henry did not finish. There could be no end to the sentence. He took a deep breath and went back in.

He emerged with a fuel can, shears and secateurs. They walked down to the secret harbour, Aragorn running at their heels. The Lady Ffiona's outboard was slung up over the stern and he inspected it quickly from the dinghy. The orange net, torn and shredded, twisted like a dervish around the propeller's blades.

"Can you pass me the shears."

He hacked at the swirls of nylon. Great lengths of it unravelled and came away. With the secateurs he cut the last thick strands, unwinding them.

"That should do it. Let's see if we still have a shear pin."

With his hand, he tried to turn the propeller, but the blades resisted him.

"Thank God for that. It's a good job they were running slowly when they fouled."

Now Henry boarded the larger boat, lowered the outboard and locked it in position. He filled the fuel tank, adjusted the choke and pulled the cord. The Evinrude engine started without complaint and he let it run for a few minutes.

"OK, it's ready if we need it," he said. "We should be able to get everyone across, shouldn't we?"

"If they all come," said Anne-Marie. "I don't know if they would."

"Are we going to get our boat and the Lizzie round here?"

"Maybe we should just leave them at the pier. Mehau understands the tide. He's taking care of the ropes."

Henry looked up at the sky, overcast now. The wind was picking up from the south-west and small crests were forming on the waves in the Sound. The first few drops of rain fell, one this side of the boat, one that, each one seeming heavier than the one before.

"You're probably right," he said. "Seems like there's a storm coming in anyway."

# CHAPTER XXXVIII

THE STORM built. Wind raced up the sound. It was visible, almost, as it scoured the waves and bent the trees.

Through the murk, Henry could see, from the battered window, a drone fighting against the gale. It seemed to lean in to the wind, stationary for a moment as the motor held it. He could almost imagine the operator —he, she or it, whoever or whatever it was - wrestling with the controls. Then, suddenly, the thing buckled, flipped on its back like a boxer finally out for the count. It tumbled and span in hectic motion, bounced twice on the water, and crashed against the rocks on the shoreline.

Inwardly, Henry cheered. The elements had beaten this thing. Now they had to do the same. He pulled out four packs of cards.

"Racing Demon," he said loudly, trying to make himself heard above the pounding of the rain. He laid out his cards on the carpet. Shani and Anne-Marie followed suit. Rabiyah sat quietly in an armchair, cradling Noor.

"How do you play?" said Lou.

"It's patience war. You have four cards laid out, thirteen in a separate pile. Aces in the middle. Get rid of your thirteen and you're the winner. Kings score ten."

She watched the first round intently. It did not take long for her to pick up the game.

"King!" she shouted, diving across the floor to place the King of Spades on the Queen before Shani could get hers down.

The kitchen woman walked in.

"Is there any fish for tonight?" she asked Anne-Marie.

Anne-Marie pointed outside.

"Not the weather for catching mackerel."

"We brought over whatever we had left in the Landcruiser," said Henry. "Where did that stuff go?"

"Eaten, mostly. I have to feed seventeen people tonight, and all I have is some rice and two or three mackerel."

'A loaf and two small fishes,' thought Henry, but did not speak.

"We can hunt for a deer or rabbits tomorrow. Maybe there are some horses," said Lou. She looked towards Rabiyah as Shani translated.

"It's tonight I'm worried about."

"Well, there's the girl. She may not be quite ready yet, but the meat's there."

\*\*\*\*\*\*

Leah screamed.

Lou, dripping from the rain, walked into the kitchen with an entire leg. It looked like a mannequin's leg, flat flesh at the top of the thigh and bent at the knee. Silvery glitter still clung to the girl's toe nails where the earth had not smeared them.

"I had to use the bow saw to get it off," she said.

"You can't!" cried Leah. "You can't just eat a person."

She paused and seemed to take control of herself.

"Are you really sure about this? Are you that hungry?"

"What do you mean?" said the kitchen woman.

"Normally…I mean, we're not starving. You don't read about people eating other people until they're dying of starvation. You don't just eat someone because there's nothing else in the fridge."

"Well, you don't have to eat it. There'll be rice. Please yourself."

Lou pulled out her knife and quickly sliced the flesh off the bone in large steaks. The meat was lean. She diced it into smaller pieces. The little fat there was she trimmed off and threw in a large frying pan along with some olive oil, ready for cooking.

"What else do we have? Is there any stock? I need onions, tomato puree, garlic and cornflour," she said.

The kitchen coordinator rifled through the cupboards.

"There are some stock cubes," she said. "And onions. No tomato puree or garlic, but there's some plain flour."

"That'll do. Give me a few minutes."

The rain was just a drizzle now and the sky was clearing from the west. Lou picked up a wicker basket and went outside again.

******

The basket was full on her return, roots and leaves wet with the sea water she'd washed them in.

"What have you got? Is that dandelion?"

"Yes," said Lou. "Thistle and mallow roots, young nettle shoots – should make her a bit tastier."

They heated the fat and oil in the pan and browned the meat, then transferred it to the chipped enamel dish. Lou prepared some roots while the kitchen woman sliced the onions. These too were fried gently and transferred. Lou threw in some dandelion heads and leaves and the young nettles as she poured in the stock.

"OK, bring it to the boil, then cover it and leave it in the oven for about an hour and a half," said Lou. "Is there enough wood in the aga?"

\*\*\*\*\*\*

The storm moved East and the evening sun warmed the grass.

Puja over, some of the devotees cleared the wet ashes from the makeshift barbecue, rebuilding the fire. The kitchen woman came out and put the rice on the grill. She returned with the casserole.

"Life is suffering," said Mira, as she sat down next to Shani. "There is birth, sickness, and then death, with a few interludes in between. And in those interludes, we have to practise devotion. This is what Baba Ji teaches us."

Shani looked across at her. If this was sympathy for Sam, then this woman had no grasp of sympathy.

The aroma of cooking lingered in the air, a smell that Shani thought she recognised, though she could not place it. She walked over to the fire.

"What is that?" she asked the kitchen woman, pointing to the casserole. The meat had the consistency of chicken breast, but darker.

"It's from the shot girl. I...I tasted it. It tastes a bit like, maybe, pork, but different, wilder. I didn't really know how to cook it. Well...I've never cooked it before."

"No, I don't suppose you have," said Shani.

She turned away. She felt light-headed, as if she was walking through some awful fantasy land.

"Final touches," said Lou, returning. She was mixing flour and water into a paste in a cup. She spooned it into the casserole, stirred it in and added pepper.

Across the lawn, a group of the devotees sat cross-legged on the ground, ignoring the damp. They were laughing and talking loudly. Mira called Daniel over.

"Daniel, what is going on over there? Baba Ji says unconscious chatter is a waste of our precious time."

He walked over to the group.

234

"Mira is not happy with this noise. She says Baba Ji …"

One of the people held up a small bottle. Shani recognized it - it was a miniature from the hotel. Daniel took it and studied the label.

"This is whisky," he said. "You know Baba Ji does not permit alcohol on retreat. No alcohol and no sex."

His eyes flickered towards the blonde girl.

"And no meat, fish or eggs," said one of the group triumphantly, his words jumbling. "But we've eaten fish and she's cooking meat. Human steaks!"

They giggled nervously.

"Mira has allowed these things at the moment," said Daniel. "Baba Ji is playing an extreme lila on us. It is a test of our devotion. Where did you get this bottle?"

An unsteady palm pointed towards a blue plastic supermarket tray that sat between them. It was the one that Lou had transferred to the Toyota with the remaining food from the motorhome. On it lay an assortment of bottles and miniatures, some still standing, several lying supine at random angles, as if waiting to be spun in some form of drinking game.

A woman began to whimper. She produced an unopened miniature of white wine from her smock. On her knees, she scrabbled at Daniel's feet, looking fearfully up towards Mira.

"Forgive me, Baba Ji, my mind took me from consciousness of you," she slurred, then fell sideways across the grass. Daniel removed his foot. He picked up the tray and carried it towards the house.

"If you only fuckin' knew," said Lou as she passed the drunken devotees.

She speared a piece of meat from the pan and took a bite from the tip of her blade. She considered it for a moment, then nodded to herself.

"Quite bloody tasty," she said to the kitchen woman, ignoring her glare. "Five plates please."

She passed them to Shani and Henry, then to Rabiyah and Anne-Marie. She sat down herself with the last one, forming a circle. Daniel held two plates. One had only rice on it, the other both rice and casserole. The one with only rice he took to the blonde girl, the other to Mira.

Henry picked up some meat in his fingers and ate. On the other side of the lawn, Mira took a mouthful of the casserole.

"We're all animals now," said Henry softly.

# CHAPTER XXXIX

HENRY and Anne-Marie sailed back into the bay in late morning. The shoal had been large and the Lizzie was laden with mackerel.

As they walked up to the house with the buckets of black and silver-barred fish, Henry was impressed by the diligence of the devotees. Some were cutting wood, some clearing the latrines, some digging the vegetable garden. He watched as Rabiyah, the .22 over her shoulder, handed Noor to Shani, then walked off with Mehau and Lou.

"We're going to look round the perimeter," Lou called. "And then we'll see if we can get a deer or some rabbits or something."

Henry made his way down to the shoreline where the drone had crashed the day before. Pushing yellow gorse aside, his arms scratched, he found it not far from the old pier at the back of the scars of rock that led to the headland. One leg was ripped off, the composite material gashed, dented and torn. He caught a glimpse of the mother board inside – the guts of the thing. With the circular lens of the camera slung below the body, it resembled a giant bluebottle lying grounded, its wings folded. He stepped around it warily. He half-expected the camera to swing in his direction, or the whole thing to right itself and wrap its blades around him.

But it was not armed, he noticed.

There were no markings on it, no registration number, no manufacturer's name. He decided to take it back to the house. Perhaps one of the younger people would be able to glean something more from it. Circumspectly, he put his arms out to lift it. It was not heavy – perhaps ten kilos.

Cold salt water spilled onto his stomach as it tipped. Something rattled inside. It was already too much for his febrile mind. He hurled the drone away from him and ran back. Logically, the thing was harmless. Water had got in, something had broken away in the crash. But what if there was an explosive device inside? And even if it was harmless, entirely disabled, did he, did all of them, really want a reminder of their plight, this threat, sitting on the lawn?

Henry walked up to the house unencumbered. The afternoon was muggy, with only the lightest of breezes blowing off the Sound. No helicopters or live drones disturbed the screeching of gulls and the hum of insects. In a quiet corner of the rose garden, he closed his eyes. The weight of the past days carried him to a deep sleep.

******

It was after six when he woke.

Anne-Marie pulled out the old plastic garden table. It was rickety about its legs but somehow remained standing. Henry placed the matching chairs, white and discoloured, green moss gathering on the arms, around it. He stretched and looked at his sister.

"D'ye have any of that 200-year old single malt, lassie?"

"Och aye, laddie, I think I might find a wee bottle."

"I think I deserve some."

"I think ye do."

It was an old family joke. Not even a joke. A tradition that had survived the sad times and the tough times at Balmanie. And this time was the saddest and toughest by far.

Strains of evening puja rose into the sky as Anne-Marie brought a bottle from the house, Shani behind her with a tray of tumblers and a jug of water. Henry called Lou and Rabiyah over. He poured the Scotch, passing the glasses across the table. He raised his eyebrows to Rabiyah. She shook her head as he expected, and he passed her water.

"These Baba Ji's – can we trust them? This Mira?" asked Lou. "She seems to control them."

"She is aloof, almost robotic," said Anne-Marie. "She is shackled by her devotion. But I have seen a human being in there."

Mira herself walked towards them. She looked somehow wearied. Henry waved a greeting, offering an empty chair with his outstretched arm. The plastic picnic chairs were not conducive to an upright posture, but Mira contrived to hold an almost military poise. He raised the bottle in her direction.

"Scotch?"

There was a hint of hesitation.

"Baba Ji does not allow us to drink alcohol…despite last night."

"Ah yes, of course," said Henry. "Sorry…if you change your mind."

Mira nodded. Daniel, Leah and Mehau appeared from the far side of the house.

"There are more chairs over there," said Henry, indicating a terrace almost submerged in geraniums.

Mehau disengaged the chairs from the green and red foliage and brought them to the table. The heady scent of the plants, released by their movement, filled the air around them. Henry addressed Anne-Marie.

"The boat you talked about, the RIB that you saw when you were fishing with Mehau. Were they armed?"

Anne-Marie thought for a moment. She glanced across at Mehau.

"Actually, they didn't seem to be."

Henry took a sip of the whisky, then looked around the whole table.

"No, nor was the drone that crashed so far as I could tell. You know what I think – I think this whole business is technological superiority gone out of control. Technological genocide. Whatever, whoever, these people are, they hold the wheels of power for now. We, here, are irrelevant pawns on the edges of their reality. We must be - if they wanted to get rid of us, they could have done so ten times over."

Two hooded crows settled noisily into the top of the Cedar of Lebanon, shuffling their wings in the ink green fronds and branches. A red squirrel, disturbed, perhaps, in its evening meditations, leapt gracefully down to a lower branch, its tail streaming behind it. It made its way back to the trunk, then scampered upwards, an occasional glimpse of rufous until all was quiet again.

"But perhaps I am completely wrong. Perhaps they will attack tonight or tomorrow with guns or missiles or nerve gas. With drones or helicopters.

"And, if they do, Anne-Marie and I have come to the conclusion that there is just one place we could escape to – just one place. If we can escape at all."

"Where?" said Leah.

"The white house that you can see across the Sound from the point above the secret harbour. It belongs…it belonged to Fraser, the man whose boat you came on. There is fresh water there. Would it be any different to here, any safer? I doubt it. But it is a thought, an option. If we come to that."

Mira cleared her throat, looking across at the whisky.

"I…"

Henry picked up the bottle again.

"You're more than welcome to a glass if you'd like one."

Leah took a tumbler and held it towards him.

"Thanks."

Daniel and Mehau held back. They glanced across at Mira. She heaved a deep sigh.

"They call it the Spirit of Life," said Henry.

She nodded and cupped a tumbler with both hands as Henry poured. He offered her water, but she declined. He turned to Daniel and Mehau and there was no hesitation now.

"You were saying?"

Mira took a sip. She allowed the whisky to course through her veins. She was in no hurry and no one rushed her. It was a road, Henry thought, down which she'd travelled before.

"By Baba Ji's grace your theory will be right, Henry," she said. "And before I say anything else, I would like to apologise for the attack on your boat. We had no idea…"

Henry cocked his head to the side in acknowledgement. She took a deep breath. Her hands were shaking. She was fighting for control.

"Some of my people, our people," she said, looking at Daniel, Leah and Mehau, "came to me after evening puja. They are worried.

"These new people, they said, have guns; they shot that woman, then they ate her. Yes, I know I ate some too, many of us did. But we are staying in the same house, they said, we are not safe here, we should leave."

Henry looked at her, unbelieving.

"I…I'm so sorry …"

"She were already fuckin' dead!" said Lou.

"Mira," said Henry, gathering himself, "Perhaps in the next days – if the drone people let us - I will have a chance to get to know you better, and to tell you the story of how we got here. The twelve bore is my father's gun and we have used it only in self-defence since we left our home.

241

The rifle we found at a farm on our journey. Rabiyah is a lethal shot with it and has protected us from all sorts of dangers."

He waited while Shani translated. Rabiyah's face exploded in wide-eyed shock at Mira's fears. She shook her head violently from side to side and waved her arms.

Henry stood up, holding his glass to the sun settling above the mountains inland. A raven flew low overhead, the beat of its wings rhythmic through the evening air. He looked Mira in the eye.

"I give you my word that the guns will be used only to protect ourselves or to hunt for food. Noone, and this includes your group, noone, even if the rest of us are dying from starvation, will be shot by either gun for food. I promise."

Henry crossed his arms against his chest. Rabiyah, Shani, Anne-Marie and Lou stood and followed his movement.

# CHAPTER XL

*IT WAS nearly dark when the sound crept into the room. Just a hum at first.*

*I was slumped, half asleep, in the armchair that had been my father's favourite seat. Its brown leather was cracked now like an arid field. Upstairs, Rabiyah and Noor slept.*

*The sound grew louder, a measured thud-thud-thud through the sky. We looked at each other, a small candle flickering between us. A beam of light burst through the undrawn curtains, focussing, for a moment, on me, then moving left across Anne-Marie, Lou and Shani. Lou went over to the window.*

*"Two," she said. "Close, really close. Hovering."*

*The searchlights from the helicopters swept across the house and the garden. The serpentine branches of the Cedar of Lebanon appeared suddenly from the darkness, then, as quickly, disappeared again.*

*"This is it, then, I suppose," I said.*

*Anne-Marie nodded. I patted the chair.*

*"Bye, Dad."*

*I loosened my jaw and shook my head from side to side. A sound churned from my mouth — fear and grief and curse and prayer rolled into a primordial cry of pain.*

*"OK," I said, when I was done. I picked up the twelve bore.*

*"Lou, can you get Rabiyah? We'll go back to Fraser's."*

*Downstairs there was pandemonium. Devotees were running in every direction. Some had packed rucksacks on their backs. The lights played in and out of the rooms like a strobe. Rabiyah came down the stairs. She held the baby in her left arm. The rifle was slung across her right. Noor began to scream. Mira stood at the window of the drawing room, looking out impassively.*

*"We're pulling out," said Anne-Marie. "We're taking two boats. Henry will go from the pier and I'll take the one from the harbour through the woods. You and your group are welcome to come. We'll try and make a go of it over there."*

*Mira turned. She nodded in thanks. She called Daniel. He shouted to the devotees to stop and listen to her. For a moment they quietened.*

*"This is the most extreme lila that Baba Ji has ever played on me. I am praying to Him to tell me which way to turn. I do not know myself and I do not know how to guide you. What I can tell you is that you have three alternatives.*

*"The family, and those who are with them, are leaving in two boats. They are going back to the mainland to a remote house. One boat will go from the pier where we attacked them, the other from a harbour through the woods that some of you may know. They say that we are welcome to join them.*

*"You can go inland and take your chances, but you saw what happened to Scott and Damian, who left us earlier."*

*The sound from the sky was deafening now, even in the house.*

*"Or you can stay here," Mira shouted. "May Baba Ji protect you. I now declare this retreat at an end."*

*I heard a frenzied muttering all about me.*

*"They ate that woman… they have guns."*

*"It wasn't just them that ate her."*

*"If we go together in the boat … can we risk it?"*

*A man walked towards Mira. He knelt on one knee. He kissed her hand and spoke. She looked down at him, disdain painted on her face. She slapped him so hard that his head buckled.*

The sound outside echoed off the walls, more intense, forcing a choice. One of the helicopters was landing. Mira stepped out of the drawing-room onto the edge of the lawn.

"No, Mira, please," said Daniel, his hands folded in front of him. But she did not move.

Rabiyah handed the baby to Lou and followed, rifle in hand. I could make out the figure of the pilot in the cockpit. Rabiyah knelt and took aim. Mira turned.

"Put down your gun. We cannot defeat them with guns."

Rabiyah looked at her blankly. Mira said it again, but this time she took the barrel and held it to the centre of her chest. She crossed her arms over the gun, shaking her head. Now Rabiyah understood. She lowered the gun.

Mira looked back at Daniel, still guarding behind her.

"Go," she shouted, her palms open, pushing backwards. "Go. Do not wait for me."

She walked forward across the grass. Two devotees followed her. I paused for a moment, mesmerised.

The lights that had played all around now fixed on her. She moved into the centre of the lawn, spotlit like a rock star, her hair blown wild by the sweep of the rotor blades. She raised her arms in a shape of neither surrender nor glory.

The cabin door of the helicopter opened. Inside, I glimpsed a figure swathed in a white robe. An arm waved her forward. Mira prostrated herself on the damp grass, then stepped into the darkness of the cabin. The two devotees followed and the door swung closed.

A third helicopter came from the West. I saw lights flashing in the sky — two more were coming across the Sound.

They formed a circle hovering above the lawn, their searchlights patterning the night sky like lasers. The unmown grass, the rhododendrons, the old brick walls of the rose garden, laced now with the blue of forget-me-nots, appeared and disappeared in fractured frames. Mira's helicopter tipped forward slightly, its rotor blades scything through the air, then lifted off. In seconds it was just a tail light flashing in the distance.

Fear hit me like the cold shiver of a half-heard footstep in the night.

*"Go, go, go," I shouted in the darkness at the back of the house. "Follow me to the pier."*

*Bodies raced this way and that across my vision, criss-crossing, illuminated, for seconds, by the lights skimming through the bay windows, then extinguished again. A cluster of devotees clung close to me, shaking, waiting to follow.*

*"Leah!" I heard. It was Daniel.*

*"Where are you?"*

*"Here, by the rhododendrons." But Daniel's voice was drowned by the jet engines.*

*Lou ran past.*

*"This way, Lou," I shouted.*

*She held the baby in her arms. She said something but I couldn't hear her.*

*Josephine was in the boat already when I got to the pier. A trickle of blood still fell from her wrist, but her face was calm now.*

******

*It were fuckin' chaos. Fuckin' baby screaming in my arms. Can't bloody blame it. I saw Rabiyah out there on the lawn. One minute she were there, and the next she weren't. Thought it would be safest to head for the pier, but she weren't there, so I went back. Henry were coming out of the house. Where's Rabiyah, I shouted, but I don't think he heard me. I were worried. And then Leah was there. She put her mouth right to my ear. Daniel, have you seen Daniel? No, I said, he must be at the pier. He's not there, nobody's there, she said. I've got the fuckin' baby, I said. They must be at the other one. Where is it? Come on, I know the way, she said. She led me through a wood. We were half running. That baby were heavy after ten minutes. Couldn't see a fuck except when the moon came from behind the clouds. Could smell it though. Soft and sweet and a hint of wild garlic. I tripped on a root or something. Nearly dropped Noor. We came to the water — a boat in the middle. Rabiyah was there, and Anne-Marie and Shani. Thank fuck, I shouted. Rabiyah was just fuckin' trembling. She said something in that language of hers — Allahu Akbar! - as I handed the baby back to her.*

But now Leah were screaming "Daniel, where's Daniel? Isn't Daniel here?"

"He'll be in the other boat, love," called Anne-Marie.

Leah just turned and sprinted back. I couldn't fuckin' stop her.

"We'll give them five minutes," said Anne-Marie. "See if anyone else comes. Unless…"

I can tell you it were a fuckin' relief to be away from those helicopters. You could still see the light playin' above the trees, but the noise were only a rumble now. You could hear yourself think.

"Be ready to push her off," said Anne-Marie. And I were. I were in water up to me fuckin' fanny. I were ready to push off right away. We listened. Someone was coming down that track in the dark.

"Wait. Wait for me. Don't leave me behind again."

It were Stef. She was still stark naked, bruised all over now.

\*\*\*\*\*\*

The clouds had cleared when we set off. Just us girls. Moonlight skithered across the sea like the torch of a blue dawn.

Anne-Marie steered the boat out of the little harbour between two tall rocks. I could see the outline of the mainland across the water. I thought I could see the curve of Fraser's bay, even the white smudge of the house. But Anne-Marie did not turn towards it.

"Why are you not crossing?" I asked.

"I'm going to hug the shoreline for a while. Further up the sound is narrower. We can get across more quickly. Try to escape their attention."

She turned the engine down so low the boat was barely moving. Behind us, I could hear a steady thrum. I looked back. Heading across, nearing the middle, a boat moved forward in the moonlight.

"That must be Henry," said Anne-Marie.

He was dead-heading for Fraser's house. Behind us we saw a beam rise and fall and sweep around Balmanie. A helicopter was taking off again. Another followed. Anne-Marie steered the boat even closer to the shore.

"Lou," she said, "Look ahead for rocks or anything."

*Lou pushed that brown shoulder bag of hers behind her back and leant forward over the bow.*

*Two helicopters began to criss-cross the Sound. One of them banked. It was heading straight for us, the searchlight delving the water in front of us. Closer and closer it came. We all ducked. I held my breath. I was ready to jump. And then, just before the light hit us, the helicopter turned again and flew further south.*

*"Rocks ahead!" Lou shouted. They were so close she could push us away from them with an oar.*

*The moon did not help Henry. He was there in the middle, exposed, like a young plant without shade or water in the blazing glare of the sun. The helicopters did not take long to find him. Their lights pounded on his boat, blinding and circling it.*

*We could hear now an alarm, a siren that rose and fell, and a voice behind it, echoing across the water. Henry's boat changed course but, in an instant, a plume of water rose twenty, thirty feet in the air. The explosion, muffled, reached us a second later.*

*"No!" said Anne-Marie, barely a whisper.*

*I could hardly breathe. Dry gulps of fear clutched at my throat. Still the helicopter engines thudded in the night air behind us. Still Anne-Marie clung to the coastline.*

*A point of land pushed us further out.*

*"This is the closest we can get," she said.*

*She turned off the engine and we waited in the lee of the point. The boat rocked in the swell, and all we could hear was the rise and fall of Noor's breathing.*

*Hide and Seek. It was the final Hide and Seek. But Anne-Marie's hiding place was good. More clouds came in from the west. When she saw a big heavy cloud cover the moon, she fired up the outboard to full power. It took only fifteen minutes to get across. We could see the lights of one of the helicopters to the south of us, but it didn't come close.*

*Fraser's house was just as we had left it two days previously. The Toyota was still there. We tied up the boat and went in. My legs were shaking — I could not cast off the fear. Anne-Marie slumped down on Fraser's sofa. I think everything finally bore down on her shoulders.*

"He's gone," she said. "Gone like Henry, gone like whoever else was on that boat – Leah probably, Daniel, perhaps Mehau."

We heard a noise outside like the roar of a sea lion. Rabiyah pulled the gun to her side. I shone the torch across the bay. I could see only the beach and the boat in the water beyond. There was a hammering on the door. I froze. Rabiyah held the gun ready.

"Who is there?" I shouted.

There was just a groan. I don't know why, but I opened the door. A man fell forward onto the tiled floor. He was dripping wet, his muscular chest heaving for breath. His feet were bare; furrowed ridges tore through his thigh, exposing white bone. His left side was black.

I pulled Sam over and lay with him.

"Beautiful woman – still stonkingly beautiful – check," he whispered.

# CHAPTER XLI

HENRY walked over to the window. He could hear Anne-Marie, Shani and Lou talking downstairs in the kitchén. He could hear the occasional cry of Noor, and Rabiyah's soothing voice. The hum of puja rose and fell from the other side of the house.

He stared outside. The image of Josephine lingered - she sat in the boat with him still. He wanted to hold onto the dream, but already the dream was fading.

A meadow pipit flew up from the rough ground that lay at the back of Balmanie, beside the meadow. It grabbed a mayfly from the air and settled on a rock, the mayfly clasped in its beak. It bobbed its head and looked left and right. It did not see the hen harrier, a large female, quartering low and hungry across the bracken behind the clump of trees. Henry did not have the language to warn the meadow pipit. He could have thumped on the window to frighten it away, but he didn't. He simply watched as the cycle of life revolved on the other side of the glass.

A thrash of wings - and a few feathers fell softly to the earth.

# ABOUT THE AUTHOR

After graduating from St Andrews with a degree in Modern History and Moral Philosophy, Tony Lindsell joined the Hertfordshire Gazette. He went on to write for, and ultimately edit, an alternative newspaper in London before becoming managing editor of Samsom Publications, a business newsletter publisher in the days before the internet.

He later moved out of journalism and publishing and followed an eclectic career that included selling custom interiors and interior components for upmarket business jets and forming a company specialising in the sale of equine hoofcare products. He continues to write the occasional feature article and has written for such magazines as The Lady, Trainer, Horse and Hound and Warwickshire Life.

He has also published a collection of short stories and poems entitled Days in the Life.

He lives in Warwickshire and can be contacted on email: lindsell@clara.net